IN THE WEEDS

A WHITE HOUSE PROTECTION FORCE ROMANCE
NOVEL

M. L. BUCHMAN

Buchman Bookworks

Other works by M. L. Buchman:

The Night Stalkers

MAIN FLIGHT
The Night Is Mine
I Own the Dawn
Wait Until Dark
Take Over at Midnight
Light Up the Night
Bring On the Dusk
By Break of Day

WHITE HOUSE HOLIDAY
Daniel's Christmas
Frank's Independence Day
Peter's Christmas
Zachary's Christmas
Roy's Independence Day
Damien's Christmas

AND THE NAVY
Christmas at Steel Beach
Christmas at Peleliu Cove

5E
Target of the Heart
Target Lock on Love
Target of Mine

Firehawks

MAIN FLIGHT
Pure Heat
Full Blaze
Hot Point
Flash of Fire
Wild Fire

SMOKEJUMPERS
Wildfire at Dawn
Wildfire at Larch Creek
Wildfire on the Skagit

Delta Force
Target Engaged
Heart Strike
Wild Justice

White House Protection Force
Off the Leash
On Your Mark
In the Weeds

Where Dreams
Where Dreams are Born
Where Dreams Reside
Where Dreams Are of Christmas
Where Dreams Unfold
Where Dreams Are Written

Eagle Cove
Return to Eagle Cove
Recipe for Eagle Cove
Longing for Eagle Cove
Keepsake for Eagle Cove

Henderson's Ranch
Nathan's Big Sky
Big Sky, Loyal Heart

Love Abroad
Heart of the Cotswolds: England
Path of Love: Cinque Terre, Italy

Dead Chef Thrillers
Swap Out!
One Chef!
Two Chef!

Deities Anonymous
Cookbook from Hell: Reheated
Saviors 101

SF/F Titles
The Nara Reaction
Monk's Maze
the Me and Elsie Chronicles

Strategies for Success (NF)
Managing Your Inner Artist/Writer
Estate Planning for Authors

It was still confusing. *Major* Ivy Hanson—recently promoted to White House Liaison to Marine Corps HMX-1 squadron—didn't match the woman inside her head. She brushed the cool metal of her golden oak leaves and they were definitely on *her* shoulders: not captain, major. For the tenth time she double-checked that the Eagle, Globe, and Anchor insignias on the collar points of her Marine Corps dress blues were fully upright.

They were.

She really had to calm down about this. She was a Marine—though at the moment it felt as if that was the only thing she knew for certain.

The VH-3D White Top helicopter eased out of Joint Base Anacostia-Bolling, gaining altitude slowly. The President's helicopter—which would be designated Marine One if he was aboard—was a strange, anachronistic beast of a machine.

For years Ivy had flown one of the newest helicopter types there was: the massive and highly innovative MV-22B Osprey tilt-rotor. And now she was aboard the President's vintage helicopter: a fifty-year-old machine that was somehow maintained into a far more perfect condition than her prior ride. The ancient White Top also carried more armor than her MV-22B and was far more luxurious. Instead of the sharp bite of hydraulic oil and unrelenting reek of jarhead sweat, the cabin smelled of lemon furniture polish and fine leather. Which, to a former combat pilot, was wrong on so many levels that it was better not to think about it.

Despite the soothing, air-conditioned, and well sound-insulated environment keeping the heavy load of rotor noise at a comfortable distance, her nerves continued flying sky high just as they'd been ever since she'd gotten dressed this morning.

There was a feel to dress blues that no amount of wear or dry cleaning could remove. From the steam-ironed pants' crease to its brass buttons to the gold of her major's oak leaves on her shoulder boards, blues were something special—somehow *other*. The stiff collar reminiscent of the high leather collar that had earned them the nickname "leathernecks" over two centuries ago was a badge of honor every Marine wore proudly. She always felt stronger, more powerful in her dress uniform. And far taller than she was—which was especially neat as at five-four she didn't come up to most Marines' shoulders.

Her full flight gear from her eight years piloting the MV-22B Ospreys came a close second as her favorite clothing, but there was a small and very egotistical part of her that loved the dress blues: all of her service ribbons on display, her aviator wings flying high above them—the Corps in all its righteous glory. No ceremonial sword today, but hers was so short to match her frame that she always felt a little foolish when she brandished it. She was fine without her sword.

But she was sitting in the observer's seat rather than the pilot's. That too was intensely disorienting.

A glance aft didn't reveal thirty Marines loaded for bear or a 155 mm howitzer ready to unleash havoc thirty kilometers past wherever she dropped it. Instead it revealed the President's armchair, another facing his, and a long bench seat for six aides.

Directly behind the President was a seat for his personal aide. And at the back corner, just aft of the rear door, was one last seat for the head of the Presidential Protection Detail. At the moment, Ivy was the only person in the cabin other than the Marine Corps crew chief who sat in the seat closest behind the pilots.

She was seated sideways, instead of facing ahead. Coming at her new assignment sideways was okay, as long as she got there.

Because it was *exactly* where she wanted to be.

REX ALWAYS WANTED to be somewhere else and constantly hauled at his leash to prove it.

Colby guided him down the South Lawn of the White House, leaning back against the leash's pull. His German shepherd was on the hunt for any hint of explosives and he was one hard-charging canine Secret Service agent.

Rex cracked him up.

He treated sniffing for explosives as if they were the most important thing in the world, which was exactly what he'd been trained to do. The joke was that he was a dog. EDT—Explosive Detection Team—dogs didn't really care crap about explosives. They just knew that they got a treat if they found some or checked a whole area and found none. Rex was super smart about everything except his treats—which had almost flunked him out of the Secret Service's dog school. It had taken Colby a lot of work to teach him that giving false positives didn't earn him more goodies.

Colby scanned the grounds. Two floppy-eared dogs working the outside of the fence line, checking on tourists. From here he could make out two of the three vans that housed ERTs—Emergency Response Teams of dog and handler. The handlers would be watching everything using binoculars through the tinted windows, ready to release their dogs if needed. Those dogs made

Rex look mild by comparison. An ERT dog would go after explosives, but that wasn't their primary job. They trained to take down fence jumpers—hard. He traded waves with another ERT team strolling the close perimeter around the White House itself.

He and Rex had risen to the top of the puppy pile, earning them the informal title of Lead Dog. Colby had come to enjoy wrangling the various handlers and types of dogs. But his favorite were times like this, when it was just him and Rex checking it all out.

The one thing he'd never let go of as he moved up the ladder was the South Lawn patrol. They'd been doing it together for the last four years of the six they'd been working together. He'd gotten Rex when he was two years old and they trained together, then started over at the Capitol. For a while they'd been loaned out to different teams: the Speaker, the home of the Vice President, and visiting dignitaries.

Four years ago they'd made the grade and been advanced to the White House. Now they both had the routine down. Zigzagging back and forth, they crisscrossed any possible path the President could take from Marine One to the White House. Every line from the South Portico of the Residence over to the outside door of the Oval Office.

Even though Colby knew it was just a training flight coming in this morning—he didn't bother telling Rex or taking it any less seriously. Though this flight would be a pain. Some new honcho was coming in on a free ride and their undue pride was always hard to swallow, but Colby timed it just like normal anyway. He and Rex worked their way down the lawn until they arrived in the landing zone itself at the same time as the groundskeepers. They were rolling out the trio of two-meter aluminum disks to protect the lawn by making temporary landing pads for the helicopter's three landing gear.

A quick sniff by Rex to make sure that someone hadn't jumped the fence in the night—undetected by patrols, rooftop snipers, or the array of motion sensors—to plant a bomb under Marine One's landing pads. It was all clear and the big red disks with their white crosses at the center were flopped into place. Fast work with a tape measure assured the guys that they'd dropped them spot-on to match the helicopter's undercarriage. A quick glance at the spacing told him they were expecting one of the VH-3D Sea Kings rather than a VH-60N White Hawk, the only two types of aircraft authorized to land on the White House lawn.

"Hey, one of these days, you should set them up for something huge like a Chinook or maybe a tiny Little Bird and see what those flyboys do."

"You want to piss off a Marine Corps pilot, I'll leave that to you." Jonesy, the head of the groundskeepers, grinned at him. He also kept a watchful eye as his crew pinned down two six-inch-by-twenty-foot strips of canvas in an L-shape that would give the pilots their centerline and final nose position.

"Hell hath no fury like a pissed-off jarhead," Colby agreed.

"Ain't that the truth, bro. You up for poker on Friday?"

"Sure. I need some easy cash." He guided Rex in an expanding spiral around the helicopter's landing zone until they reached the trees.

"Too bad you still owe me twenty from last week," Jonesy called.

Colby pretended he hadn't heard as he guided Rex through the last lap of the spiral.

Nothing to report, boss, Rex's expression said as he looked up at the end of it.

Colby lobbed a couple of treats and Rex snatched them out of the air with sharp snaps of his big jaws.

He gave Rex the hand sign to relax. He couldn't see the inbound helo yet, but if they were on time, they'd be here in two more minutes. And one thing could be said for Marines, they were always on time—no matter *what* was in their way.

TODAY'S FLIGHT was only three miles. But those three miles were along the *most* highly-engineered, regulated, and secure flight route in the country. Which might be exactly why Ivy liked it so much.

For every pilot who made the grade to fly to the White House, hundreds applied. The posting was considered the highest honor for a Marine Corps flyer. These were the very best pilots in the entire Corps, meaning the best in the world—no matter what any other unit thought.

She'd always dreamed of being a Marine One pilot—a member of the most elite flying team anywhere. But she'd found something even better. Only one flight officer at a time made it to being the HMX-1 liaison to the White House Military Office.

And that was her.

Newly promoted Major Ivy Hanson. A field grade officer. Her parents had nearly died with pride, especially Mom. One more rank and she'd be the same grade as Lt. Colonel Marina Hanson (retired).

The pilots were hers—not to command, that was still General Arnson's billet—but she would be assigning all of their missions.

Starting today.

From the *White House!*

In charge of all operational planning for the unit. She'd tell them where and when she needed heliborne assets and General Arnson would make sure that they delivered every single time.

She kept her breath under strict control, because she was a Marine and never showed nerves or doubts. The overwhelming excitement was harder to keep hidden. She was a professional and that's all her team would ever see. But she could hear her heart pounding louder than the muffled rotors. And the adrenaline was almost as sharp at the back of her throat as the lingering hints of the half-burned kerosene from the cold engine start.

Once off the tarmac at Anacostia-Bolling Air Base, they turned due west. A quarter of a mile across Hains Point—the southern tip of East Potomac Park—to the middle of the Potomac River.

"Any problem, Captain?" She called forward to the pilot. It was weird that the sound insulation was so good she didn't even need an intercom headset. There was something intrinsically wrong with that; it hardly felt like a helicopter at all.

"Why do you ask, Major?" She knew Walters well enough to hear the amusement in his voice.

"Your rate of climb is below simulator profile. Just wondering if there's a reason."

"No reason that I can think of, Major." But neither did he begin to climb more rapidly.

The crew chief pointed out the side window. She turned and looked down at the island below just as one of the two decoy helicopters—Presidential helos typically flew in packs of three, constantly shuffling places to keep the President's actual position hidden—flew by them even a little lower.

The thirty-six holes of Hains Point Golf Course covered this entire end of the island. They were low enough that she could see the main rotor's downwash blow away one golfer's hat and another's umbrella. They passed so close that she could see players shaking their little putters at them as their balls were rolled about the green. At least that explained why the pilots chose to fly so low. In addition to the rough and sand traps, this particular golf course had the occasional air hazard.

It reminded her of the day she'd found out that Drill Sergeant McKinnon, much to her surprise, wasn't a sadistic asshole. Or perhaps that he wasn't *just* a sadistic asshole. On graduation night from Officer Candidate School, she'd spotted him drinking quietly in the back of a Marine bar while her class was whooping it up in the front. He'd waved her over. She could still feel the nerves that had shaken her as she crossed the room, but it was one of what she'd come to think of as McKinnon's Laws.

Being a Marine doesn't mean that you're not afraid. It means that you don't give a damn if you are.

Once she sat, he'd looked at her a long time in silence, but she'd waited him out until he'd finally acknowledged her with a nod of what actually looked like satisfaction.

"You're gonna be one hell of an officer, Second Lieutenant Ivy Hanson. So let me tell you all the things you're going to want to do wrong." And they'd talked right through last call; she'd still been on her first beer after many of her classmates were face-down on the floor and being shoveled out the door.

Another of his laws was: *You're going to want your people to behave perfectly. They're Marines, so they will when it matters. Don't sweat the small stuff. They'll respect you for letting them be human. But you draw the line and don't let anyone cross it. Ever! Or they'll run right over you.*

Batting down golf balls with a twenty-million-dollar helicopter struck her as small stuff. But they already knew that General Arnson expected them to land inside a ten-second window every time—even on a training flight like this one—and that she'd expect no less. The Army's Night Stalkers said plus or minus thirty seconds in any battlefield, and they delivered. But these were the fliers of Marine One and nobody kicked ass like the Corps.

Across the golf course and over the Potomac, they finally reached the mission profile's altitude. There was nothing like the DC skyline from five hundred feet.

COLBY GLANCED up at the snipers on the West Wing roof.

Two of them had their rifles aimed high and due south. With their spotter scopes, they were always the first to see the approaching helos. By their very steadiness, he knew the guys had picked them out. That placed the helos out over the Potomac and just turning north.

He wondered how the Marine Corps pilots felt, knowing they were in the sights of the snipers. Wouldn't be his first choice, but they were Marines, so what did he care?

Four years—more importantly four DC springtimes—and he still wasn't used to working here. The Presidential Park was stunning this time of year. The new-mown grass smelled rich with May sunshine. The trees were all leafed out, but still brilliantly green—the darker shades of summer were a month away yet. The morning breeze was out of the west, from over the vegetable garden. Nothing much to smell from that quarter yet, just lots of green shoots; though there was a hint of chlorine from the freshly refilled swimming pool. The Rose and Kennedy Gardens lay to the north of his current position so he couldn't smell them even though they were already rich with lush flowers.

Perfect season to take a girl for a walk through them, except he didn't have a girl since Elsie had given him the heave-ho. And escorting a congressional secretary around the White House grounds like it was good place to bring a date wasn't exactly the best idea…no matter what Elsie had thought.

Just as well. Rex had never liked her much, which should have told him something a lot sooner than 20-20 hindsight. Rex was happy now because he'd gotten back his spot on the couch. And Colby was done with clubbing, never a big hit with him anyway, and was back to his ESPN and action flicks. He knew it was a stereotype, but anything was better than pounding sound systems among bodies so tightly packed together that they were indistinguishable— when the whole point of going in the first place was to "be seen."

"Need to find us some girls, boy." Not that Rex had the anatomy to care about those anymore.

Colby wasn't sure how much he himself cared either.

Elsie had been fun, and watching her dance never failed to fire up his libido. Too bad that was all she'd fired up. They'd been good together in bed, but not much heat otherwise—either good or bad. They hadn't fought often, but they hadn't done the whole close-couple thing either.

He looked aloft and spotted the trio of helos as tiny black dots. That placed them even with the Pentagon.

Colby still felt the thrill every time. It didn't matter if it was the President himself or an empty training run, there was something majestic about watching them approach that he'd never tire of.

This time they'd told him to there was a sole passenger for him to escort to security. Captain Baxter—the head of the Secret Service Uniformed Division for the White House—wasn't big on extra words, like who the hell Colby was meeting. Just some officious official who'd finally earned enough rank to con a ride on the helo. He would be so totally full of himself after the HMX-1 ride that Colby suspected he'd want to unleash Rex on the pompous jerk by the time they had crossed half the lawn.

Colby backed off from the three landing disks and watched the helos come in.

<hr>

IVY COULDN'T DECIDE where to look. The crew chief was grinning at her, but it was impossible to be blasé about the ride or the amazing view.

There were a few days that particularly stood out in memory: her first ever solo in a Bell UH-1 Huey, four combat missions that she wished she didn't remember quite so accurately in her nightmares, and a few others. She knew today would join those.

Once they were at altitude past the golf course, the flight had smoothed out as a serious focus took over. She checked the time mark on the dash when they crossed above the Arland D.

Williams Jr. Memorial Bridge. Just five seconds early for this particular profile—her kind of flight.

The Pentagon dominated the view to the west. To the east, the Tidal Basin cherry trees bloomed like a bridal bouquet gone madly pink—past their peak but still radiant in early-May glory. Then the majestic turn that placed the Jefferson Memorial due east and the Washington Monument dead ahead.

Pilots flew it a hundred times in the simulator before they were allowed to even fly as copilot. She had "ridden" along on twenty of those simulations herself so that she could witness all of the primary emergency scenarios.

But to be able to fly the route itself, even as an observer, was like a miracle. Never expecting to command them, she'd been gunning for the post of Presidential pilot since boot camp, a fact she hadn't even told Drill Sergeant McKinnon. Though proving that nothing ever got by him, just this morning she'd received a text from him, his first contact in years. He'd spared two whole words for her: *Go Marine!*

She'd been shocked that her heart hadn't blown right out the chest of her dress blues. In an excess of pride, she'd sent back *four* words that, of course, he hadn't replied to: *For the Corps, Sergeant.* In hindsight, she should have sent *Semper Fi!* Short for *Semper Fidelis,* always faithful. Two words for two words.

She'd broken McKinnon's Law of: *Never use extra words. They only serve to cloud the communication.*

Tough! She was damn proud of what she'd done and she was a major so she'd use four whole words if she felt like it. If McKinnon had ever laughed, she could imagine him laughing at her. But it was impossible to imagine he ever had, so she was safe on that account.

They crossed the middle of the National Mall between the very top of the Washington Monument and the World War II Memorial at the foot of the Reflecting Pool three seconds behind schedule. No one but a Marine would notice.

McKinnon had been right. Let the boys have a little fun when it didn't matter and they'd perform all the better when it did. The pilots wanted this flight to be perfect as badly as she did.

Nothing had prepared her for the real view of the White House from the air—something so few ever saw. In the simulator it had looked amazing: interactive video simulated from high-resolution 3D imaging. But that was nothing compared to the real thing. Now she was looking down on the South Lawn from above as the pilots eased between the trees, doing the trademark quarter turn down between the treetops to turn the President's helo door so that it faced the White House. There it was, the center of government—the home of the Commander-in-Chief himself.

And her new office.

She'd probably never get to take this ride again, so she'd promised herself to pay attention to every detail, every moment. Yet between one eyeblink and the next, they were settling down on the lawn, landing on the trio of six-foot aluminum disks rolled out to protect the lawn.

Of course, during the last few meters of the landing itself, the pilots were unable to see the disks themselves. But no Marine pilot would take that as an excuse to miss landing precisely on those hidden disks. No signalman stood by waving batons, just those two strips of canvas. Marine Corps pilots didn't need anyone else's help to nail a landing.

Contact two seconds early—dead zero as the shock absorbers fully took the weight of the seven tons of helicopter, fuel, and extra armor. She thumped a fist on Captain Walters' shoulder and she heard his pleased chuckle.

They went through the full routine: cycling down the engines before the Marine crew chief opened the forward door and lowered the stairway. He then did a military march, three steps out, six steps to the rear, and three steps in to lower the rear door and stair. The front door of the helo was reserved for the use of the First Family and the crew chief. All others used the rear stairs.

So she placed her white, field officer cover squarely on her head and walked down the length of the cabin. At the rear stairs she made her own neat right angle turn and descended down onto the grass of the immaculately manicured White House lawn. Per protocol, the crew chief had returned to stand beside the forward stairs. There he stood at parade rest with his hands clasped behind his back, ready to aid or honor the President. As she stopped two steps in front of him, he saluted sharply.

She couldn't resist looking down at the wheels first. The center of all three white crosses were hidden by the black rubber of the tires—hitting the marks within six inches in the blind on a six-foot disk. She returned the sergeant's sharp salute, then shot a thumb's up to Walters, who grinned in relief. *Go Marines!*

McKinnon's Law: *Let them know when they done good and you never have to tell them when they done bad. They'll know.* His corollary, which she'd also proven many times: *Tell them about the second screwup. Third time ask yourself if they're really Corps material.*

"Thank you, Sergeant Mathieson." She automatically checked the crew chief's uniform. He was one squared-away Marine. Too bad about the officer-enlisted gap, because he was also damn fine looking in his dress blues. He had three bronze hashes on his sleeve, marking twelve years of service. He'd earned his right to stand there and look magnificent.

"A pleasure, Major." His smile said that he might be thinking the same thing about her. Nothing would ever happen there, but it didn't hurt her ego in the slightest.

She almost wished the Press Corps was around so that someone would get a photograph of her striding this one time across the South Lawn in her uniform.

When she turned to walk up the lawn, Ivy nearly tripped over one of the biggest German shepherds she'd ever seen. He was wearing a US Secret Service vest and a giant-sized doggie smile that revealed equally large teeth.

"Hey there, Saint Ives!"

Ivy sighed. Only one person had ever called her that.

COLBY HAD TAKEN his normal station on the back side of the helo's landing area, between there and the distant fence. This was his station, keeping an eye out for any last-minute fence jumpers. Once the helo was down and stopped, he'd circled around the tail, arriving just in time to see the back of the officious official.

Except the officious official was a pint-sized Marine in full dress blues, a female one. As trim and perfect as a wind-up doll, complete with her hair wound into that donut-shaped bun that female Marines wore. They never had a single strand astray because that would be against regulations and even a Marine's hair follicles followed regulations. She looked a hundred percent delectable and he no longer minded having to escort her to the White House. Maybe she'd like a personal tour of the White House.

He hadn't been ready for when she turned to salute the sergeant by the front stair. It was a profile he'd know anywhere. Moving closer didn't change who it was. Their families were neighbors and her older brother was still his best friend. But when did Ivy Hanson start to look like this? She'd been overseas so much these last several years that he'd only seen her in passing.

Rex moved in to sniff her just as she did a military about-face and almost trompled him.

"Yipes!" Her cry of surprise as she stared down at the dog and fought for balance was pretty funny.

"Hey there, Saint Ives."

She closed her eyes in a deeply pained expression.

When she'd turned to face him, it was like being hit by a taser blast. Little Saint Ives transformed into a Marine Corps officer in her dress blues was messing with his head. She carried a dark blue leather-encased tablet computer that managed to make her look even more official and impressive.

That's when he noticed her shoulder insignia.

"Major? Whoo-hoo! When did you get them pretty little leaves on your collar?" He had to say something to distract himself from the conflicting thoughts she was firing into his brain. Little Ivy and sexy Marine Corps major was a very weird juxtaposition.

"Last week," she heaved a sigh. Even the dress blues couldn't conceal the very pleasant movement of her chest. Then she opened her eyes again, which were bluer than the DC springtime sky.

"Would you mind getting your dog out of my way?" Rex had sat after giving her a good sniff.

Colby looked down at her. He'd always remembered her as a little bit of a thing, three years younger besides. She'd always been cute as hell, but she was completely under the best-friend's-little-sister rule: no touch, no look, no think. Hell, he'd practically helped raise her. It was a rule he'd always been fine with, mostly. He'd certainly never told Reggie about any stray thoughts to the contrary. Or Ivy. She'd have flattened him even if he could have picked her up one-handed.

But she didn't look like anybody's kid sister in her Marine Corps uniform. She was breathtaking.

"Colby," she let a Marine growl into her voice, sounding almost as gruff as Rex, who cocked his head to listen to her. That was funny enough to give him back the power of speech.

"Afraid not, Ives. Rex is sitting for a reason. Want to explain it to me or should I frisk you?"

"You. Wouldn't. Dare!" She shifted her weight to her back foot. The Secret Service had given him enough hand-to-hand combat training to recognize a fighter's stance when he saw one. That's when he remembered that one teased Saint Ives at their own risk. She'd been a taekwondo black belt by junior high and judo black belt in high school. Or was it jiu-jitsu? Dangerous as hell either way. More than once she'd taken him down despite the age and size difference. Even before she'd become a Marine, she'd always fought like a girl—to win.

"It was range work and you damn well know it. He's looking right at my sidearm." And Rex *was* staring at her holster. Detection dogs triggered to spent powder. Then she pulled out her White House ID, looped the band over her head, and held it out for Colby to see. She had full Proximity Clearance—which meant that not only could she stand beside the President unescorted, but she was also one of the select few outside the Secret Service who were authorized to be armed in his presence.

He should read her badge, but he couldn't look away from her photo. Not even for a White House badge had Ivy been able to lock down that brilliant smile of hers. It was like she was looking right at him, as if he was a ray of sunshine on a winter's day.

Then he managed to look up from her photo and into her face. Not so much with the smile—sunshiny or otherwise.

His leaning down had placed their faces entirely too close together. She didn't get this close to anyone.

Typical jerk, leaning in so close. Colby knew he was a handsome SOB, but the emphasis was on being a son of a bitch—and not in the good, Marine Corps sense of the word. He looked really good and…she'd clearly lost her mind.

The last year that she'd spent with HMX-1 had been brutally hard, trying to live up to the impossible standards that challenged every single jarhead in the squadron. General Arnson drove his Marines just as hard as he drove himself. She'd never served with such an exceptional team before. But it had also meant she'd had no time for more personal liaisons.

And now Colby stood so close that she could smell—

McKinnon's Law: *Marine first, second, and third. Everything else comes fourth.*

"Back off, Thompson." He jolted away as if she'd slapped him, his eyes a little wild.

So much for her dignified arrival at the White House.

She glanced back and caught Sergeant Mathieson's smile as he marched the six steps from closing the rear door of the White Top and returned to the forward stairs. He turned to climb the stairs himself and his smile was hidden from view. Then she spotted Captain Walters' grin through the pilot's side window. She really didn't need this.

Ego don't mean shit in the Corps. And McKinnon's wisdom wasn't helping her ego at all.

"What are you doing here?" Colby said it as a whisper.

"I'm the new HMX-1 liaison to the White House Military Office."

"The WHMO?" That earned her a whistle of surprise. "You know that those guys are a little freaky, right?"

Hard challenges are what Marines live for!

"Damn straight!" Ivy wasn't sure if she was answering Colby or an imaginary McKinnon. Though Colby was right. The WHMO was one of those quiet agencies that almost no one had ever heard of. Yet Marine One, Air Force One, the ceremonial Marine sentries, the Nuclear Football with the President's launch codes—all that was only part of what they did.

"What are *you* doing here?" She tried to step around Rex, but he shifted to keep giving his warning signal. Colby put on his best innocent look, which never fooled anybody.

"Any landing of the Marine helos on the South Lawn is part of Rex's and my patrol. We secure the passage, the landing area, then act as backup on standby. If I'm right there," he pointed off to the side as if she cared what he did, "then I'm not in any Press Corps photos either."

Overhead, the helo's engines began whining to life. The rotors swung through their first lazy turn. Then another. Burning kerosene replaced the smell of fresh-mown grass.

When Ivy again tried to step around Rex, the low growl that emanated from his chest was loud enough to be easily heard despite the escalating noise of the twin turbine engines. She froze in place. In fact, she was fairly certain that she stopped breathing entirely. He really was huge; his shoulders practically reached her waist.

Colby flickered a hand sign to Rex to ease off. But the dog was too busy pointing his nose at her sidearm. He tried again. Still nothing.

Ivy offered him a smirk. Still the same old Colby, never having his act together.

IVY'S SMILE wasn't all happy and friendly like the one on her ID—it was more, *What a goon!*

He signaled Rex one more time, but he was too busy looking at Ivy. Who could blame him? Somewhere over the last few years while he hadn't been paying attention, she had tipped over from being a cute, feisty, pain-in-the-ass to being a gorgeous Marine warrior. He finally had to call out, *"Gute Hund."* Rex looked up at him but didn't move until Colby remembered to fumble out a dog treat.

Once he had happily chomped it down, Rex sprang to his feet and let Ivy step past. She didn't scowl at the dog, but she did scowl at him. Not his best day's work.

Behind them, the helicopter's rotors wound up to full speed. But he didn't look. He was too busy trying to catch up to the striding Marine a head shorter than he was.

"Such," he told Rex with the hard German ch. *Seek.* And they were alongside Ivy in a moment.

"Because of course a German shepherd speaks German," Ivy

didn't ease up from her military perfect posture as she strode across the lawn. Her voice carried easily over the roar of the departing helo. She'd never been soft-spoken, but the Marine Major carried an authority that he wasn't sure what to do with.

"Of course," he agreed amiably. Actually, it was a very common practice among military and Secret Service dogs to train them in German. It avoided confusion in a crowd. The number of German words spoken by the Secret Service in general conversation were few and far between, so it also decreased the chances of a false signal to the dog.

But what Colby was wondering about was if Ivy's perfect posture was a leftover from all the ballet she'd done as a kid or martial arts as a teen? Or was it pure Marine? Whichever it was, she was making it damn hard to remember the best-friend's-little-sister rule at the moment. Major Ivy Hanson was a serious woman who looked amazing in her dress uniform.

"Don't you have something else to do?"

"Nope, can't think of a thing." Rex was tugging ahead, sniffing the air that he'd just checked coming the other way before the helicopter had landed. Unlike the friendly, floppy-eared dogs who patrolled among the tourists on the outside of the White House fence line, Rex was eighty-seven pounds of hard-driven canine who had never learned to be easy on the leash when he was on the job. He'd dump someone as small as Ivy right on her face as he charged ahead.

Then Colby looked over at her again.

Marine tough. Not a button or hair out of place. Enough ribbons on her chest to tell him that she wasn't good at what she did—she was exceptional. Of course he wouldn't expect anything less from Saint Ives.

Maybe she'd be just fine handling Rex.

"Colby, I know how to walk to the damn White House alone."

"You can try, but it's not gonna happen."

"And why not?"

"Because for roughly the next ten minutes, I've been assigned to be *your* liaison to the White House."

"For reasons beyond understanding."

"For reasons of security. You've entered the White House grounds without passing through Security. Just because they let you onto the Anacostia airbase and aboard a White Top helo doesn't cut it with the United States Secret Service. That means that you have an escort until you're registered as being on the grounds. Think you can put up with me for that long, Saint Ives?"

"I don't know. It will be hard. But we Marines are used to shouldering heavy burdens." She delivered it in a flat tone, but that smile of hers slipped out and lit up her face.

It was a good thing the White House kitchen was in the basement of the Residence. That's where her brother, Reggie worked —so he wouldn't be able to see what was going on.

What was going on?

Colby didn't know. But he knew he wanted to see Saint Ives smile at him like that again—really soon.

Then Rex swung left as Colby stumbled off to the right. He was thinking of Saint Ives *how?* Reggie would kill him.

Off balance and looking the wrong way, Colby went down on the South Lawn—face first. Leftover grass clippings were plastered to his face and he brushed at them frantically.

Rex spun to look at him in surprise. He heard a sharp laugh from one of the Delta snipers on the roof of the West Wing.

Saint Ives didn't even break her stride, but it was easy to imagine her eye roll. Easy money said she'd make a point of rubbing in his clumsiness as well.

THE WHITE HOUSE LOOMED. Ivy had been here dozens of times working with the White House Military Office as part of her training, but she'd never stood on the South Lawn before. She'd also never arrived by helicopter, but it was still the same White House. It was still the same WHMO.

Except it completely wasn't.

It was as if she'd teleported down onto another planet and was caught in one of those *Star Trek* back-in-time episodes.

Here she was, walking across the South Lawn. The long arms of the East and West Wings wholly overshadowed by the towering white facade of the Residence. Fifty meters wide and twenty high, it looked as if the mass of sandstone was going to tumble down the gentle slope and crush her.

Overseas, she'd seen far too much of Libya and plenty of Iraq and Yemen from the air. Her Marine Expeditionary Unit—MEU —had gone on to Syria at the same time her requested transfer to HMX-1 had come through. She still felt bad about that. However, after the recent attack on the Presidential Motorcade, she was feeling less guilty. The President needed the best protection there was. That's why the Marines were on the job.

But now she was a sole Marine—without the two thousand other Marines of her MEU—walking toward the most imposing facade in the nation's capital. Perhaps in the world.

Walk like you own it!

Yeah right, Sergeant. It was an act of sheer will to remain upright despite her knees gone to liquid.

She held the line set by Colby. The South Portico with its twin sweep of stairs was off to her right. And to her left, the Oval Office dominated the South Lawn from its corner. It actually didn't look like much, a curved wall with a lot of windows and several tactically placed trees that would mask the Oval Office from a distant shooter. But even though the President was at Camp David with the Australian Prime Minister, the Oval Office was there and she could feel the windowed eyes watching her every step.

Colby had been guiding her toward the Rose Garden. The entrance there led into the hall that ran between the Press

Briefing and Cabinet Rooms. Past those lay the main floor of the West Wing, but there was a stairway around the first corner that would allow her to descend into the far less scary ground floor of the West Wing.

"Does it still spook you every time you walk here?" Ivy whispered her question to Colby as she crossed the paved circular driveway for the South Portico.

When he didn't respond, she looked over at him, except he wasn't there. He was behind her, trotting to catch up. Rex had a happy smile and lolling tongue as he had a chance to move with a springy lope rather than dragging at his leash.

"What happened to your knees?" His dark slacks were brightly grass-stained along with one of the elbows of his white shirt.

Colby just glared at her like he was some kind of pissed. About what, who knew? Or cared? Not her.

Ten minutes. That's what he'd said. *Fine!* She was a Marine. She could cover a kilometer wearing a forty-pound rucksack in under ten minutes—she could certainly deal with Colby Thompson for that long. Thank goodness they didn't have to work together.

She turned back just in time to plow into a small Shetland Sheepdog that yipped in surprise as a young voice called out, "Zackie!"

***

COLBY MANAGED to grab Ivy's arm before she plummeted to the ground. As a result of his grasp, they performed a small whirling dance. He almost had their balance right—except Rex, as he'd been trained to do during the unexpected, firmly braced himself to act as a support if needed.

Instead of support, the sudden tightening of the leash in his hand tipped Colby's own balance past recovery. If he'd let go of the leash or Ivy at that moment, she might have been fine. But some part of him hadn't cooperated and he was dragging her down with him.

With a sharp twist, he managed to get his back to the lawn and take the brunt of the fall—squarely on his spare: the Glock handgun that he kept at the small of his back. Pain sliced up his back.

The rigid black brim of Ivy's hat cracked him sharply enough across the bridge of his nose to bring tears to his eyes. And the impact of her fist, tightly clutched around her tablet computer, nailed him in the solar plexus.

"What the hell?" Ivy shouted at him from an inch away.

All he could answer with were small *whoop* noises as he desperately struggled to take a breath. That Ivy continued to lie full upon him made it even harder to recover.

He'd only ever let himself think about how goddamn cute Ivy was—and even that little bit only on rare occasions before he caught himself. He'd never thought of what it would be like to actually touch her or...

Lying full upon him, she didn't feel like a best friend's little sister under a no-touch-no-think interdiction. She was no longer the little girl he'd practically helped raise.

Colby inhaled through his nose to force his breathing to slow down. It was the fastest way to recover from a solar plexus hit. But it also filled his senses with her scent. She smelled of glory and gunmetal, of spring grass and not even a little bit of the teenage girl running down the beach in a hormone-busting sleek one-piece. As she struggled to free herself, she nearly cut off his nose with one of her collar-point insignias. She felt so light, except against his diaphragm, which was registering a weight somewhere between elephant and lying under one of the wheels of Air Force One. *Whoop. Whoop.*

"Let. Go. Of. Me." Ivy ground out the syllables like a military command.

It took him a moment to identify that his hands were still

firmly clenched about her upper arms. Serious biceps and triceps there for a woman. Rex was sitting off to the side holding his own leash, which Colby had finally dropped, between his teeth.

It took Colby several moments more to unclench his grasp without setting off more spasms in his chest.

In seconds, Ivy's weight was gone. She now stood, brushing at her immaculate uniform. No grass stain would dare impinge on her perfection.

Perfection. That was Ivy Hanson's specialty. That's why he'd tagged her as Saint Ives when she was all of five. The nickname had worked on several other levels as well—particularly in that it had always irritated her.

Saint Ives *lived* to be in hot pursuit of the absolute perfect. Nothing less, in herself or others, was ever tolerated. As a kid he'd first thought it was ridiculous. Then later, a little terrifying.

By the time she'd hit high school and was entering state-wide martial arts competitions, he'd wondered what he'd been missing by not trying harder to achieve something—anything. He was smart enough that he'd been able to loaf through high school without much effort. With Ivy jarring his attitude, he managed to kick a little ass in college with solid grades and a state swimming championship.

He'd always been a good swimmer. The Thompsons and the Hansons had side-by-side cabins near Ocean City on the Maryland barrier islands. They'd all been swimming through the breakers since the time they could walk. College had simply honed that natural ability until it felt as if he owned that skill.

By the time he made the Secret Service, it felt as if he was in control of his life. Dog handler at the White House totally rocked.

Then Saint Ives shows up. She'd driven him to become who he was, even if she didn't know anything about that. But instead of living up to that standard, suddenly he was in high school not-living-up-to-his-potential mode again. It wasn't fair.

He sat up once his gut muscles could tolerate a sit-up. A sit-up square into a giant face lick by Zackie.

"Dilya! Get your dog off me!" But he smiled and scrubbed the Sheltie on the head, making her wag her tail happily, to show there were no hard feelings. It wasn't the First Dog's fault that it was so excessively cheerful; just part of the breed.

"She's not my dog."

"As good as."

He looked up at Dilya. The teen was the First Dog's handler as well as the on-site babysitter for the former-President-turned-Secretary-of-State's child. And now with the First and Second ladies both pregnant, she was soon going to have her hands full. It was a good thing she was finishing high school a year ahead next month.

"You hear from the schools yet?"

"Georgetown. Political science and international affairs double major. So, I still get to play part-time nanny and dog sitter here."

"Wow! You go, girl. Too bad you weren't born in the US. I'd vote for you for President." Dilya was seventeen, brilliant, and—he had to blink a few times—fast becoming a gorgeous young woman. Her Uzbekistani medium-dark skin and long black ruffled hair were offset by brilliant green eyes. She was taller than Ivy, but gawky-teen slender rather than Ivy's ever-so-nice, hyper-fit, Marine Corps trim. The guys were definitely going to be hounding her heels.

Though Dilya also mysteriously seemed to be at the center of everything that happened around the White House.

"President is too visible. Maybe I'll run the CIA instead. Or maybe the Secret Service, then you could work for me." Then she bit her lower lip, clearly something she hadn't meant to say.

Dilya had that same driven enthusiasm that had always made Ivy such a standout.

She hurried on, "I was just walking Zackie when I spotted the helo. She wanted to say hi to Rex."

Colby rose to his feet and gave Dilya the same treatment he'd just given the First Dog: a big head rub to mess up her hair. Though he wouldn't be trying that on Major Ivy Hanson.

"Hey!"

"You heard the helo, knew the First Family wasn't due back yet, and were in too much of a hurry to grab Zackie's leash as you used her as an excuse to rush and see what was going on."

Dilya just grinned at him and held out her empty palms.

"I shouldn't even introduce you."

"Oh, she's Major Ivy Hanson, the new HMX-1 liaison to the WHMO," Dilya *did* know everything. "Hi, I'm Dilya. Sorry about Zackie."

Ivy scowled at him rather than the dog.

"Are you okay, Ives?"

"Little slow with that question, Colby. This is your idea of a welcoming committee?"

"No, Rex and I typically reserve this particular type of greeting for visiting heads of state. The Pope and I had a nice roll around the fountain one particularly sunny afternoon." He pointed to where the big fountain splashed cheerfully farther down the South Lawn. With the helo gone, it was the loudest sound there was. The traffic on Constitution Ave beyond the Ellipse was muted by comparison.

"I'm thinking that my brother wouldn't hold it against me if I killed you right now."

"He still owes me fifty bucks from poker the other night, so he might offer to hold me down. Just saying, in case you need to take up a posthumous collection for my funeral expenses. Of course, then you'd have to put up with Rex. He'd whine pitifully if something happened to me."

Ivy looked down at his German shepherd. "You sure about that?"

Rex sent him a questioning look, like: *What are we standing around for?* Or perhaps it was a doubtful look, like: *Miss you? Maybe yes, maybe no.*

COULD she have found any less dignified approach to her first day? Thank God there *hadn't* been a Press Corps photographer around. Ivy brushed at her uniform again, but couldn't find any grass stains.

Rex didn't look like a whiner. More like a furry, four-footed Zulu Cobra attack helo—lean and lethal.

She really needed to have a long talk with Reggie about his choice in best friends. Colby Thompson was definitely a lower life form, the kind a woman scraped off her boot after stepping in it accidentally. He'd always been a lazy, arrogant jerk wholly convinced of his own self-worth with little to no justification.

Then he leaned down to pet his dog and take the leash from the dog's mouth.

But he didn't look useless. Nor had he moved like some bumbler. Her martial arts training let her understand the move he'd done to take the hit of the fall himself. It wasn't something he'd thought about, then done; there wasn't time. It had been an instinctively trained act, trained to the point of reflex, to protect those around him. The fact that it was also a decent and selfless act must be strictly a coincidence.

And lying on him, he hadn't felt useless. Instead he'd…

As he turned to chat with the teen, she could see the grass stains on his white Uniformed Division shirt: both elbows, one shoulder that must have dug in hard to get so green, and a clear imprint of the backup piece at the small of his back that had to really hurt to land on. But no complaints. Instead he'd asked if she was okay. This wasn't any version of Colby Thompson that she recognized. This wasn't the boy who'd taught her to read one moment and started a food fight that she'd been the one to get in all the trouble for the next moment.

Watching his back, she could appreciate other changes in him. He was no longer the whip thin Colby she'd grown up next door to. Somewhere along the way he'd earned himself seriously broad swimmer's shoulders. The rest of his body showed that he made his living on his feet: powerful legs, trim waist, tight—

She was *not* looking at Colby Thompson's glutes.

But she could still feel the strength of his arms as he wrapped them around her to protect her from the fall.

She was a Marine Corps major. She didn't need anyone to protect her. Her aircraft had often been the tip of the spear—first on the ground delivering forward teams beneath the watchful eye of the leading gunships. The only protection she needed was provided by the Corps.

Colby and Dilya appeared ready to chat all through the sunny morning. Zackie and Rex had sat close beside their handlers and were holding a tongue-lolling contest.

Ivy punched Colby on the shoulder, the unstained one to avoid staining her knuckles. Not hard enough to knock him off balance, but hard enough that she double-checked to see if she'd just punched a brick wall. Again, solid muscle and Colby Thompson, hard to equate the two.

"Right. Sorry. Later Dilya." He reached out and messed up the girl's hair again.

He tried that on her and she *would* kill him. Why did guys always think that was so cute? She shared a glance of commiseration with Dilya as the teen struggled to get her hair to lie properly again.

Ivy punched Colby's shoulder again—hard—on Dilya's behalf.

"Hey, what was that for? We're going already." He began leading her once more toward the West Wing.

Ivy glanced back to see Dilya shove enough hair aside to

uncover a wide grin. Ivy found it very easy to smile back before she followed Colby.

Today was supposed to be about stepping into her new job and confirming relationship roles. She checked her *Star Trek* wrist watch—its silver face etched with the lines of the top of the NCC-1701 Enterprise's saucer section was sufficiently elegant and understated to be permissible with her uniform—stated that she still had fifteen minutes before her meeting with Major General Markham, the director of the White House Military Office.

Yet against all common sense, she had the sudden notion that perhaps she'd just had the most important introduction she'd have today. The President's dog walker had known who she was, had the run of the grounds even during an HMX-1 landing, and her innocent teenager act didn't fool Ivy for a second—though Colby appeared to have swallowed it whole.

Or…Ivy was imagining everything and there was a force field around Colby Thompson that projected mental aberrations on unsuspecting Marine Corps majors. That hypothesis at least had a higher degree of plausibility.

As they crossed through the Rose Garden, she glanced back once more.

Dilya had produced a tennis ball from somewhere and was heaving it far out onto the South Lawn. The Sheltie went bounding after it. It could have been any girl playing with her dog. But it wasn't. This was the White House and everything here had more meaning than it would anywhere else. Just as Ivy was turning away, Dilya's bright eyes swung to inspect her again. Focused. Thoughtful.

Yes, the girl was not what she seemed.

The Rose Garden itself was something of a disappointment. In none of her prior visits had she actually been out to see the gardens. The Jackie Kennedy Garden on the far side of the South Portico was a riot of brilliant blooms. The Rose Garden itself was a broad, rectangular expanse of perfectly trimmed lawn. Only the border had trees and flowers. The bright pink of the magnolia tree blossoms were brilliant, but the narrow border of roses and immaculate box hedges didn't impress her much. It was so formal. A rose garden should be a lush affair that abounded with masses of blooms, not some carefully constrained study in rectangles.

Hopefully she wouldn't be disillusioned by trading her chance at being an HMX pilot for the WHMO position.

Colby led her up the broad steps at the far end of the Rose Garden. Atop the steps they crossed the West Colonnade and Colby held the door open for her into the West Wing.

Did that have more meaning too? Colby Thompson had never held a door for her once in all the years growing up together. She'd have remembered if he had, just because it would have been so unusual. He'd been far more likely to "accidentally" let one close in her face. And she'd been just as likely to "accidentally" kick him in the shins shortly afterward.

He had also managed to keep her from disgracing herself and her uniform on her first day. What meaning did that have?

Facts are all that count. Marine officers love conjecture, but never lose sight of the facts! McKinnon had been mostly right about that one. She'd learned that there *were* times to ponder an enemy's intentions, but never to lose sight of the facts.

Fact: She knew Colby Thompson's failures as a human being far too well.

Fact: None of those appeared evident in the man holding the door for her.

Hypothesis: Maybe he was a pod-person, a secret alien substitute in Colby clothing.

Conclusion? She was flying deep in a total brownout.

2

"You're a sad case, Thompson." Captain Baxter's bullhorn voice echoed through the big Secret Service Ready Room in the West Wing's ground floor. It made every agent look up, first at Baxter, then invariably following his glare (as clear as a laser on a foggy night) to the green grass stains all over his clothing.

Colby groaned. He just wasn't going to get a break today. He'd handed off Ivy to security and was gunning for the clean shirt he kept in a desk drawer. The Ready Room was the largest contiguous room in the West Wing. Only the Situation Room was bigger, but it was chopped into eight or ten spaces, or so he'd heard. Even though he walked by it every time he came in the west entrance, he'd never walked through those guarded doors—which was fine with him. He'd seen the looks on the faces of the people headed in and out of there. Merely grim meant it was a good day.

"My office. *After* you've changed." Baxter bullhorned again, then withdrew into his tiny cube of an office at the far end of the room.

The head of the White House Uniformed Division—which

included all of the dog handlers—was a fixture. Rumor was that, when FDR had the West Wing basement dug and built out beneath his fifth cousin Teddy's original structure, they'd unearthed the Captain already at his desk—and built the Ready Room around him. Of course there were also rumors that he'd served in every conflict since the days of Genghis Kahn, so it was hard to tell if the basement rumor was true. Either way, he was as formidable as the bedrock he'd been carved from.

Rex stretched out on his dog bed after Colby stuffed a couple of treats inside a Kong toy and then dropped it for the dog to wrestle with.

Colby dug out a fresh shirt and stripped off the soiled one. He didn't keep extra slacks here, so his knees were just going to be grass-stained all day. He got a round of applause and some catcalls from the eight other agents currently in the room as he stood bare chested by his desk. *Whoops!*

He took a bow.

And stood up to look directly into Ivy's eyes as she passed by the Ready Room door on the way to the White House Military Office that lay another fifty feet down the hall.

Her gaze on him lasted only for the two strides it took her to pass by. Not even a hesitation in her step despite her head turned sideways.

As he was pulling the fresh shirt over his head, he heard a male exclamation of surprise. When Colby dragged the shirt down enough to see, he spotted a staffer now standing framed in the doorway, still stumbling to regain his balance. He looked as if he'd just been rammed by a pint-sized Marine juggernaut who hadn't been looking where she was going. Colby found that strangely encouraging, though he had no idea why, as he hurried to Captain Baxter's office while still tucking in his shirt.

Two offices defined this end of the Ready Room: Baxter's, the lair of the all-seeing eye; and the office of the head of the Presidential Protection Detail, which seemed to be rarely occupied.

Harvey Lieber traveled with the President but also wasn't an office sort of guy; he was always stepping out for meetings or to check on his detail. Colby saw far more of Harvey while he was on grounds patrol than he ever saw of Baxter—which was fine with him. Colby had worked for Baxter for four years at the White House and, still, he was scary.

Colby knocked on the door and Baxter looked up from some report to eye him. "Yes?"

"*You* wanted to see *me*, sir." *Correcting Baxter? Smooth move. Real smooth.*

The captain's office was a study in military precision. His steel desk had precisely one file on it, closed automatically at Colby's knock and exactly centered in front of the Captain. There was an inbox that was empty and an outbox in the same condition. Six secure file cabinets and a single folding metal chair for guests. One wall had portraits of the Captain with the last six presidents —all shaking hands, all signed—and the other had a small shelf bearing an American flag folded into one of those triangular wood-and-glass display cases. There'd been a lot of speculation among the agents about whose coffin that flag had originally covered, but no one knew. And sure as hell, no one asked.

"And why would I want that, Thompson?"

Colby had long since learned that Baxter hated people who spent too much time thinking before replying; he wanted his agents to move fast and decisively at all times. But Colby could think up no quick answer so kept his silence. Apparently it was the right choice as Baxter continued one breath later.

"Now that you're done rolling around on the grass and making a disgrace of the uniform..." His baleful gaze didn't make it clear whether he was merely interpreting the stains on Colby's uniform or had somehow used his all-seeing eye to glare when Colby had taken down Ivy Hanson.

Baxter often displayed an odd sense of humor in unlikely situations. Not the least hint of a smile this time. So he probably hadn't been witness to the situation where he had totally embarrassed himself, otherwise Baxter would have made something more of it.

"Sorry, sir. I snagged Rex's leash and—"

Baxter made a pinching motion to indicate Colby should close his mouth. As it seemed likely that Captain Baxter would consider it beneath contempt to have picked up the gesture from a Bruce Willis movie, Colby was left to wonder how Bruce Willis might have picked up his trademark hand sign from Captain Baxter.

"You've been on site at the White House for four years with Rex, and one year as the head of the White House grounds dog teams."

"Lead Dog, yes sir. Four years here as of tomorrow. And four fine and fun years they've been, sir." And when was Colby going to learn to keep his trap shut? Apparently on the twelfth of never. But he hadn't thought that anyone would notice the anniversary except him. He'd been thinking about taking Rex out for a beer and two burgers to celebrate. He should remember that nothing got by the captain.

"Sit down and shut up."

Colby double-checked that Rex was still on his dog bed. He wasn't yet done wrestling the Kong toy into submission. The big boy really was a laugh riot—a dog as smart as Rex mesmerized by a toy that resembled a six-inch-high black-rubber snowman.

He sat and Baxter kicked the door shut.

"You've been a real asset, Colby."

The captain's tone sent a chill up his spine. He'd been fired once in his life, from a teenage summer job doing pool maintenance. It didn't get much lower than that. But now Baxter's tone—

"As much as I hate to do this…"

Colby could feel his breath going arrhythmic, as if something far worse than Ivy Hanson was punching him in the solar plexus.

"I'm taking you off Lead Dog."

Colby froze—afraid to move because he might shatter. Like

really might. Making the Secret Service was the one thing he'd ever done really right. To leave, to lose Rex—who belonged to the Secret Service, not to him—meant that...

"I need you in foreign travel."

"You need...what?" He felt whiplash as the conversation veered in a wholly unexpected direction. Baxter's grimace said that he just might be enjoying himself.

"Agent McPhee's Rusty is retiring. He's eleven and should have been retired two years ago, but he's the kind of dog who hates to quit. Rex has proven that he doesn't spook. The helos don't throw him. You've had him around jet transports several times and the reports say there were no issues."

"There weren't." Colby was still as befuddled as his dog was by food hidden inside a toy.

A lot of dogs, even the ones who had been trained to keep working through gunfire and explosions, hated helos and flying on jets. Colby often wondered if it was the high whine of the turbine engines—which hurt his own ears badly enough, never mind giant doggie ears—or perhaps they thought that an aircraft was like a car that was too big and fast to chase so they must be, plain and simple, wrong. Whatever it was, Rex seemed to look at any aircraft and just shrug.

"Also, you're single. Heading up the dog teams for the Presidential travel detail is brutal enough without maintaining a relationship in the middle of them. You're not paired up with anyone I don't know about?" Baxter, of course, knew everything about everybody.

Colby could only shake his head. Elsie had given him the boot several months back because he "just wasn't a long-term kind of guy." *Hell!* He could have told her that...if she'd ever cared to ask.

"McPhee broke his ankle stepping in a gopher hole out at Camp David about an hour ago. I was going to overlap you for a week, starting with the President's return this afternoon, but that's out. Effective immediately, you're transferred. I've got

Malcolm sniffing for the Motorcade, but I need someone on the helos. And I need someone to keep all the travel dogs out of my hair. That's you and Rex. Here's your primary contact." He handed over the file he'd been reading. "Read that before you head over."

"Who will take over my former role?"

"I figure Linda Hamlin and Thor can't do any worse job than you two do."

Ouch! Thor was a scrawny mutt. Though Thor and Linda had saved the President's life in his first month at the White House—which proved they had the chops. There were also a lot of other things to like about Linda, but she'd married the White House chocolate chef, so he'd been careful to only admire her from afar.

"You'll show her the ropes. Any questions?"

"Yes, sir. No, sir."

"Out, Thompson. And try not to disgrace the Secret Service any more than usual."

"I wouldn't ev—"

"Out."

Colby got out and headed to his desk to study the file. Rex had finally freed his snack from the toy's interior and made quick work of it. He now watched Colby intently as he crossed the room.

"It's gonna be good, boy. It's gonna be good." He knelt down to give Rex a big scritch. And it *was* going to be good. Presidential travel. That meant he and Rex would be off to see a bit of the world, domestic and foreign. "Sounds like an adventure."

Rex didn't seem upset by the change. Of course, he had always been the steady one of their team—the elder statesman. He'd left puppyhood behind while he was still under a year old and now took everything right in stride.

Colby was less certain. He'd been born and lived his whole life in Maryland. College had been in Baltimore and his Secret Service training had been at the James J. Rowley Training Center just outside DC in Laurel. Other than the two three-month trips to FLETC—the Federal Law Enforcement Training Center in Georgia—he'd never been out of the state.

"About time we did a little adventuring, huh, boy? Stretch our legs? Maybe ride the big plane with the main man? Could be fun."

Rex appeared ready for it.

Colby glanced at the file Baxter had handed him.

No *way* was he ready for it. He didn't need to open the file; the label alone already told him too much about who he was reporting to.

Colby didn't turn to look at Baxter. He didn't need to see or hear him. Colby could *feel* the captain laughing his ass off.

3

Major General Markham of the United States Air Force offered a "Welcome Aboard" greeting that Ivy quickly discovered was indistinguishable from a Drill Sergeant's first day briefing of new recruits, except with less yelling. He was concise, to the point, and he required one hundred and twenty seconds to impart his sage wisdom. Even appropriate "yes, sir" and "no, sir" comments were superfluous and she abandoned them inside the first fifteen seconds of the one-twenty.

Three minutes after entering the near silent White House Military Office, she was sitting at her desk—one cubical in a pod of four—and feeling a case of vertigo. Her head spun like she was the first-ever person through a starship's experimental transporter. One moment she'd been flying aboard an HMX-1 Sea King. The next wondering if this...*this* was what she'd been looking forward to?

Markham had made it clear that HMX-1 should do its job and not bother him because he was busy with "important" matters. The fact that she was female was a crime. The fact that the Marines had allowed her in was a travesty. The fact that she had served four tours flying forward combat with the most decorated and most blooded Marine Expeditionary Unit of the seven MEUs was irrelevant. She was in the White House now and was not to disturb him with such minor shit as Marine One—a job that should belong to the Air Force anyway as they were the ones who were supposed to do all the flying for the US military.

She'd barely managed to *not* point out that the Army, Navy, Marines, and Coast Guard had all fought hard with Congress to keep flying elements because the Air Force was such a pain in the ass to work with. The USAF was territorial, officious, and...

Ivy sighed.

And Markham was a prototypical two-star general in any service. Too old and passed over too many times to ever make three-star except as a retirement bump, which should have been done a decade ago no matter what the man's age was. He was old-school military, with no respect for anyone who'd come on board since the elder Bush's war to free Kuwait from Saddam.

There was a line of demarcation in the military. Oddly, it wasn't at the end of the Vietnam War—they'd all hit mandatory retirement by now and even fossils like Markham didn't go back that far. Rather it was at the start of Afghanistan and Iraq Wars in 2001. The earlier Desert Shield and Desert Storm conflicts had been traditionally fought battles for the most part. Fought with equipment not all that different from Vietnam—heavy bombers and massive troops with Special Ops mostly under the radar.

But in Afghanistan and Iraq, tanks and Humvees fell to cheap-ass, homemade IEDs, and it was up to the MRAP to change ground warfare. Marines and Special Ops stalked in where Army grunts used to stroll. The Air Force found no major military installations to bomb in those pitifully downtrodden nations. Helicopters had taken larger roles than jets, and air-to-air dogfights were a thing of the past because it was only a matter of a few minutes' work before neither country had any air force at all. The allies quickly achieved supreme command of the air—if you didn't count surface-to-air missiles—leaving the Air Force with too little to do. Few of the old-schoolers understood the fundamental changes, and officers like Markham denied the shift with every breath and action.

Ivy had never known anything else. She'd joined the Corps years after the jets flew into the Twin Towers and the Pentagon to light the fuse in Afghanistan. There, the Marines led the way with the unstoppable kind of force only they could bring. They also led the way on innovative technology like her MV-22B Osprey tilt-rotor aircraft. At long last, a full decade behind the Marines, the Air Force was finally getting serious about the best helicraft in the sky.

And HMX-1 was the best helicopter squadron flying anywhere. *That* was the reason they were entrusted with the President's life. The USAF's 1st Helicopter Squadron—who'd once shared the Presidential transport role with their even more ancient Hueys—had been given the boot decades ago. So long ago that only the Air Force even remembered it or kept mentioning it. She'd damn well make sure that HMX-1's reputation continued no matter what the director of the WHMO said or thought. She was going to ram the Marine Corps right down the throat of every stuck-in-the-mud, narrow-minded, misogynistic—

"Don't let the old man get to you."

Ivy flinched. Despite being a Marine, she actually flinched.

"Hi," a handsome blond man held out a hand as he sat in the chair across from hers.

She gave it a Pavlovian shake, still too jarred from her unexpected dismissal to respond normally.

"Major Steve Curnow. Air Force One liaison. Don't let the old man get to you. He doesn't micromanage unless you screw up."

"I'm a Marine."

"Which means when you screw up, you do it at full speed. Good. That's the way we like it here. Special Agent Tish Tolman, there to your right, is Motorcade and Secret Service liaison. McPhee is our traveling dog man, but he's out at Camp David with the First Family so we usually just ignore him. As long as the four of us keep our noses clean and get the President where he needs to go, Markham leaves us alone."

Ivy allowed her shoulders to sag with relief as she shook Tish's hand and it earned her a laugh from the other two. She didn't like ignoring a superior officer unless he was a superior asshole. Actually, they were the most dangerous to ignore as they typically took offence so easily.

Tish could be short for Morticia from *The Addams Family.* Her hair was straight and dark and her complexion fair enough that she'd burn instantly if ever exposed to the Maryland sunshine. The fact that she *wasn't* burnt told Ivy just how many hours this team spent at these desks. After nine years of working and flying more outdoors than in, she wasn't sure that she liked the sound of that.

Was it too late to approach General Arnson about dropping into the pilot's seat the next time one opened?

No challenge is too tough for a Marine. Not one of McKinnon's Laws, it was a Marine law, ground into her soul by the bootheel of nine years of service and a twenty-five-year Marine Corps mother.

Their four cubicles were all open toward a small table that would automatically be the center of any conversation. It was just a chair spin from her own desk to the team desk. There were a dozen pods like it crammed into the room. What she'd first taken for Markham-cowed silence, she could now hear was the soft buzz of professionals doing their jobs. That made her feel much better.

"So, what's on the boards?"

"Are you always all business?" Tish asked in a surprisingly high and sweet voice, making her seem gentle and soft. But she was Secret Service, so the soft part was probably only skin deep.

"I'm a Marine," Ivy repeated her earlier answer. It was a

Marine Corps trademark: absolute focus and commitment to each and every task.

"Yep! She's a laugh a minute," a deep voice sounded behind her.

Ivy closed her eyes. She really didn't need this.

"Go away, Colby." She opened her eyes and looked straight into the deep brown gaze of Colby's German shepherd. His breath smelled like doggie treats. "I don't need you either."

The dog rested his muzzle on her knee, probably shedding a million hairs that would never come out of her dress uniform slacks.

"Apparently you do. Have they told you about McPhee yet?" Colby stepped into the small circle but did nothing to call off his dog.

"What about him?"

"His dog's retiring. So, he's going to get reassigned. I'm his replacement. Except he broke his ankle in a gopher hole—McPhee, not his dog—about an hour ago, so I'm your man ahead of schedule."

Exactly what she didn't need. "Can't he just get another dog?"

Colby sauntered over to the only open chair and dropped into it as if he was at a backyard picnic. He stretched his legs out far enough under the table that they were nearly touching hers. She was grateful for the thick-soled Oxford shoes that were part of a Marine's dress uniform as she kicked him in the shins. Only after she did so did it remind her of old times. He jolted but pulled in his feet only a few inches. Then he grinned just as goofily as his dog—who she'd started scratching between the ears without thinking, creating yet more dog hair.

"Minimum six months to train up a new animal. Besides, it doesn't work that way. One agent, one dog. In the entire history of the Secret Service dog teams, there've only been one or two times an agent got assigned a second dog. That's probably half the reason McPhee and Rusty hung on as long as they did."

He sounded so casual. He even looked casual, slouched in his chair with his fingers laced together and resting on his stomach. But she knew Colby Thompson, and while he might be fooling everyone else, maybe even himself, he wasn't fooling her for a second. Colby was only truly still when something was freaking him out.

She remembered Colby as a kid, when their families went to a restaurant together. He'd start by balancing a knife on his fork like a teeter-totter to find the center of balance. Then he'd stack on a spoon and have to reconfigure the balance points so that everything rocked on the back of the fork. Then he'd slowly spin test his assemblage. She used to wait until he almost had it, then subtly jar a table leg with her foot while innocently looking the other way. He never complained amidst the clattering collapse of his silverware arrangement, instead merely started over. He didn't fidget so much as tinker, but he was never truly still.

Except now.

Was it his presence here? Or hers?

"You know," he turned to Steve and lowered his voice confidentially, "when Major Hanson was younger she'd—"

This time she kicked him hard enough under the small table that he yelped. It was also enough of a jolt for Rex to lift his nose off her other knee and heave a sigh before moving to curl up at her feet. She brushed at her trousers, but the attempt was wholly ineffective. At least he didn't drool. So far. Tish reached back to her desk and tossed over a lint roller, which helped a little.

"As I was saying earlier… What's on the boards that I need to know about?"

Steve and Tish were smiling at each other. Neither of them had missed what had happened either. Maybe she'd lost some of her subtlety the day she became a Marine. Steve gave her the login to the scheduler for her tablet.

"Meeting at Camp David ends in two hours," Tish began rattling off from memory even as the information populated Ivy's screen. "Marine One scheduled back here in time for a lunch meeting with senior staff. Next travel is tomorrow morning, all fairly routine. A one-dayer. Landing at Cape Canaveral, Florida. An HMX out-and-back to the Gulf Coast Conference at a hotel in Orlando with Mexico, Cuba, and the five surrounding states' governors attending. Motorcade on the ground just in case. Then HMX back to Canaveral for a nighttime satellite launch. It's one that the President sponsored while he was still VP. Back in DC by two a.m. if all goes to plan. In our beds by three. Cut and dried, as much as these things ever are."

"Ouch!" Colby still hadn't eased up despite his whole casual act. "Not exactly a tourist timetable."

Thankfully, Steve laughed in his face, sparing her the need to.

Ivy couldn't believe this was happening. Cape Canaveral? Had she just died and gone to heaven? A shot at seeing an actual launch? She'd always promised herself that one day she'd make it down there for one…except she'd be stuck here at the White House.

"Looks like Rex and me are gonna be doing some runnin' about in some purty interestin' places."

Ivy considered kicking him again, just for vengeance. He'd always been the brains of the Reggie-and-Colby show and spoke perfect English when he cared to.

Rex had shifted without her noticing and was now asleep with his chin resting on his crossed paws—which were crossed on her shoe. Her right foot was tingling its way to falling asleep. She wiggled her toes, which earned her a happy sigh before Rex rolled his big head against her shin. Oh, fine! Now she'd have dog hair there as well.

It was unfair that Colby was going to get to see all of those things, and she wasn't. It was *her* dream, not his.

Except…

"What's after that?"

"Three days after we get back, there's a day trip up to Ottawa for trade talks with their prime minister. Then, the week following, we've got a France, Germany, UK round robin. It's fully scheduled, advance teams are already in place. Then quiet until Memorial Day, when we're scheduled for a trip to the First Lady's family farm in Tennessee—that one we have down. So, planning is good on at least that one for the moment."

"Perfect," Ivy wasn't above a tiny bit of subterfuge. "I'm going to take Marine One logistics local."

"Huh?" Steve and Tish looked at her in surprise.

"I've reviewed the last two years of operations reports and I want to try taking the liaison team on site for maximum efficiency. Our problem isn't data coordination back to this office. Once the trip has begun, our problems are out there in the field: communications delays, rapidly evolving scenarios that we don't have eyes on, and the like." She liked the way that sounded. Ivy almost believed it herself.

She checked in with her inner McKinnon while the others at the table exchanged puzzled expressions. Not a single McKinnon Law came up that she was violating. She might be stretching the *Trust your own impressions over everyone else's facts* law to her own purposes, but not by much. Besides, it *sounded* right—something she'd learned to trust.

"We'll set up a standard speed-dial conference number. Anyone hits it and our other three phones ring. Steve travels with Air Force One. Tish gets out there with her motorcade advance teams."

"Oh boy," Tish rubbed her hands together. "There's got to be better pickings out there in the world than here."

"Pickings?"

"Men," Tish looked at her as if she was a dunce. "Cute ones, like Colby. But there's no way he's going to look at me with you in the room."

Colby shrugged a "Maybe so."

"I'm with the helos," Ivy blocked anymore comments on such a stupid topic. There was no way that there was anything between them—ever! "And Colby is…" She wasn't sure where.

"I go in with the helos' transport. Jim Fischer and his dog Malcolm travel as part of the Motorcade, but McPhee was always on the helo advance team."

Ivy hadn't intended to force herself closer to Colby; farther away would be definitely preferable.

Treat your planning screwups like they're genius master strokes. Your instincts may be smarter than you are—lord knows I've done what little I can to train them. Besides, it saves you sounding like a damn fool when you try to unravel one. Great! Thanks, Sarge.

"Let's do it."

"You *are* a Marine!" Tish grinned at her. "I'll get us a speed-dial conference number," she headed over to the desk for the White House Communications Agency, another arm of the WHMO.

Ivy checked her master schedule.

"The advance helos for tomorrow's flight are shipping out this afternoon. Colby and I will hop a ride back on Marine One after it delivers the President." If a chance to take that flight again meant she had to travel with Colby, she'd even do that.

STEVE TURNED BACK to his desk and got on the phone setting up his own travel arrangements. It left just the two of them, and Ivy was bent over her tablet computer, clearly trying to ignore him.

"You just want to see a space launch," Colby guessed.

"Not so. It will offer me an eyes-on analysis of HMX-1 operational processes in the field." But a bit of a blush colored her cheeks and she was careful not to look up at him. She'd always been a crappy liar. Even her fibs as a kid had never flown. Well, they worked well enough on Reggie, but Colby had always been able to spot them.

"You were hyped on Star Trek reruns since you were two."

"I don't remember that far back," she kept her face down but Colby had the impression that she wasn't making much progress on reading her screen.

"I do. One of the best ways Reggie and I had of dumping you. You'd always be following us around—like that's what a pair of five-year-old secret agents wanted, a two-year-old brat chasing after them—unless we found you some television show or movie set in space. Didn't matter. *Star Trek, Star Wars,* one of those awful 1950s things. You loved them all."

"Colby!" Her voice was practically a hiss. "It's a good thing that your dog is sleeping on my feet or you'd get a busted kneecap and spend the next month in physical therapy."

"He's *what?*" Colby ducked down to look under the table. Sure enough, he wasn't just asleep on her feet. He looked like he was moving in to stay. "Well, that's weird."

"Why? Dogs like me. I'm likeable."

He wasn't going to comment on the second part of that. He was still having problems with the best-friend's-younger-sister-who's-really-a-pill memories that seemed to be bounding to the fore. It was far easier to recall her thrashing him in miniature golf or taking flash pictures at precisely the wrong moment of what was supposed to be his and Reggie's double date-first kiss with the Ivanov sisters. It was harder to remember from moment to moment that she was a Marine sitting in the White House West Wing. With his dog asleep on her foot.

He looked again, but Rex absolutely was.

"He's not generally a big fan of women."

"Maybe it has to do with the *kind* of women you bring home."

He just raised an eyebrow at her.

"That wasn't an offer, Thompson."

"Yes, ma'am." He wanted to snicker, but it seemed to get caught in his throat. So he saluted her instead.

"Will you just go get ready? We're out of here on Marine One at 1230 hours sharp. Go away! I have work to do."

He clambered to his feet, but had to nudge Rex awake with his boot to get him moving. Not even a pat from Ivy, though Rex was looking for it. One thing he had to say for Ivy, she didn't offer either of them any encouragement.

———

"YOUR SISTER'S HERE." Colby leaned against the doorway into the White House Kitchen.

"Uh-huh." Reggie was sprinkling herbs he'd just minced into a giant soup pot as if one shred more or less was going to make or break the soup.

Colby had parked Rex in the small Secret Service office in the basement of the Residence and then ducked around the corner to harass Reggie while he mooched a meal. He'd done it so often that even Chef Klaus, the executive chef, did little more than offer his customary Teutonic scowl at Colby's arrival. Colby was careful to always throw a five or ten into the jar to cover food costs—Reggie had lectured him the first time about taxpayer costs, even on leftovers, and Colby had never forgotten.

The White House kitchen was in full swing, but just for a luncheon so there were only four chefs working at the moment. A knife hammered against a cutting board, mincing garlic faster than his FN P90 submachine gun on full auto. There was a sharp sizzle of bacon on the griddle that made Colby's stomach growl—he'd have to snitch a piece for Rex or he'd never be forgiven. A rattle of plates being stacked on the warming shelf as someone else hustled by on their way into the produce fridge. Overall pretty quiet. If it was a state dinner, he wouldn't go near the place.

"Ivy looks hot in her dress blues." Colby wasn't quite sure how he'd ended up here on such a crazy morning, but he had a free half hour and no longer had a patrol duty to fill it with.

He'd gone to his truck in the Secret Service HQ garage and snagged his emergency go-bag. Then he'd tracked down Linda and Thor, her scraggle-haired mutt with one of the best noses in the business, to discuss her taking over the Lead Dog role at the White House. Linda had been a little startled—apparently Baxter hadn't warned her. Typical.

Linda was still new enough that he had to explain that was Baxter's idea of a rip-roaring, hilarious joke. Thor had been fine with it though. Colby had given her access to all his files on the dog teams and then felt lost and at loose ends. Until it was time to go, there was nothing more for him to do.

So he and Linda had walked and talked their way to the White House Chocolate Shop, which was run by her husband. The Chocolate Shop was about twenty feet from the kitchen so Colby had dropped in on Reggie.

"Ivy's really grown up. She's changed a lot." More than he'd ever imagined possible. Yet in other ways, she was still that same driven girl he'd always known.

"Uh-huh." Reggie's attention had moved from his soup to cutting up a loaf of sourdough bread, totally missing that Colby had just said his little sister was hot. Which she was, but he wasn't going to actually think about.

"I've decided to marry her."

"Uh-huh." Reggie stacked the slices neatly in a lavender-colored glass serving bowl so that it looked more like a flower arrangement than food.

"We're going to name all of our kids after you."

"Sure."

"Even the girls."

"Fine. Wait… What?" Reggie blinked at him in surprise.

Colby did his best to keep a straight face.

"Ivy's here?" Reggie looked around the kitchen as if he expected his little sister to pop out of a cabinet the way she used to when she was trying to scare them. It had never bothered Reggie, but Colby had jumped every time. She'd loved that. The time she'd jumped out of the refrigerator when he'd been after a soda had almost given him a heart attack. Only belatedly had he noticed all of the shelving and contents neatly stacked off to the side. She wasn't above elaborate preparations for her traps—she'd been wearing long johns and a parka while she waited. He'd also spotted a book because Ivy never just stopped. He'd never again opened a refrigerator without first checking for the slightly open door providing an airgap.

Colby put on his best smirk for Reggie.

"Oh right. She starts today." And just that fast, Reggie was gone back to his lunch prep.

Colby should know better than to bait his best friend when he was cooking. They'd cooked together a lot growing up, but for Reggie it had always been a thing. For Colby it had been an excuse to hang out with his friend and eat amazing food.

"You're getting married, huh?" Reggie was often tuned in, even when he was tuned out. "How did she take the news?"

"Like the trooper she is."

"She's not a trooper, she's a Marine. And you'd be all black-and-blue if you'd tried suggesting anything as stupid as marriage because she'd have kicked your ass."

"I've got grass stains on my knees," he went for pity points. Except, he'd kept a fresh pair of pants in his go-bag, so there was nothing to show.

No deal. Reggie didn't spare him a glance anyway. "Let me guess, you tripped over Rex and did a face plant."

Even best friends weren't supposed to know things like that.

"So, what are you really doing here midday?"

"Grade bump. At least I think it is. Presidential travel detail."

That actually got Reggie's full attention. "Hey, Colby, that's great."

"Hope so." A pinch between his shoulder blades made him shrug.

"Seriously! Don't you get it? Lead Dog at the White House is great and you earned that. But you just got bumped to the Presidential Protection Detail. That's huge."

Colby hadn't thought of it that way. Did that mean he now reported to Harvey Lieber, the head of the PPD, rather than Baxter? Was he supposed to trade in his slacks and jacket for a black suit? The captain hadn't said anything about that.

"You always were the slow one of the team."

"As if you're such a genius. Your little sister's sharper than you."

"Ivy's sharper than both of us put together."

Right next to the no-touch rule for little sisters was the always-agree-that-they're-exceptional rule. Of course, in Ivy's case, that was easy because she absolutely was.

Reggie had cut some more bread and was throwing together a massive BLT sandwich.

"Better make a pair of those. Ivy and I fly out together in about fifteen minutes."

Reggie's hands froze halfway through slicing a tomato. Then he very slowly looked up at Colby. "You *and* Ivy?"

"Uh-huh," he did his best to echo Reggie's earlier distracted tone.

"You and Ivy." Somehow the paired sandwiches had tipped Reggie's internal alarms where a tease about marriage hadn't. He'd always been a food guy. Colby remembered having to explain how girls flirted—in foodie terms—for Reggie to get it.

She's not going to offer you the main course of steak unless you go through the minestrone soup first. And you're not going to get the minestrone kiss without some major antipasti. Before that, you've got to have hors d'oeuvres to convince her she even sits at the table with you.

Explained that way, Reggie's success rate had risen, as had Colby's. Though the Ivanov sisters had ultimately slipped away unkissed.

"As part of the bump, I got assigned to the White House Military Office. We're headed out for a couple days. Together." He did his best to drop the last word suggestively, but he could feel his voice shift strangely. He and Ivy together for a mission. Two days was more than he'd seen her in the last five years.

In silence, Reggie finished the two sandwiches and wrapped a napkin around a few extra bacon slices for Rex. Colby would have been happier if Reggie was groaning or slinging some shit back at him. Instead he handed over the wrapped sandwiches with a look that said one thing very clearly: *You go there and I'll kill your ass.*

Colby shrugged like: *as if that could ever happen.* Besides, Secret Service training versus chef training, he wasn't worried. Though Reggie did have access to some seriously sharp knives.

4

"*W*hat's in the bag?"

"What's it worth to you?"

"Rude," Ivy commented with no heat. She stood in the West Wing Colonnade and had been watching the sky even though it was still too early for the Marine One flight returning the President from Camp David. This time the Press Corps had piled out of the West Wing and were ganged up along the rope line.

But now she was looking up into Colby's dark eyes...and would rather she wasn't. He was very hard to look away from. He was so unexpected that she—

"Hold it, would you?" Colby handed her the bag, dropped his satchel at her feet, then stepped away to join a female dog handler who had just walked past.

Ivy watched as they walked together along the rope line that kept the press gaggle at bay. Several of the reporters greeted Colby and Rex, though none reached out to pet the dog as he sniffed them. She could hear the greetings for the other agent and dog as well: Linda and Thor.

Ivy watched as Colby instructed Linda on the proper search pattern, starting at the West Wing doors and working their way down to the landing area. There was a kindness that surprised her. Not that Colby was an unkind man. But it was easy to see the calming effect his instruction had on his teammate. They finished their patrol just as the groundskeepers rolled out the aluminum disks for this afternoon's flight. Introductions all around: friends with the groundskeepers.

That had always been Colby's trademark: Mr. Easygoing. In high school, the girls had flocked to him. Not because he'd been anything special in those years, but because he'd been friendly and kind. He'd always been attractive, really attractive, and he'd always known it, which was a major turnoff to her. Except, where it had once been the only card he had to play—and why not? It had worked on flocks of high school girls—he didn't seem to be using it anymore.

He escorted Linda to a position that would be between the helo and the fence, gave a final instruction, then shook hands with her before striding back across the lawn toward her. The tall man and his huge shepherd walking across the White House lawn as if they belonged. It was a walk worthy of a Marine.

Walk any turf as if you own it. That places fear in the enemy's heart, especially if you do it on their home soil.

Colby followed McKinnon's Laws instinctively, without any training by the Corps.

She remembered the bag she was holding and looked inside so that she wasn't watching Colby as he returned to her side. Two sandwiches. She hadn't even thought about food. A Marine Corps major having a major blood sugar crash on her first day would not be a good thing. Her flight suit had a small pocket that she always kept stocked with energy bars. She hadn't even thought about needing to do that in her dress blues even if there was a place. Her metabolism didn't have a lot of leeway and Colby had remembered that about her. She hadn't even been aware that he knew that.

Colby arrived and reached into the bag without ceremony. He

snagged one of the sandwiches and a folded paper towel. He unwrapped several slices of bacon for Rex, then bit down on his own sandwich. "Damn, your brother even makes a sandwich something special."

"You saw Reggie."

He glanced up at the roof of the West Wing and nodded—more to himself than to her. "Better eat fast."

She pulled out her own and bit into it. BLT with avocado and the special mayo spread that he'd invented just for her. "A little chili for zing because it's so you, slivers of tarragon for your sweet heart—" a *so* big-brother-got-it-wrong detail (more than one boyfriend had labeled her heart as pure steel…with wire barbs) "—and a touch of lemon juice for the sunshine you bring." It was sufficiently the taste of home that it almost brought tears to her eyes.

"Sure I saw him. Told him we were getting married."

"How did he take it?" Colby wasn't the only one who could deliver a straight line.

"He thought it was a little odd that I wanted to name all our kids Reggie, but other than that he was cool with it." Colby's voice always gave him away. He'd tried to make a joke and Reggie hadn't been amused. Her brother was always so serious. It had definitely made Reggie and Colby an odd pair growing up.

"Works for me."

Colby choked on his sandwich.

Whereas having an older brother and Colby to practice on, she'd learned to never give away anything she was feeling.

They finished the sandwiches just as the White Tops flew into view beyond the Washington Monument. Three Sea Kings in a shifting group—even *she* couldn't pick out which was Marine One at the moment—and a pair of heavily armed Black Hawks flying overwatch patrol. Those were the pitch black helos of the 160th SOAR Night Stalkers who were best known for being lethal, even by Marine standards.

"Though maybe we should name the dog Reggie instead of our kids," she continued as much to distract herself as anything else. Her nerves were attempting to rematerialize. "Wouldn't want my brother getting a swelled head, thinking he was important or something."

She could feel Colby's shock take another hit.

This was even better than jumping out of cabinets to get a reaction out of him.

HIS JOKE HAD DIED TWICE NOW and Colby didn't know what to do with it.

Reggie had taken it seriously, when he was supposed to laugh.

And Ivy, its real target, hadn't reacted at all. Instead she'd talked about what they should name their dog as if she already had pictured their whole life together.

Did he even know her?

He considered asking her what she was actually thinking or feeling…but he decided that he didn't need that kind of joke backfiring on him a third time. And what if suddenly it wasn't a joke? He definitely couldn't deal with that.

He stuffed the empty sandwich bag into his gear while the President, his entourage, and the press did their dance and cleared off. Then they left the shade of the big magnolia and headed down to the helo. Once aboard, he dropped into the first seat and suddenly the Marine crew chief was glaring at him.

"What?"

The Marine's scowl grew darker.

Ivy sat in the armchair opposite him, but her smile was wicked.

Now what?

"You might want to look at the seat back you're sitting against so casually."

He leaned forward enough to turn and look. There, like a target at the middle of his back, was the Presidential Seal woven right into the fabric.

"Holy shit!" He jolted out of the seat, stumbled over Rex, who had laid down in the aisle, and plummeted onto the bench seat on the other side of the aircraft as the helo lifted.

Ivy burst out laughing.

The lethal-looking Marine Corps crew chief did not. Colby had clearly desecrated a holy sanctuary.

"Give him a break, Sergeant McShea. He's merely Secret Service; he can't help screwing up."

And Baxter had told him not to embarrass the service. Not much luck so far.

Rex looked at him as if to say to get his act together, then settled into his standard helicopter mode—naptime.

"Fine. Do that. I won't tell you that it's only a three-minute flight."

Ivy patted Rex's head and he sighed happily. "I think that renaming him Reggie isn't very fair to such a nice dog."

Between Rex's size and typical unrelenting drive, most of Colby's past girlfriends had been afraid of the German shepherd. Not Ivy, of course. She'd never been afraid of anything.

Ivy Hanson. A dog. Kids. It was a crazy image, but that didn't mean he hated it either. Maybe that was the problem. It was surprisingly easy to imagine waking up next to her—which was not where his thoughts about women typically started. His imagination was far more about the lying down together part. He'd found his share of attractive women over the years, but—

Hold on a sec!

Now he was thinking of Ivy as an attractive woman?

Not just pretty or good-looking, but actually attractive? Literally? Like he was attracted to her? That was so strange that—

The helicopter began descending rapidly. He glanced out the window. They were flying low enough over a golf course that he could easily read the flag numbers on the greens as they flapped in the wind off the rotor. *Crap!* He'd just missed his one-time-ever chance to see the White House takeoff from the other perspective.

But it wasn't the image of the South Lawn that stuck in his mind. It was the image of Ivy lying down next to him that was occupying his thoughts. Of course, he'd never be stupid enough to suggest such a thing seriously. Because Reggie had been right, Ivy would kill him if she found out.

As he watched out the window, he saw a blur flash close by the window. Like a giant bird. Or a tiny F-14 Tomcat fighter jet.

It seemed impossibly close, yet looked as if it was far away to be so small. Before he could make sense of it, there was a loud crunch like a pure steel gull hitting the side of the helicopter.

He was about to ask Ivy if everything was okay when the helo lurched sideways.

An ear-shattering scream pierced even the presidential sound insulation!

That definitely wasn't normal.

5

*I*vy knew the motion the instant they entered the sideslip. An engine's cry was bad news, but an auto-rotation landing could always be achieved.

This wasn't an engine failure sound.

The sideslip was the loss of the tail rotor followed by the rending steel of the transfer shaft blowing through its bearings. They weren't going to be landing under any sort of control.

"Buckle up! We're going down."

They tightened their seatbelts in unison yanks.

She tried to figure out what she could do for Rex when Colby scooped the big dog into his lap and clamped his arms around the German shepherd. Despite his size, he'd picked Rex up as if he weighed nothing.

It was crazy at this moment, but it was a visceral reaction—a body memory of how solidly he had held her as they fell on the South Lawn. Of his strength and power in ways that she'd never experienced in a man before. The fact that it came from Colby Thompson wasn't something she had time to consider at the moment.

Colby looked right at her, but didn't say a thing. Good man, the Marine in her thought. No scream. No questions she couldn't answer. No panic.

She glanced out the window and was impressed at his lack of panic, because she could feel her own adrenaline kicking into high gear as the breath choked in her throat.

Without the rear tail rotor to counteract the spin, the helicopter had begun a death spiral. The rotors turning one way and the helicopter itself forced to rotate in the other. Normally the tail rotor pushed the tail sideways against the engine-induced spin to hold the helo in straight-line flight. Not anymore.

Flashes of the golf course.

Anacostia Air Base so close, but completely out of reach.

The blue slash of the Potomac.

The trees between the golf course and the park at the south tip of the island.

A radio call by the pilot, "Marine 173 going down, south end Haines Point." His voice calm and clear, but he didn't waste time repeating the call. Other than that, he and the copilot fought the controls in silence. The crew chief braced himself and kept his silence as well, knowing their fate was out of his hands.

The Air Base.

Blue water.

Because the pilot had been flying so low over the golf course, they were below fifty feet when the failure had occurred. It had sounded like a bird strike. Out of the death zone. The death zone for a helicopter started at fifty feet and ended at four hundred. Below fifty, you mostly fell out of the sky. Above four hundred, you could set up an autorotation (unless you lost your tail rotor), and have some choice in where you came down. Even without the tail rotor there were some things that could be done with enough altitude.

In the death zone…

Well, it was aptly named and she was glad to not be in it.

Didn't mean this wasn't going to hurt.

Ivy's body instinctively strained against the controls—controls that she didn't have. Her left foot jammed into the plush carpet, just in case some bit of the tail rotor still existed. She rocked her non-existent cyclic to the right in hopes of using the airframe's body angle to some advantage against the increasing spin.

She looked up and saw Colby clutching Rex to his chest.

But he was watching her.

As if he wanted to say something.

As if he didn't know what to say.

Maybe he—

They slammed in.

Momentum heaved her against her seatbelt.

Her hands, clutched to the seat arms, were torn loose as the helo flopped about like a dying fish.

Colby twisted, taking the brunt of the hit for his dog, just as he had for her forever ago on the South Lawn.

REX KNOCKED the air out of Colby's chest just as effectively as Ivy had earlier. Only this time it was much less fun. He couldn't even make a small *whoop* noise as the helo tumbled through a full roll.

He held Rex tightly so that he didn't drop his dog down onto Ivy as she was momentarily directly below him. Then struggling not to drop him on the ceiling as they both dangled from his seat-belt. Finally he crashed onto his back with eighty-plus pounds of dog flopping into his chest.

Struggling dog.

Wet dog!

Water poured into the cabin and in moments he was not only breathless, he was also underwater.

Rex kicked free, landing a few final injustices on Colby's body that might have made him scream if he'd had any air and not been underwater.

Finding his seatbelt, he struggled free and popped to the surface, banging his head on the helicopter's entry door as the helo now lay on its side.

He managed a small *whoop* for air just as Ivy surfaced inches from him.

Some joke about how good the wet look was on her, darkening her sun-bright hair to a rich gold, didn't have the air to be voiced. It had always been a good look on her when their families went to the beach—something he'd definitely looked forward to each summer.

Then a large wet muzzle surfaced between them, driving them apart.

Colby grabbed Rex again to protect them both from the dog's swimming feet. His paws were big enough that it was surprising he wasn't walking on the water, not that there was much room as the cabin kept filling with water.

Ivy popped the latch on the door and pushed it up.

No more water poured in—though small waves slopped in over the edges filling in the last of their air gap. The door was up in the air or she wouldn't have been able to swing it open against the water pressure. He managed to get his feet on the edge of the bench seat below, but by the way Ivy kept kicking his shins, she was treading water.

They stuck their heads out.

The helo lay on its side in the Potomac shallows off the south point of the island. Water lapped around them.

He gave Rex a heave up and out. After a brief scrabbling of claws on metal, he was gone with a splash that sloshed water back over his and Ivy's heads in a wave.

"Thanks," Ivy sputtered out a mouthful of Rex-flavored river water and glared at him.

"Aim. To. Please," he managed to gasp out on three micro-breaths. Then he reached out underwater, wrapped his hands around her waist, and heaved her upward as well. His hands could practically wrap all of the way around her waist. So trim, yet so brilliantly fierce. He'd always enjoyed that contrast in her.

He managed to place her high enough that she was able to sit on the edge of the doorframe. Unable to resist, he grabbed her by the ankles and flipped her off the helicopter and into the river.

She flopped back-first into the water and sloshed her own wave into his face just as the crew chief surfaced beside him.

"Pilots are clear, out the front windshield," Sergeant McShea announced with a sputter.

They shared a nod, then boosted themselves up and out of the helicopter together.

Their door was about all that showed above the choppy water. Just that and a single rotor blade sticking straight up—giving the world a twisted, twenty-foot middle finger for dumping it into the Potomac.

The beach lay fifty feet away and a crowd was already gathering.

Rex had reached the shore and was keeping the crowd back by shaking off great clouds of cold water. Ivy hung on to one of the wheels that dangled just below the surface and offered a smile at seeing the two of them emerge safely.

This time, Ivy *was* unleashing that big smile of hers in his direction and it felt damn good. As if he'd never done anything so right as being alive at this moment.

"Apparently they all think," he nodded toward the shore, "that a crashing helicopter is somehow unusual in these parts."

"A crashing HMX-1 helo is unusual. It has *never* happened before in our entire history." And that big smile of hers switched off. He was gonna miss that unless it came back for a spell. Colby decided that he was good with working on that.

He and McShea slid down into the water together, just as the pilots swam around from the other side of the aircraft. One had a bloody nose, the other was grimacing and appeared to be swimming one handed, but they'd all survived.

"Nothing like a minor miracle on a Monday morning," the crew chief revealed a sense of humor that Colby somewhat suspected was unbefitting a Marine. Colby chuckled to promote his bad behavior.

"Miracles? I always blame those on Saint Ives," Colby called out as they swam ashore together.

"Saint Ives?" The bloody-nosed pilot burst out laughing—which was cut short when he swallowed a mouthful of the Potomac. No question, that nickname would be traveling around.

"Colby!" He could hear Ivy's teeth grinding.

Very near the shore, they plowed into a raft of duckweed. In moments, their every surface was covered in the tiny tri-petal plants until they looked like they'd caught alien-green measles or something. Getting their feet down in the shallows, they waded the rest of the way to shore, raking handfuls of plants off their faces, hands, and clothes. At least they weren't slimy, merely infinite in number.

He reached over and hauled handfuls of the water weeds out of Ivy's hair, then wished he hadn't. A man only got to handle a woman's wet hair if they showered together. It was a shockingly intimate feeling—until she slapped his hands away hard enough to sting.

The one-armed pilot had a broken wrist, but they were all alive. As one, they clambered across the steel railing that the helo had flattened in its death roll and sat on the grassy bank facing the one-bladed protest of the otherwise submerged aircraft. A weekday morning crowd of thirty or so people kept a respectful distance.

The other two helicopters in the flight had been in the lead when theirs went down. One continued to base, but the other circled back and was descending to land on the lawn above the beach. The crowd was brushed back even farther as the five of them huddled to keep their backs to the blast of rotor-driven wind and grit. Rex ducked low in their wind shadow and closed his eyes.

As soon as the helo was down and the blast abated, Rex rose to his feet in front of them. He gave another shake, finding yet more water in his thick coat to spray in all of their faces. It was mixed with gritty sand and a jillion more tiny duckweed leaves.

A chorus of complaints sounded.

"Hey, you can't get any wetter."

As if to prove him wrong, Rex walked into his arms, licked him in the face, then gave himself a final shake.

At least, because this time Colby was hugging Rex's head, most of the spray went sideways—into Ivy's face.

"Good boy," he whispered in Rex's ear.

6

"Turnabout is fair play," she warned Colby as they stepped off the Sea King helicopter that had fetched them across the narrow Washington Channel to Anacostia.

She was wet, dirty, had lost her cover, and could only hope that the dry cleaner could deal with the damage done to her uniform—dress blues were hideously expensive. Her return to Joint Base Anacostia-Bolling was far more ignominious than she'd imagined possible. For over seventy years, HMX-1 had never had a flight failure or other accident. They had the best service record in the world—and she'd been on the flight that had just ruined it with their plunge into the Potomac. Forever after, from this moment on, the Marines Corps would always have to say, "Zero mission failures...except this one time when the new White House Military Office liaison was aboard and—"

"What do you mean: turnabout is fair play?" She'd forgotten about Colby and Rex as they stood close beside her.

"Meaning, if you leave my side, someone actually *may* shoot you."

"After being knocked out of the sky, I'm not in much of a

mood to be shot. Guess I'm glued to your hip." He offered her one of his teasing smiles. Two could play that game.

"Good thing we aren't getting married or I might read something into that." As she turned away, she caught an odd expression on Colby's face. But by the time she turned back it was gone and the cocky dog handler was once more in place. Now it was *her* mind that was playing tricks on her.

"What's your clearance?"

"I'm Lead Dog, or I was," his face fell at that.

Surprise. Surprise. Colby Thompson had actual feelings. She almost ribbed him about it, but couldn't get past the sad face.

"Which means what?"

"It's not an official title, but it still has a lot of meaning inside the team. I was head dog handler on the White House grounds. They didn't work for me, but if they had a problem, they came to me first and it was my job to solve it before it hit the Captain's desk."

"Which tells me nothing about your clearance."

He flicked his badge at her, which had somehow survived the crash and their swim on its lanyard. "I've got armed proximity to the President status, just like you. Anything that isn't code-word classified or eyes-only I have full access to, if I was dumb enough to want to read any of that crap."

She had to respect that. It took over a year to get that clearance as she well knew; *if* you could get that clearance. Now that she thought of it, she remembered the FBI interviewing her about Colby some years ago in her role as friend (yeah, right) and neighbor (not by choice). It had taken all the kindness she could muster at the time to not shout "Hell no! Not him!", figuring someone else they interviewed would take care of that. Apparently no one had and he'd made it in.

Ivy didn't like being wrong, but looking up at the man beside her made it difficult to argue. If it was anyone other than Colby, she'd be respecting the hell out of him at the moment.

Had he been interviewed when she'd earned her clearance? Probably. She decided not to ask what he'd said. And definitely not what he thought about saying but hadn't.

They weren't authorized to move away from the Sea King, so she kept them standing out under the midday sun as they dripped. Even soaking wet, one didn't just unbutton a dress jacket. You wore it or you went and changed. *Spit and polish all the way down to your soul.*

"HMX-1 has a split personality." Ivy spoke up to fill the weird silence between them. Besides, split personality was the best way to describe what newbies were walking into here.

"Like you and your big brother?"

"Hey, he's your best friend. I'm only related to him because we accidentally have the same parents."

"Yeah. That and he'd kill someone with one of his chef's knives if they even looked at you funny."

She glanced at Colby but he didn't seem to be joking. "Really?"

Colby just scoffed at her. "I made that joke about naming our kids after him and almost got a ten-inch Wüsthof up my nose."

"Huh." Reggie had never seemed like the protective type. More like the quiet, overly-serious chef, leave-me-alone type. Yet he'd always hung with Colby, which had never made sense to her in either direction, even if it had to them.

Colby and Rex were looking around the airfield. Rex shook himself again, but was thankfully out of water to shed.

"This used to be a big airport back in the day," she explained. "The runways and hangars have all been filled in with office buildings now, except for this one hanger and the helo landing area." Six helicopter-sized squares bordered in yellow-and-brown lines were painted on the bare concrete. All of them empty except for the bird that had just ferried them onto the base. Even now, a team was prepping it to tuck away into the hangar.

"You have your own dog team," Colby was watching the team that first went through their rescue helicopter. "Guess they want to make sure I didn't smuggle any explosives or bacon aboard on the thirty-second ride over from Hains Point beach."

"Don't even joke about explosives around here."

Then they came over to inspect him. Rex took one sniff of the new dog and turned his head away.

"What was that?"

"Dogs have always confused Rex. He thinks he's human and is never sure what to do about lower life forms except to ignore them."

The Marine's dog sniffed Colby with no interest at all before moving off.

Now that they'd been cleared, she led him toward the hangar.

"Split personality," he reminded her.

"Right. Three bases, two classes of birds, two birds in each class. We keep White Tops based here for fast access to the White House, a few more over at Andrews, but our main installation is forty miles downriver at Quantico."

"Three airfields. Check. And you guys own the landing pad on the South Lawn since you chased away the Army and Air Force back in the '70s. That makes four."

"Okay, four."

"Except that we at the Secret Service only set it up for you temporarily. Then we take it away and roll it into storage. So we're the ones who control whether you have four or three."

"Shut up, Colby."

"Yes, ma'am."

She'd never really noticed what a great smile he had. Had he always? She tried to remember, but that all seemed so long ago.

They stepped through the open hangar door into the cool shade. Eight helicopters were stowed there. The tech team was fussing over the engine of one. Two others were being waxed. When she needed to check her uniform, she could see her reflection in the shine of any HMX-1 helicopter—except the one now crashed into the river. Despite that, at the moment she strongly suspected that she'd be smiling and didn't want to be caught doing that by Colby Thompson. Bantering with Colby had always been fun.

"White Side and Green Side," she focused once more on her introduction as she headed to a supplies shelf to find Colby some spare clothes. Size Marine large to span his chest and height.

"Couldn't you just call that top and bottom of the helo? Why do you paint the helos two colors anyway?"

Ivy considered picking up a handy crescent wrench and going after him with that instead.

<hr>

COLBY LOVED MESSING with Ivy's brain. He'd done it a thousand times growing up. She was just as focused and almost as serious as her older brother, which had made her an easy target. Reggie just shrugged off Colby's best digs like a duck and rainwater, but Ivy's revenge was always charmingly devious.

When Ivy had been trying to learn her single-digit addition and subtraction, he'd asked her what was "two minus three." That had shut her up for a good long time. Later he'd asked her, "Why does swimming have a double m, but dancing only has one c?" And a myriad of other traps that he'd learned first by being three years older. Though in later years, she'd pulled ahead of him and he'd had to get more creative—like picking her up over his head and throwing her into the ocean right after she'd stretched out to sunbathe on the beach. Which he'd had to leave off doing as her martial arts skills had improved.

Of course he knew that the two colors of the helo wasn't what she'd meant about White Side and Green Side, but he wasn't going to tell her that.

Ivy skipped the teeth grind and went straight to malevolent glare just as he'd hoped.

And his would be a reasonable assumption to anyone who

didn't know better. Each of the helos was painted a glossy forest green except for the very tops, which were painted a white that reflected the errant sunlight beam coming in one of the high windows so strongly he was surprised that the crews didn't wear sunglasses to work on that aircraft.

"White Side," her voice sounded as narrow as her glare, "are the White Tops for transporting the President and other heads of state. Top secret clearance, with presidential special access or better, is required to even enter this hangar. We have a desperate time getting pilots and service personal because of how long it takes to obtain that level of clearance. Green Side are the civilian transport aircraft—which are painted all green. Here we're White Side only. At Quantico, there's a patrolled security gate between the two. They can't even hand a part or a tool across the line because it might have been tampered with."

Colby felt a bit of a chill and it wasn't just because his soaking wet clothes were now cooling rapidly in the hangar's shadowed interior. He wished he was standing back in the sunlight. It was a given that these guys were serious, but now maybe he understood the reaction of the crew chief at him even sitting for a moment in the President's seat.

"White Side flies the Sea King and a modified Black Hawk called a White Hawk. We're replacing the Sea Kings with VH-92 Superhawks, but those are still in testing for another few years. Green Side flies MV-22B Ospreys for missions like transporting the Press Corps and senior staff. They just retired the other aircraft."

"Which makes it two sides, but one of them has three aircraft and the other only has one. Doesn't seem very fair to me."

"Shut up, Colby. This new anal side of you isn't charming."

"I'm completely charming. Just ask me."

Ivy didn't take the bait. Instead, she punched a finger at the floor close by a bathroom. "You. Sit. Stay."

Rex's look said, *She's talking to* you, *buddy. I've already got my butt on the floor.* He'd sat down as soon as they'd come to a stop. Colby didn't sit, but he did stay.

Two minutes later a woman walked out of the bathroom and Colby almost didn't recognize her.

The wind-up-doll perfect Marine Corps major in her dress blues was gone. The white cover—as Marines insisted on calling their hats (which was probably now at the bottom of the Potomac or flowing out to sea)—was now a Marine-green garrison cap with its little ridgeline running front to back. Shoes to boots, trousers to camo pants, and the dress jacket with all of its ornamentation was now a USMC drab green t-shirt that clung tightly enough to show a perfect outline of her sports bra. In addition to her earlier sidearm, she now wore a KA-BAR knife almost as long as the thigh it was strapped to. A camo jacket hung loose off her shoulders, which also bore a small pack. If not for the wet dress blues in a plastic bag, he might have thought she'd done one of her parallel-world alternate-self things.

Protocol perfection had switched over to down and didn't-mind-getting-dirty Marine.

"Well, that's a relief," he told her.

"What?"

"*This* Ivy Hanson I recognize."

"Is this gonna be some crap about the past?" She waved him toward the bathroom to change.

"Absolutely!" Then, instead of explaining, he handed her Rex's leash and went to change. It was easy to see the parallels between Ivy and the squadron she flew with—lovely but hard.

"So what are you on about this time, Colby? What's this old crap you want to dredge up now?" She shouted through the door.

"Well," he considered and decided what the hell, she could only kill him once. And if she busted in on him now, he'd be naked and who knew what interesting places that might lead. "Now that you're dressed to get some work or ass-kicking done, just seems more like you."

"I can kick your ass just fine in my dress uniform."

"Don't doubt it. But your dress uniform is so goddamn impressive that it distracts from the amazingly beautiful woman wearing it. Your working gear lets me see you clear as day."

For once, she had no snappy comeback to that. Maybe he should try telling her the truth more often. Though he wished the door wasn't separating them so that he could see her stone silent reaction.

***

THE FOUR OF them stood in a line on the tarmac of the HMX landing field at Anacostia: her, Colby, Rex, and General Edward Arnson—commander of HMX-1.

"Well, that's not something you see every day," the general's tone was certainly drier than she was, despite a change of clothes and two hours listening in on the debrief of the pilots.

One of the VH-60N White Hawks hovered above Anacostia. At the lower end of the cargo line, it dangled the battered Sea King helicopter it had just fished out of the Potomac.

"There goes our perfect no-accident record," Ivy couldn't believe that she'd been on the flight that had destroyed a seventy-year Marine Corps tradition.

"Don't blame it on the Marines. Blame it on whoever was flying the F-14."

She turned to Colby, as did the general. He clearly didn't know what Colby was talking about either.

"It was odd." He cocked his head much the way his dog would as he studied the descending helo—the helo they could have so easily died in.

They all kept a respectful silence as it came to rest on it wheels not twenty meters away. Within seconds, the lines to the hovering White Hawk were released and a phalanx of mechanics moved in to see what had happened.

"Just before the impact—" Colby resumed.

"What impact?" She didn't remember any impact, just something broke with a bang followed by an awful rending sound as the rear rotor ate itself.

"The F-14."

"Colby! What are you talking about?"

"Well, that's what I'm trying to tell you."

"Could you do it in a less of your typically laconic manner?"

"Could, if you'd hush up some."

She could see General Arnson on the other side, grinning down at her. He wasn't much given to grinning in her experience. She bit down on her tongue—hard—to make sure she kept her silence. It wasn't an easy thing to do around Colby. Something in him just made her want to keep poking at it to see what hid underneath.

"Just before we went down, I spotted an F-14 coming in fast from," he hesitated and looked across the Washington Channel and the Anacostia River to where the helo had plunged into the river not a quarter mile away. "It came from our back quarter, out of the northwest."

"I couldn't have missed an F-14," Ivy's tongue ached from her hard-clamped teeth as she released it and blood flow resumed, reminding her why she'd been clamping down on it in the first place.

"You must be mistaken, son. I'd have noticed an F-14 in the corridor. It would have shaken us hard flying that low. I was standing in the hangar when you went down." He nodded over to the big building behind them, which would have a clear view of the accident. "First I heard of it was a shout from Jake that something was wrong with the approach. Saw you spin in. There's no way to miss an F-14. Besides, the military retired the last of those over a decade ago."

"Maybe it was a bird, Colby."

He looked down at her. "Unless seagulls have developed twin

vertical stabilizers, glass cockpits, a four-missile array under the wings, and a steel-gray paint job, I'd say it was a might more likely it was a Grumman F-14 Tomcat. Remember, we built an awful lot of fighter jet and helicopter models together after we ran out of spacecraft. You still have those?"

Ivy bit down on her tongue again. That was something else she'd forgotten about Colby, his infinite patience in teaching her how to make models actually look as good as the image on the box. He might tease, but he was smart as hell—even when he'd been lazy about everything else, his mind missed nothing. The details of that nine-inch model built across a couple of stormy afternoons had been cataloged neatly away until he needed it twenty years later.

"I couldn't figure out what was up. It looked incredibly close, but looked small at the same time like it was..." He tentatively stretched his arms out until his hands spanned four or five feet. "It still doesn't make sense."

"An RC." It was the only way that an F-14 could be that small but still have the level of detail Colby was describing.

The general was now scowling at her.

"Radio-controlled model—RC. Models come in all sizes. They sell kits that you can fly with a remote. Fly fast. Like a hundred miles an hour."

"Some pissed-off golfer with a toy took down one of my helicopters?" General Arnson's scowl was gone—and had been replaced by a dark fury. "I almost lost five personnel and a helicopter, and scrapped a seventy-year safety record, because of a goddamn toy?"

"Six personnel," Colby corrected him, cool as could be.

Ivy had been eyeing potential escape routes and wondering if there was a bomb shelter big enough to save her from one of the general's rare but legendary explosions. But Colby was facing straight into the storm.

"Six?" Arnson ground out.

Colby pointed down at Rex, who looked up eagerly, knowing he was the sudden center of attention. Probably hoping for a treat.

Instead of killing Colby on the spot with his bare hands, the general laughed (though it was a grim sound) and leaned down to pet Rex. "Six it is. Glad you made it too, boy."

The general raised a hand and a lieutenant appeared at his elbow.

"Warn the dive teams. They're looking for the remains of an F-14 model, one to two meters across. Get a team to shut down Hains Point Park and check every damn person for a radio controller or whatever the hell it is they use to fly those things. Tell them not to kill the bastard before I do."

"Yes, sir!" The lieutenant saluted.

The general snarled at him, and the lieutenant broke into a run toward the hangar.

In unison, the four of them moved forward to inspect the damage to the helicopter that had almost killed three of them.

7

Three hours later, they were little wiser.

Approximately a third of a model F-14 lay spread across three tables in a hundred pieces. The transmitter had been destroyed, so there was no information to be gotten there. The kit manufacturer had confirmed that it sold a model with that serial number five years before. The Secret Service had a field agent at the purchaser's doorstep within twenty minutes of obtaining his address. He had registered his kit to get the warranty, but sold it for cash at a RC fly-in last October because he'd upgraded to an F-22 Raptor.

"I don't know who he was. Just your average white kid with more money than sense. Said he'd never flown an RC, but wanted the F-14. Knew he'd crash it on its first flight, but he had the cash. Figured mine was the good side of a four-hundred-dollar lesson for the kid. Wish I'd kept it, though. F-14 was the last of the truly great pilots' birds." That had been in Ohio.

The opinion of the Washington, DC, RC club president, that to fly the F-14 at full speed to impact a helicopter's rear rotor was "a fine piece of flying," almost got him beaten to a pulp by the

Marine Corps forensic team. But the only F-14 model he knew about in the whole club was quickly accounted for.

Ivy definitely considered tracking him down herself and offering him a lesson or two on tact.

No radio controller had been located in the park. The plane could have been easily operated from a boat and the search was expanded to see if the controller had been dumped in the Potomac, but nothing had been found in the muddy depths.

Now they were out of time and the Marines of HMX-1 were never late. A VH-60N White Hawk was prepped and waiting for them.

As she'd grabbed the contents of their recovered go-bags from the big clothes dryer they kept in the hangar, General Arnson stalked up to Colby. She managed to blend into the background by sorting her dry clothes from Colby's into their respective packs. It was a surprisingly intimate process, unwinding one of her bras from his briefs—he was a briefs man and she'd bet that he looked good in them. In *just* them. *Whoa! Divert all power to the shields!*

It also helped that General Arnson's whispers were at a level that most officers issued commands. "I got one word for you, Thompson: *careful*. Be careful that you don't mess up my best officer and I won't be forced to make sure you get demoted from dog handler to dogshit cleaner for the rest of your natural born life. We clear?"

Colby had the good sense to reply, "Clear, sir."

Ivy had to puzzle at what the general was talking about as she handed over Colby's packed bag and they moved toward the waiting White Hawk together. There was no doubt that the general was referring to her—though as his "best officer," which was far more than he'd ever said to her face. If he'd meant it, the fact that he'd even said it made her feel as if she was in her dress blues again—with the sword this time.

But how would Colby mess her up? Irritate her to death

perhaps, but she was missing something. It bothered her that Colby appeared to have immediately understood what the general had meant.

Colby settled into a seat—not the one with the President's seal on it; actually he chose the one at the very rear of the aircraft—and told Rex he was a good boy. Ivy sat next to him in the much smaller helo for the flight from Anacostia over to Andrews Air Force Base. She'd forgotten that the White Hawk seats were narrower and they were practically rubbing shoulders. That, in turn, reminded her of something Colby had said just before they were separated by the debriefing teams.

"You called me beautiful."

Colby burst out laughing loudly enough to attract the pilot's attention from the duties of preparing for flight. "You always were a tenacious girl, Saint Ives."

"You paid me a compliment?"

"Might have. Took you long enough to notice."

If Ivy was any less of a Marine, her jaw would be down.

Colby Thompson had paid her a compliment? Several? At least two.

He'd acknowledged that despite his Secret Service training, she was still probably the more capable fighter. Which was true, she was a Marine, but it was unexpected of him to admit it.

And he'd called her beautiful.

Not cute. Because of her size, she'd heard that enough to spit fire at any guy who said such a thing.

But Colby had called her beautiful. Colby. Her.

This was a time to speculate about the enemy's intentions and to hell with McKinnon's Laws.

If Colby was just messing with her, she'd get him back but good. And why hadn't she done just that? *Well, of course I'm beautiful. But if you and your dog were in a pageant together, guess who'd win?* Though Colby had grown up to become some serious eye candy and—

She needed to make an appointment for a new brain—soon.

Ivy jolted when the crew chief came aboard and slammed the double door shut. The rotors wound up and in moments they were headed aloft to Andrews Air Force Base.

On the other hand:

Query: What if Mr. Oh-I'm-so-cute-while-I-play-with-my-dog-on-the-helicopter had meant it? What if he'd actually *meant* his compliment?

Query: What if his teasing joke about marrying her and naming all their kids Reggie hadn't been completely a joke?

Conclusion: Then she *would* have to kill him. Now would be the opportune moment. While she'd been thinking, they'd climbed up to a thousand feet over Maryland. Nobody would think anything of it if his body suddenly plummeted out of the sky. Crew Chief McShea was a Marine—he'd cover for her. Though maybe not. Colby had done one of his everybody's-friend things after their plunge in the Potomac.

Secondary conclusion: It was the coward's solution anyway, unbecoming of a Marine. No, if he actually had meant what he said, she'd kill him one-on-one with her bare hands, somewhere that she could hide the body. That would be far more fitting for someone like Colby Thompson.

So, the Marine in her understood the situation.

But the woman was just a little bit charmed by Colby Thompson calling her beautiful.

8

The C-5 Galaxy cargo jet boomed and echoed its way south along the East coast. He and Ivy weren't the only ones aboard the massive plane. Three VH-60N White Hawks, including theirs, had been loaded aboard the Galaxy after having their rotor blades folded back along the tail. The vertical rear rotor also had to be folded down, but otherwise the massive jet swallowed the three helicopters whole. That hadn't even *begun* to fill the cavernous interior. Their crews, plus a ground team with their service truck, plus seven vehicles for the Presidential Motorcade and all of their personnel were aboard as well.

The upstairs seating, which spanned the rear third of the plane above the cargo deck, wasn't even full. He could tell the old hands: most of them were asleep before takeoff. He'd heard that about the top soldiers—they could sleep anywhere. It was only the third flight of his life—one of his Georgia training trips, he'd gone by train—so there wasn't a chance he was going to be sleeping anytime soon. He wished there were windows so that he could see, but there weren't so he couldn't.

Pure willpower had fought off the intense wave of claustrophobia. That, and he didn't want to embarrass himself in front of Ivy.

Because of Rex, Colby and Ivy had claimed front row seats to get some extra foot space where Rex could lie down. Of course Rex was a dog, which meant he automatically filled every available inch. As a result he and Ivy had no room at all for their own feet. Their front row was actually at the very tail of the plane because all the seating was installed facing backward.

"They put it this way so that our backs are padded for nose-first crash landings," Ivy was smiling. Smiling!

He had to assume it was a joke—hoped to hell it was.

Then on takeoff someone whooped out, "Hey! A C-5 that's actually working." That earned laughter and catcalls from others.

"Actually working?"

Ivy leaned in close enough that her scent filled his brain and he could hardly understand her words as she spoke barely louder than the roar of the four massive engines. "The aircrews have nicknamed the Galaxy as FRED—short for Fucking Ridiculous Economic Disaster. C-5s aren't exactly known for their maintenance and reliability record."

Just what he didn't want to hear.

Unable to stand it, as soon as they were at cruising altitude Colby unbuckled and descended the steep stairway into the cargo hold. An air pocket almost flipped him off the side of the ladder even though he was clutching both handrails. The South Lawn never did that to him, except when Ivy Hanson was walking across and sending her own shock waves into his world.

No windows here either, but at least he could pace around the perimeter.

The helos and other vehicles were chained down to the deck in a double file in the plane's belly—as tightly packed as a Dupont Circle traffic jam. Down past the three Beasts—as the President's limos were known. Up the other side past the Halfback, Watchtower, and Roadrunner SUVs—protection detail, electronic countermeasures, and the mobile communications platform that could be used to run a war if necessary. Last in the row was the elite counter-assault-team SUV codenamed Hawkeye Renegade. The CAT guys were sitting in the flip-down seats built into the plane's side.

No friendly waves and trades of dog sniffs. Just a terse nod, so expressionless that he didn't know how to interpret it. They were close beside their vehicle and methodically stripping and cleaning their weapons. They looked more lethal than even the Delta Force snipers who manned the White House roof.

Finally, he lapped around the three helicopters with their folded-up rotors and then once more past the Beasts.

The earplugs made all but the simplest conversations impossible. He traded grunts and a wave with the CAT guys on his second lap. By the third lap they were ignoring him as a fixture of the flight. Maybe he'd just walk across the country, one plane length at a time.

Near the end of his third lap, someone grabbed his arm.

With little ceremony, he was shoved into one of the parked White Hawks. Unable to focus his eyes on the two facing armchairs to determine which was the President's, he collapsed across the aisle onto the bench seat that ran the length of one side. Rex hopped up into the open space for the President's legs. Ivy dropped into one of the armchairs, yanking the doors shut behind her.

His dog was following *her* around—just goddamn perfect.

She pulled her earplugs.

He did the same. Because of its presidential sound insulation, the inside of the helo was blessedly, almost painfully quiet. His ears rang from the sudden silence after wading through the C-5's roar.

"What the hell is wrong with you, Colby?"

"Wrong with me? There's nothing wrong with me. I've been on a plane twice in my life: for the flight down to the Federal Law

Enforcement Training Center in Georgia and back. Twice. My entire life. It would have fit in this cargo hold. It was just a Boeing 737 so it probably would have fit with its wings still on. But *that's* not the problem. That makes this all old hat to me. Did you know that the C-5's hold is longer than the Wright Brothers entire first flight at Kitty Hawk? There's something really unnatural about that, too—just saying. Though that isn't my point either."

He wasn't sure what his point was, but he couldn't seem to stop ranting at Ivy.

"This morning my life made sense. White House perimeter security. Lead Dog. Keeping it all safe. Now I'm bouncing around the country to protect a President I've never actually met. Rex trusts me, but who the hell am I supposed to trust?" He might have been shouting a little by the end of it. It was hard to tell.

"This is only your third-ever flight? How did you get between states and countries in the past?" Like *that* was the important question.

"I fucking walked, Hanson!" Now he was definitely shouting, but was helpless to do anything about it. "I'm not some ultra-decorated super-duper Marine Corps pilot genius who has flown all over the world, okay? I'm not used to sitting backward for when we come crashing down out of the sky." That just *had* to be a joke. More likely no one survived if one of these monsters crashed. "I'm just a guy who's been to Georgia a couple of times. What the hell are we flying toward?" He waved a hand toward the nose of the helicopter. "I don't know! I've never been there! And what the hell am I supposed to be doing when I get there? I don't know. I've never done this. You're the big hot-shot liaison. Care to explain my job to me in some brilliantly anal retentive administrative detail? Huh? Huh? I'm just a high-paid dog handler. And you are so…" *Shit!* There was no safe way to finish that sentence as she watched him intently with those lovely blue eyes of hers. Watched him like a bomb with the timer fast running down to zero.

"That's the back of the plane. That's the front," she pointed toward the tail of the helicopter.

Right. This helo had been loaded backward to save space, overlapping tails with the White Hawk parked in front of it. *Crap!* He didn't even know which way he was going. He had to clench his jaw or he was going to be sick.

"Who are you, Colby Thompson?" Like he was some sort of total loser.

"Eat shit, Hanson!"

NEVER IN A HUNDRED years would the Colby Thompson she knew have admitted a weakness. And whoever this man was sitting across from her, he had just told her he was terrified!

Actually, Ivy had met so few men who would admit to feeling vulnerable—no matter how out of their depth they actually were—that she couldn't come up with a single name.

"Colby?"

"What?" He snapped out more sharply than his German shepherd.

"You're spooking your dog." Rex was indeed looking at Colby with alarm written clear across his furry face.

"Aw shit," he knelt down on the carpet and grabbed Rex's head, then rested his own forehead against the dog's. "I'm sorry, boy. This isn't about you. You're doing great." And he kept his forehead there until both he and the dog seemed calmer.

Which was about the sweetest thing she'd ever seen. It felt as if she should look away because the moment was so private. But she couldn't.

After Colby returned to his seat, he rested his foot on Rex's side. She was about to protest at how crass that was, using his dog as a footstool after the beautiful moment they'd just had, when

Rex flopped on his back in the narrow aisle. Colby began rubbing his dog's belly with his foot.

Neither of their families had been dog people. By all rights they should have been, growing up in a kid-friendly neighborhood and having side-by-side cabins at the beach. But they hadn't. Yet Colby had finally found something to care about. And he appeared to be a natural at it.

Ivy wanted to slap herself. She needed to stop seeing Colby through the lens of the past. She didn't know what Lead Dog really was, but if what he'd said was true and not just bragging, it meant that he'd become one of the very best at what he did. He was the guy the *other* Secret Service dog handlers came to with their problems.

The past didn't fit the present man at all.

So, discard the past. Think of the man. Competent, but out past the stretch zone and into a hot-landing-zone type panic.

"Colby—"

"I'm not some goddamn idiot, Ivy. I know I'm in over my head. I've onboarded enough new dog teams to know irrational panic when I see it. I just don't know what to do with it."

"You act as though everything is fine."

He squinted at her.

"You think I've never been scared? Freaking out is part of being a pilot. When tracer fire is punching holes in your fuselage and your Marines are stuck inside, taking the hits with no way to fire back, and you're just praying to the gods the enemy fire doesn't punch out a critical system and bring your whole aircraft down out of the sky in a ball of flaming fire. Right then? Trust me, you're freaking. Training kicks in. You do the next task that's right in front of you. Chaff release, restore failing hydraulics, evasive maneuvers—whatever you can."

"Whatever's right in front of me?" Suddenly Colby had that half smile he always wore just as he was about to zing her. She'd learned to let him have his teasing moments. Partly because it was usually fun, partly because it made the revenge so much sweeter. But the shift this time was so fast.

"Exactly!"

"No matter what the consequences?"

"Well, hopefully it will fix things, but sometimes not."

"And you're sure about this?" That half smile was still growing. That was one of the things about Colby's teases—she could see them coming, but even with all the years of practice she could never predict what they'd be. Something about aircraft. Or flying.

"Worked every time so far." Maybe about travel.

"Fine, let's see how your luck is holding."

"*My* luck? You mean *your* lu—"

And Colby leaned across the narrow aisle and kissed her.

She'd guessed wrong again.

COLBY HAD EXPECTED any number of possible results: top of the list being a head-twisting slap. In anticipation, he'd casually rested a hand on her shoulder, placing his arm as an effective block. Because she was sitting sideways in the armchair, her other hand would be blocked by the back of the chair.

Instead, her burst of laughter broke the kiss. In seconds, he joined in. There was no way to stop it.

He and Ivy. There wasn't a more unlikely couple on the planet.

It was like they were sixteen and nineteen again, but it felt more as if he was eight and she was five. Except they'd never "stolen" a first kiss from each other. They both would have screamed "Cooties!" and run in opposite directions. She'd grown up sleek and beautiful and he'd really enjoyed watching her once she had.

Actually kissing her had never been part of any program.

Ivy managed to catch her breath first. She held out a hand as if to shake his.

Unsure what else to do, he took it and shook it firmly once.

"Hi, I'm Major Ivy Hanson." *Not a kid anymore.* He heard the unspoken part clear as day.

"Lieutenant Colby Thompson at your service, ma'am." And suddenly he wasn't holding her hand prior to some martial arts throw or grabbing her to heave her overboard. Instead he was holding the hand of a beautiful woman.

Using their clasp, he slowly drew her back in. She watched him carefully with those wide, blue eyes, but neither did she resist when he kissed her again.

This time it wasn't at all about who they'd been.

Somehow, at least for today, Ivy had become the only sensible thing in his world. A day that had begun so normally had spun out of control. And when she'd explained her theory of panic was the moment he'd understood what was really throwing him off his usual even keel.

His problem wasn't all of that other noise—that was merely making him a little nuts. His problem, since the moment she'd stepped off that helicopter onto the close-trimmed grass of the South Lawn, was Ivy Hanson.

He'd sworn at her, cursed her right to her face, and her response had been to sincerely try to help him. Cool under pressure he didn't doubt. But there had to be a woman in there somewhere.

And here she was, clear as day physically—an exciting combination of lovely and lethal. And so straight-ahead. No wonder she was a Marine Corps major. It was as if they'd invented the Corps for people like her—focused, straight-ahead thinkers. That trait was what had always made her so fun to tease: her absolute willingness to walk right into any trap he set for her.

The combination was amazing, but it was the woman who was dazzling him. He'd never have pegged Ivy Hanson as having kindness.

Or such a taste. Each moment she let his kiss continue added another layer of richness, of depth, of wonder. He'd been "lucky in love" and knew it. He'd had some fine women share his bed. None had tasted so vibrantly alive as Ivy.

Her hand pressed against his shoulder as a slow, steady pressure, driving him away even as she leaned into the kiss. Finally, she pushed enough farther with her arm than she leaned in that the kiss slipped apart with just the slightest tug of her teeth on his lower lip.

Anime girls didn't have eyes as big as hers were at the moment. Their brilliant blue shone brighter than a DC summer sky.

Continuing to use her arm as a lever against his shoulder, she slowly pushed herself back into her seat.

"I could ask why…" But she didn't.

He was glad she didn't, because he had no good answer to that. Any glib response had been erased by the surprising depth of that kiss. Her brow furrowed as she puzzled at it. Ivy really *was* the cutest thing on the planet. Not physically cute, which was how she would take it if he said anything, even though it was true. But linear, hyper-rational cute. That kiss had just dropped his prior experiences of women right in the deep end of the pool where they'd all sunk with no idea how to swim. And she was busy thinking it through.

"I think instead I could ask, 'Since when?' "

"Well, since you're asking questions instead of running your pig-sticker into my gut, I s'pose I should try to answer that."

"Please."

It took everything he had not to laugh in her face. Her eyes were still unnaturally wide, her breath was running in short hard gasps, yet her voice was perfectly calm. Marine training he supposed.

"At first I thought it might be the moment you stepped off that helo this morning without even a hair out of place."

"So, it's just lust." As if she could deal with that.

"Then I recalled that red-white-and-blue one-piece you wore

at the beach for July 4th the year you turned sixteen. Please tell me you still have that swimsuit. You looked beyond amazing in that."

"So you're just interested in my body."

"But now I'm thinkin'," he stretched out the moment by leaning down to rub Rex, who sighed in his sleep, "I'm thinkin' that it goes back to maybe when I was five and you were two, following us everywhere. You made Reggie nuts, but..."

"You're so warped that teasing me to death was your way of saying you liked me?" Ivy concluded in a tone of judge, jury, and executioner.

"I was five. Sue me."

"And you aren't just messing with me now?"

"I'm not a big thinker, Ivy. I'm a Be Here Now sort of guy. And after that kiss, being here now sounds pretty damned good to me."

"But—"

"You're already thinking six steps ahead."

She nodded with a grimace that said it probably caused her at least as much trouble as it saved her. She'd always been the one with a plan.

"Remember what our favorite books were?"

"What are you talking about, Colby?"

"Reggie's favorite book as a child was written by Julia Child. Yours was..."

"*The Little Engine That Could.*" And it had been. He'd helped teach her to read from that book. There'd been most of six months where he couldn't turn around without finding Ivy clutching her favorite book and looking up at him with her little girl eyes begging him to read it to her. She did that long after she could read it herself.

"You were always way past the train making it up and over the mountain with a trainload of toys. I bet you have never once thought 'I think I can.' You were always 'What can I do next?'

Pretty damn humbling, Ives. Remember what mine was at that age?"

"*Winnie-the-Pooh,*" her voice was little more than a puzzled whisper. It would have been impossible to hear outside the helicopter's sound insulation.

"*Winnie-the-Pooh,*" he confirmed. "Know why?"

She shook her head.

"Because I'm like Pooh. He's the ultimate Be Here Now kind of guy, just dropping in on his other pals in the Hundred Acre Wood. So, no, I wasn't thinking ahead about messing with you, or setting you up for something. I was thinking about how much I wanted to kiss you. Enough that I didn't even care much what your revenge might be."

"At least I think before I act."

Which was true. It had taken him a long time to realize that because Ivy always thought so damn fast, it looked like simple reaction; but it never was.

"Unlike me. I just wanted to kiss you, so I did. What are you thinking, Saint Ives?"

"I'm still thinking that you're messing with me intentionally."

He raised three fingers in a Boy Scout salute. "As God and the Scouts are my witness—"

"Save the shit for someone who cares, Thompson." But she said it with a smile.

"Yes, ma'am."

He tried to wait her out, but she wasn't having anything to do with it. He looked around the helo, even out the windows, but all he could see was a black SUV to one side and the steel side of the C-5's hull to the other. That left him to think about what had just happened.

"Hell of a kiss though, wasn't it?" He'd never actually imagined kissing her, but now that he had, it was hard to think of anything else.

Ivy just nodded.

"Want to try it again?"

She shook her head.

No! She *absolutely* didn't want to try it again.

Her job, her *life* did not have any possible interpretation that allowed a kiss from Colby Thompson. The first peck, maybe. It had been almost cartoon funny—even less likely than some of the Captain Kirk kissing the alien seductress scenes.

The second one, though? Clearly, she'd slid off into some alternate reality. Who knew that hormones could shift her world track —temporarily only, she prayed—to include such a thing? It was a Jean Luc Piccard and Beverly Crusher kind of kiss, full of meaning and history and—

So not! *Where are my damn shields!*

Ivy Hanson and Colby Thompson—*that* belonged on the far side of the galaxy through a very twisted quantum space that...

She didn't know *what* it did!

But it certainly didn't leave her heart racing faster than the time she'd been shot down and saved her crew as much by luck as by skill.

That was it!

She must be injured and lying in some hospital bed again, suffering from a painkiller-fueled delusion, like the one time she'd let a handsome Austrian *oberstleutnant* convince her to try skiing. Southern women should not be made to downhill ski. It had caused her to swear off dating all Austrian military men ever since —and German and Swiss military while she was at it.

So why in the world did her fantasy include a scorching kiss from Colby Thompson?

She looked down at Rex. He was lying across Colby's boots but had his front paws and nose resting on hers. He was looking at her as if telling her to get her act together.

Ivy didn't have dreams where she could see each expression as it moved over a dog's face in real time. Her dreams were crazy, swooping swirls of adventure ever since that Saturday when she was eleven and she'd watched too many sci-fi movies in a row—only to relive them all mashed together in her sleep. Gort and Robby the Robot dancing to the *Star Wars* theme, while Princess Leia and Spock debated the nature of effective rebellion over a game of holographic chess played between *Jurassic Park* dinosaurs and *Blade Runner* replicants all singing the five tones of *Close Encounters of the Third Kind* in thirty-two-part harmony that slowly fractured as more and more of them were killed off by phaser blast and light saber-wielding Klingons.

She'd learned never to try and explain her dreams to anyone. Not since the one time she'd tried to explain one to Colby.

"You laughed in my face." He had. Years ago. But her present dream had included an undeniably real kiss.

"No, I didn't. I kissed you. Well, the first time, yeah. Besides, you laughed first. But that second kiss was no laughing matter."

"Then what was it?"

"Stupendous!"

"That's not what I'm talking about." Kisses with the Colby Thompsons of the world were *not* supposed to be stupendous, even if it had been. "It wasn't. It was just an aberration, that's all. An aberration that's never *ever* going to recur."

"Ivy, sweetie."

"Sweetie? You were doing so well, Colby, right until that moment." *Patronizing bastard.*

"You know it was an amazing kiss." He offered one of his smarmy Colby grins. "Bet you just can't wait for another."

"I... *What?*" As if she didn't *know* what she wanted. As if she hadn't had to fight every step of the way to beat her way into the Marines. She didn't deserve this kind of shit from anybody. Not her brother, not Colby, not anyone.

Ivy popped the door on the VH-60N, climbed out, and closed

it quickly—almost catching Rex's nose and cutting off Colby's attempt to backpedal. She didn't look back to see either of their faces in the window.

There was no free weight set on this plane. No punching bag to work out on. She needed to beat on something badly.

There was also nowhere to hide.

Unless…

She strode forward as if she had a purpose. As if.

"WELL, I screwed that up pretty royally, didn't I, boy?"

Rex sighed and returned to lying on his feet, sprawling out over the President's carpet.

"She smell as good to you as she did to me?"

A second sigh.

"She tastes even better."

Rex ignored him.

"And she is some kind of pissed right now. I just—" He didn't know what had come over him at the last second. He'd suddenly found himself pushing Ivy's buttons—hard—and he knew right where they were. Like he'd backslid into some past version of himself and couldn't stop it.

Ivy didn't mind being laughed with, but she hating being laughed *at*. Hate was too mild a word. He'd seen her shut out friends for life for doing that to her. In hindsight, he was perhaps the only person he knew of in her entire life who'd ever gotten away with it.

"And I just told her she didn't know her own mind. Shit! I guess I deserved her storming out on me."

Rex fell asleep.

"And now I'm sitting in the President's helicopter talking to myself because even my dog isn't listening."

Nothing was happening.

"Sitting where the crew chief will shoot us for just sitting, even if you weren't shedding all over the place." While probably not true, it was enough to motivate him to get moving. He swung open the door, then roused Rex so that they stepped down from the helo together. When neither of them was shot, he took it as a good sign. The fact that Ivy was nowhere to be seen was, perhaps, less of a good sign.

He circled around to the other side. The boys of the counter assault team were apparently done checking their weapons but hadn't gone back upstairs.

For lack of anything better to do, he flipped down the next seat that ranged along the side of the cargo jet's fuselage and sat with them. Once he introduced Rex around and had given him a treat for each "positive" he found on all the guys as they petted him, they relaxed enough to start asking him questions. A few were about the White House, most were about Rex and how he could respond to various attack scenarios. Not a single question about Ivy, which was good.

"YOU GUYS ARE ALMOST HUMAN. When did that happen?" Ivy teased the Air Force crew and it earned her a laugh and some flak about being a toy soldier. They had an entire habitat on the upper deck. It stretched from the wings forward with no access to the aft passenger cabin except through the big cargo bay down below.

It began just forward of the wings where there was a seven-seat area for military couriers who couldn't risk mixing with the general population of mere soldiers. A small living and bunk area for the relief crew. Typically they were aboard only for long missions—since with midair refueling the C-5s could span the globe. But carrying the President's motorcade and helicopters, they wanted to be prepared for everything, and an entire second crew was along even for the short flight down the East Coast. In addition to the standard four on the flight deck—pilot, copilot, and two engineers—they also had a navigator who only flew for special missions.

She'd managed to talk her way into the flight deck's observer chair by waving around her White House Military Office appointment. It was nice that it had some use other than saddling her with Colby Thompson. She'd also wager that being Lead Dog wasn't going to get him permission to climb the forward stairway. She could use the distance.

Out the front windshield, she could see that they were hugging the coast, slipping between brilliant white lumps of cumulus clouds scattered across the blue sky. She could see just a little of the eastern seaboard of the Carolinas below, dotted with giant spots of cloud shadow.

She'd somehow fallen into one of those shadows down in the cargo deck with Colby, closed inside a helicopter. Now she was once again up in the sunlight, talking about foreign missions, the lousy conditions at different overseas bases, and the food at Ramstein in Germany versus Lemonnier in Djibouti. Familiar. Competent.

How could Colby never have left the East Coast? Not even to Florida?

As she chatted with the crew, making a point about how luxurious the Air Force had it with beds and baths and room to walk around, she thought about that.

Colby had started out the conversation very differently than he'd ended it.

He'd been overwhelmed. Afraid even. Of travel. Of his new role. Of leaving the familiar grounds of the White House.

Had he let his fears show because she was the only person around? As close and he and Reggie were, her memories of eavesdropping on their heart-to-heart chats had been much more in guy speak.

"Thinking of France for a couple years." Her brother spent two years at the Sorbonne's culinary school. But she'd overheard him checking out the idea with Colby long before he mentioned it to their parents. He'd never thought to ask if she'd miss him.

"Leaving DC?"

"Yeah, need to get away from your stink. Maryland ain't half far enough."

Then they'd gotten really deep.

"You cool with it?"

Colby's manly, worldless shrug of "Why wouldn't I be?"

And yet he'd *spoken* to her. Told her he was afraid and recognized that in himself.

The Air Force guys teased her back about having an entire eight-hundred-foot Landing Helicopter Dock ship to wander around with her MEU. "Yeah, real luxurious, guys. Two thousand Marines crammed aboard and we aren't even allowed on go up on deck to see the sky most days because of constant flight operations."

It earned her the "smallest violin in the world" pity gesture.

She responded with an equally friendly flying middle finger and they moved on to reminiscing about other operations.

How had she responded to Colby's cry for help?

She'd told him to never show it. Stuff it down deep and never let anyone know.

And that's just what he'd done.

And when he'd started to say something about her, she'd told him that he was pointing at the wrong end of the plane. Real smooth.

So, instead, he'd kissed her and called her sweetie as if either of those was okay.

If he was smart, he'd never risk speaking to her again because who knew what new ways she'd find to slam him down. She was showing about as much emotional depth as her big brother. The New Colby had peeked out into view and her answer? She'd squashed him like a bug. He probably did the kiss and "Sweetie" thing just to chase her away. It was certainly something Old Colby would do. Or a Colby with the least sense of self-preservation.

Except for that kiss.

Better than she'd ever imagined possible.

Had she ever imagined kissing him?

Wait! She had the timeline wrong. Colby had kissed her, really kissed her. Then, when she'd slammed into him about laughing at her crazy dreams half a lifetime ago, he'd pushed her away hard: "Sweetie, I bet you can't wait for another."

"Assholes!" He'd been a complete and total asshole. But then… so had she. They both were.

The Air Force crew was looking at her strangely.

"What?"

She'd lost track where she was. They'd been waiting for a laugh or mock indignation or some response to something. By the look of it, it was their third or fourth attempt—then she'd called them all assholes. And not in the kindest of tones.

How could she explain…without explaining. The smiles died and the moment withered just as she imagined Colby's smile had when she'd slammed the door in his face.

"We're starting our descent," the captain finally spoke and the rest of the crew got busy. The Air Force captain had barely tolerated her up here in the first place and joined in none of the banter. Now his message was very clear.

She might pilot a helicopter rather than an airplane that weighed four hundred thousand pounds empty, but she could tell they weren't actually doing anything yet—other than *looking* busy. She took the hint and thanked them for the view.

"Anytime," and they made it sound sincere. Even might have been. Except the captain, who said nothing.

As she descended the ladder, she spotted Colby huddled up with the shooters of the Counter Assault Team. They appeared to be having a grand old time. And she'd been worried that she'd hurt him. Or not listened to him well enough or something. Nope, nothing actually upset him. Maybe the whole vulnerable thing had been the act. The kiss hadn't been part of that. It had been part of "Sweetie, I'm sure you deserved it when I laughed in your face." That was the real him.

Fine, Colby Thompson. You're on your own.

Of course, with friends like her, maybe he didn't need enemies.

She descended the steep stairs quickly and circled around the far side of the parked vehicles where he wouldn't be able to see her. When she ascended the rear ladder to the seating area, no one looked up at her except for Rex, who must have caught her scent as she went by. Colby missed the cue from his own dog.

Ivy couldn't stop wondering if that was a good thing or bad as she met with the HMX crews upstairs. Or after she strapped in alone in the front row of seats once the descent finally began.

Colby stayed downstairs with the guys.

Fine.

9

*E*verything got much more lively when they landed at Cape Canaveral. There were two runways, one in the heart of Kennedy Space Center. The other, an overlong strip built specifically for landing shuttles. Flights using the latter runway were so restricted that there was no taxiway, just the main strip— meaning traffic must not be a problem. Their C-5 Galaxy apparently rated.

The CAT guys had warned him, so he'd been waiting close by the rear ramp when it was finally lowered. He'd been told that the unloading would be a good opportunity to get run over and it would be best to just get out of the way.

When the back of the plane cracked open and the stern of the cargo bay began lowering, the heat and humidity had rolled over the top of the angled ramp and crashed into him like an unexpected tidal wave. It felt wrong and it smelled wrong. As if somehow the humidity made it achingly dry. And it was thick with sea salt against his tongue, like an ocean that someone had forgotten about and left cooking too long on the burner.

Ivy grabbed his arm and dragged him down the ramp, jumping off the side just as one of the SUVs rolled backward down the slope and onto the sizzling pavement. Even with the CAT guys' warning, he'd been stunned into place. He checked the tires of the descending vehicle, but they didn't appear to be melting when they hit the pavement. According to his watch, six in the evening was not late enough to be visiting Florida. He could feel the heat driving through the soles of his boots.

"This is insane."

"It's a heat wave. Never gets much above this. Still, it's cooler than Camp Lemonnier," Ivy didn't looked wilted at all.

"Which is…"

"Horn of Africa, Colby. You really should get out more. This is mild. And you get used to it."

"I like DC just fine." But that wasn't what Captain Baxter had set him up for. He'd set him up for travel, probably worldwide travel. "Next you're going to say that I need one of those t-shirt that says 'Whining' with a big red circle and slash over it."

"Marines never whine. I don't know what's up with you Secret Service types."

Neither did he. He never complained about anything. Of course, compared to the last twelve hours, most of his life had given him very little to complain about. Even when it had, he'd always made a point of acting as the positive force in the group. Ivy apparently brought out his dark side or something.

"You and Darth are close I guess."

"What was that?" She'd been watching the unloading.

He decided to keep his thoughts about Ivy's power and the dark side of the force to himself.

One of the Beasts eased down the ramp, the long limo carefully tended by two loadmasters and a small phalanx of Secret Service techs. It was closely followed by two more SUVs.

"Come on." Ivy led him into the relatively cool shade beneath the aircraft. They walked past the eight tires of the left landing gear, each taller than he was. Much more tolerable.

Of course she hadn't felt like the dark side of the force. Not until *after* he'd kissed her and the fury had lashed out of nowhere.

"I didn't kiss you to make you angry, Saint Ives."

"I wish you wouldn't call me that." Again, she answered the wrong part of the question.

"Goddamn it, Ivy!" Colby grabbed her arm and dragged her to a halt beneath one of the jet's massive engines, so monstrous that it felt like it was going to fall off the wing and crush them at the least excuse.

Maybe he no longer cared if it did.

"Now you're going to make me angry."

Ivy just squinted at him like he was a bug.

"Fine," he turned to continue forward when he heard her voice softly behind him.

"Then why did you?"

"I...don't know. But it wasn't to piss you off. And it wasn't a tease. I did it because...I wanted to."

"Well, don't. It's confusing."

Yeah, like that was news. He kept going, but stumbled to a halt when he and Rex reached the nose of the plane. Or rather where the nose was supposed to be.

Instead of sticking out the front of the plane, the nose section had swung up and out on massive hinges until it was three stories above them pointing upward at the hazy blue sky. In its place, a forward ramp had been extended and the White Hawk helicopters were being rolled off out the front of the plane.

"Go to work," Ivy prompted him from close by his elbow.

Of course that's all she cared about. He didn't look at her. If he did, it would just make the hurt worse.

Don't. It's confusing.

It wasn't like he knew why he kissed her in the first place. She was always too smart for him, living in some stratosphere to which he didn't belong. Too smart, too motivated, too good to do anything other than succeed.

Rex.

He understood Rex. Sniff, eat, nap, get treats. Dog actions broke down into such simple categories.

"*Such,*" he ordered.

And Rex sought.

Simple. *That* Colby could take comfort in.

They circled and crawled through each helo. They checked every technician working on the birds: the ones unfolding the rotors, others from the base who arrived to fuel the helos, two more techs doing systems checks. They sniffed at the flight crews as they assembled to pre-flight the helicopters in preparation for a test flight.

Ivy moved forward to talk to the flight leader. Thankfully Rex had already checked him and they didn't need to go near Ivy, but he could feel her attention tracking him. Like there was some sort of dog leash between them now.

Since the moment of the kiss, he'd had an incredible awareness of her.

On the flight, he hadn't been watching for her, yet had somehow glanced up and recognized her boot from all others as it hit the first rung of the ladder down from the Galaxy's flight deck. Forcing his attention back to a friendly argument with the CAT shooter's ridiculous preference for the old Colt 1911 with .45 rounds over Glock 19 pistols with 9mm was the only thing that kept him from watching how she moved.

He *had* tapped Rex's shoulder to draw his attention to her so that Colby could track her by the motion of Rex's head—up the rear ladder to the passenger deck without coming anywhere near him.

Shit!

For something to do once his inspection of the helicopters was complete, he guided Rex over to the wing shade on the far side of the C-5. The monster plane had "knelt," squatting down on its wheels until its belly almost rubbed the tarmac to make the unloading easier. It also had the advantage of blocking his sight-lines beneath the aircraft to see Ivy. He scanned the scrub grass and low brush while Rex lay down on the pavement and rolled over as if it was a comfy heating pad.

"How do you do that with all that fur?"

Rex sighed happily, laid his head back, and fell asleep with four paws in the air.

The interesting parts of Cape Canaveral lay south of the airfield, warped by the heat haze. Impossibly tall gantries were scattered about like individual skyscrapers, each missing their city. In the far distance, there was a small group of truly massive buildings. Ivy could probably tell him about each and every one: purpose, history, and God alone knew what else. Only the fifty-story tower of the Vehicle Assembly Building, where the rockets were assembled for launch, stood out clearly. At less than two miles away, it alone commanded the southern vista.

This section of the Cape was a lonely place. Due east was nothing but a line of low trees—mangrove and Brazilian pepper, one of the C-5's loadmasters had told him—cutting off any view of the nearby ocean. To the north, only a few tall condos peeked above the trees. To the west, again nothing.

Maybe he'd just act like those lone skyscrapers. Ivy hadn't been in his life or much in his thoughts for several years prior to this morning. No loss. He'd just go back to ignoring her, standing alone on the baking runway beneath a strangely hazy sky—blue, but definitely not DC blue.

Did sleeping dogs get homesick?

"It feels desolate, doesn't it?" Ivy spoke from close behind him.

Between one heartbeat and the next, Rex flopped over from upside down, dead asleep to sitting up and looking for a pet from Ivy.

She looked impossibly sad as she complied.

Colby could ignore many things, but he couldn't ignore that.

SHE HADN'T EXPECTED this feeling.

Shuttles had landed here. Right here!

Cape Canaveral.

Kennedy Space Center.

After a lifetime of dreaming, she'd finally made it to the heart of America's space program. And all that struck her was the vast emptiness.

The isolated runway.

The lone C-5 jet.

Except for the quickly assembling HMX-1 fleet and the Motorcade, the silence was echoing. Air Force One would be arriving early tomorrow and everything would be ready. Where was the drama? The excitement?

"Why didn't you ever go for being an astronaut, Ivy?"

Colby's question surprised her. "I..." She didn't have a good answer to that. Because almost no one ever made that grade? Well, she'd guaranteed that she wouldn't by never trying.

"I guess that I never really thought to try. It was all too far away, too magical."

"Reality looks a lot like hard work."

"Well, that's a downer, Thompson."

"No! No!" Colby turned to face her. "I'm fine with hard work—"

"Didn't used to be."

"Maybe you could grant that I grew up somewhere along the way."

"Sure...sweetie!" But that was wrong. Ivy shrugged an acknowledgement that felt as if she was saying he was right. Earlier today it would have been a sarcastic *Yeah, right!* But it didn't feel like that anymore. This Colby Thompson was too impressive to deny.

"I like a challenge. Gives me purpose. You taught me that."

She looked at him in surprise, but he continued too quickly for her to ask what he meant. If she didn't know better, she'd say he was sorry he'd spoken that thought aloud.

"I love working with Rex and the other dogs. Just… It seems as if there should be more, somehow. I don't know. Just whistling in the wind here." He turned back to face the low green wall that bordered the long runway. "There are hundreds of agents and dozens of dogs working to keep the President safe. That doesn't count all of the other forces we recruit from police and military. I've caught my fair share of fence jumpers, and Rex has tagged a couple of wannabe bombers, but nothing big. Which I suppose is good, but it still feels…small."

"I feel like that all the time. I think that's what makes me keep pushing."

"Sounds right. But it doesn't sound like me. Maybe it's just this place."

Colby knew her that well, to know what sounded like her even when she didn't. He knew her better than anyone other than… maybe not even herself.

The salt wind seemed to be taking the daylight with it. The sun, now a bloody orange orb, set beyond the helos as the first one lifted aloft for its test flight. Soon the other two followed.

"Shouldn't you be there?"

Where she should be was back in the White House Military Office, acknowledging the report that the HMX-1 team was ready. Here, she'd already seen that the operations team was fully prepared to carry out their tasks without her poking her nose in. She would complete the mission, but perhaps her idea of being in the field hadn't been the best. All she'd managed to do was get shot down.

"I…" the words seemed to be trapped in her chest. "I don't know where I'm supposed to be."

Colby wrapped a friendly arm around her shoulder for just a

moment and Rex nuzzled at her hand, both of which made her feel better for no reason she could identify.

"We'll figure it out, Saint Ives."

"Why do you always call me that? I'm not from Cornwall. And he's the patron saint of lawyers. So that can't be it. Tell me it isn't the dumb nursery rhyme."

"*As I was going to St. Ives, I met a man with seven wives. Each wife had seven sacks. Each sack had seven cats. Each cat had seven kits. Kits, cats, sacks, wives. How many were going to St. Ives?*"

"One. The narrator who meets the man, etc. who are going the other way."

Colby looked down at her carefully. "You've always gone your own way, Ivy. Full bore, crashing over anyone who tries to become an obstacle."

"Doesn't sound very nice, does it?" However, it did sound more than a little true. Just like her, in fact. The little engine who could...no matter what was in her way.

"It's one of the things I admire most about you. You're beautiful, funny, and you have a kiss so good that I still can't get my head around it. But your stand-out feature is your determination. It's as clear and direct as...as a rocket flight—always going your own way without any doubts or questions. I'm sure that it makes you an awesome Marine, but that's why I was wondering that you never went into space."

"I was only ever a pilot. No advanced degrees in science or robotics."

"And NASA doesn't use pilots?"

"I was only ever a *helicopter* pilot. To pilot for NASA, you have to be a *jet* pilot first. Jets never interested me."

"You're a funny woman, Saint Ives."

"Ha-ha funny?" She wasn't feeling like laughing at the moment.

The three VH-60Ns came racing in from over the horizon, high enough to glow brightly in the sun that had already left the runway in shadow. Low enough to suppress conversation for the few moments of their passage.

"Not to me, Ivy. Funny as in each time I think I understand you, I discover that I don't at all."

"Welcome to the club. I don't understand me either most of the time. I'm a Marine who doesn't fight. I'm a Marine pilot who no longer flies. How did I think that was a good thing?"

"I did learn a few somethings about you over the years." Colby's look seemed kind, which must be a trick of the fading light. She didn't deserve it after the way she'd shut him down.

"Which is?"

"Anything you do is a good thing. Anything."

His tone said that he firmly believed that. And knowing of his belief helped ease her own doubts. Made her once again remember how proud she'd been as she approached the White House.

"Colby?"

"Um-hm?"

He saw her as more capable than she saw herself. When she wore her Marine Corps cloak, Major Ivy Hanson knew who she was. The woman-Ivy was more of a total-frame-loss accident that had happened long ago. But maybe, just maybe, there was hope for a woman named Saint Ives.

And she felt that way because of how Colby was looking at her. Because of how he spoke of her. Because of how *he* made her feel.

The three VH-60Ns hammered down out of the dark, landing on the pavement to finish their test run. Maybe it was time for her to test a thing or two herself and see how they progressed.

She stepped forward into Colby's arms and pulled him down far enough to kiss him.

olby woke in the darkness with a start. The soft sound of the air conditioner said motel room. The soft snore close by the side of the bed told him Rex's location. He must be on his back again; he only snored when he was upside down.

The woman, a mere outline in the white nightgown standing close by the bed—no more substantial than a ghost—her he couldn't place at all. The red LED clock informed him it was still short of midnight.

Rex's snore cut off.

Not a ghost.

The woman...

"Ivy?" They had kissed at sunset. If he'd needed proof that the first kiss wasn't a fluke, the second one had proved that it was because it was even more incredible. Her body had tucked against his like a custom fit. Her soft moan of pleasure had nearly taken him to his knees as he wrapped his arms more tightly about her. Ivy Hanson kissed as she did everything else: with her whole being.

Then the flight leader had appeared out of the dark to report on the successful test flight. Which had led to a review of the next day's mission and the multiple sorties that would be necessary to provide for the President's itinerary. Which had looked simple on paper, but Colby had rapidly learned was anything but. Even the two-point-seven miles between the shuttle runway and the launch viewing area had to be carefully considered.

Because of the events that had landed them in the Potomac that morning, she then became involved in discussions about changed security measures in case another drone approached any of the HMX-1 flight paths. Firing a hundred-thousand-dollar Hellfire missile capable of punching a hole in a Russian tank at a small object weighing ten pounds wasn't a solution. He'd made sure she ate at one point, but she'd been so deep in it that he'd finally taken a ride to the hotel with Sergeant McShea.

"Ivy?" His room ghost hadn't replied.

There was a slight movement of the gown that might reflect a nod.

Unsure of what else to do, he slid to the far side of the bed as he folded open the covers.

The ghost took a step forward, stumbled on Rex, and flopped down onto the bed completely unlike an ethereal ghost. There was a brief scramble as Rex moved to a new location on the floor and Ivy attempted to untangle herself from her second crash landing of the day.

"So much for my dignity," she mumbled.

"Or any indecision about climbing into my bed. As you're now sprawled in it."

"I told the clerk my mag card key had died, then gave him your room number to reprogram it to. Not exactly a high security place."

"Not complaining. Surprised as hell, but not complaining." As they spoke, he tried to lean in to assist her. Instead of finding her elbow, he found something else wonderfully soft beneath smooth flannel. "Whoops!"

When he went to pull away, she grabbed his hand and kept it against her breast. "As good a place to start as any."

"Ivy? Maybe we should talk first?"

"Why?"

Of course Ivy Hanson would be as straight-ahead about sex as she was about everything else.

"Because…"

But Ivy had gotten herself straightened out, slipping under the covers and moving against him. There was something about a woman in flannel that begged to be touched. And on Ivy's body, every touch was a wonder. That lean strength of hers was unlike any woman he'd ever been with. She had the strength of a body-builder and the lithe slenderness of a dancer.

This was, uniquely, Ivy.

Little Ivy—who didn't feel little at all.

Reggie's little sister—but Reggie was a thousand miles away.

She was—

Her kiss removed his last attempts at rationalization.

He scooped her against him and groaned at the feel of her so close, so real. There would be no shedding of her nightgown, they were already too tangled together. He wanted to feel her flesh to flesh, but through the ever so slight barrier of flannel, she also felt enticing and fantastically exotic as he stroked up and down her body.

EACH SLIDE of Colby's hands seemed to peel a layer off her skin. This HMX-1 liaison to the WHMO had just spent five exhausting hours in an intense review of procedures. So immersed that she hadn't even noticed when Colby had left. One moment he'd been there, with Rex asleep at her feet, the next they'd both been gone. There hadn't been a moment to miss them, but she did.

His hand stroked down over her behind and tugged her thigh

up to drape over his legs and the Marine Corps major washed away faster than her thirty-second combat shower had rinsed off the Potomac.

She liked that he slept without pajamas or even underwear. Someone as male as Colby Thompson would of course sleep in the nude. Studying his body, as he was clearly doing to hers, revealed so many things she already knew but hadn't known.

Colby's strength had been breathtaking when he'd caught her on the South Lawn this morning. Again when he'd lofted her out of the sunken helicopter as if she was weightless. But it was also reminiscent of the visceral thrill when he would sweep up a young girl and heave her into the ocean. He'd always been the strong one of the three of them.

Lazy and directionless, sure. Though he wasn't directionless at the moment as he shifted to take her breast with his mouth through the thin cloth, forcing her to arch into the powerful sensation.

She could get past his guard with subterfuge, but never with strength. Now he was using all that glorious muscle to keep her tight against him. The hand at the small of her back that said she wasn't going anywhere, not that she wanted to. Even the leg, which had slid between hers until she'd clamped it between her thighs to hold tight to the sensation, was solid with the muscle of a man who walked for a living.

When he finally peeled the layer of flannel, one slow, agonizing, spectacular inch at a time, she finally lost all track of Ivy Hanson. In Colby's arms she was simply a woman. Not just some girl. Not a mere crazy-hot kiss—emphasis on the crazy if she was in bed with Colby Thompson.

In Colby's embrace she felt more female than with any other lover she'd ever had.

Most lovers made her painfully self-aware. Each move, each touch considered and measured. There was no flight plan with Colby. Every touch was natural, normal, unplanned, and a nerve-tingling escalation over the one immediately before, which had been an escalation of...

The first waves slammed through her and she felt no embarrassment that she climbed the peak alone. How could she, with Colby's hands upon her in the most personal ways. Without her noticing, he had spooned her back against his chest. The arm her head pressed against continued around her so that she was completely pinned. His other hand had drifted down between her legs and driven her aloft without her even noticing what he was doing.

She had no metaphors for the sensations. She should. Flight, combat, something. But she couldn't recall anything except for the intense blasts from her nervous system as she gave herself completely over to him.

Control. She *always* had control. Was always the one *in* control. Could always—

But not this time.

Everywhere Colby led her, she was helpless to do more than follow.

When he slid on some protection, she tried to ready herself. Ready for power. Ready for rough handling and hard driving.

He eased into her so gently that she almost wanted to cry. As if he worshipped her, rather than just finally taking what he really wanted. The climb this time was so much slower and so much more certain that when she crested it was like a long, smooth ride home after a dangerous mission.

When they were both done, he didn't roll away. He didn't just collapse on her either, though she'd have welcomed the weight of him. Instead, he simply held her, kissed her neck, and whispered her name in her ear as she drifted away into the silence of space.

COLBY'S first sight was a puzzled frown on Ivy's face. Morning had happened outside the curtains and enough light entered to see her clearly. She sat cross-legged on the bed, once again shrouded in her snow-white nightgown. It wasn't her anger frown—which brought a chilly winter snap to her light blue eyes.

"Sadly, that doesn't look like a frown of considering how soon we can jump each other's bones again."

"What?" She'd been concentrating on something so deeply that she actually startled when he spoke.

"Good morning, Ives. Where did you go?" He brushed a hand over her cheek and enjoyed the impossible softness of her fair skin.

"Good morning." She neither leaned in nor flinched away. Back to being unreadable.

And, typically, she didn't answer the more important part of what he said. He wasn't going to let her dodge it this time. "Ivy?"

"What?"

"What are you thinking about so hard?"

"The President's flight schedule."

"Bullshit."

She shrugged, but this time there was a hint of a smile.

"Well?"

"I'm not a very sexual person."

Colby couldn't even manage a *bullshit* remark. His jaw wouldn't retract enough for him to form any words.

"I just assumed I was broken somehow. Inside."

"So not," he managed. "By the way, it feels awesome to be inside you. Just in case I didn't make that clear last night. Need another demonstration?"

"Not just yet," she shook her head. Her fine blonde hair, out of its Marine Corps bun, danced around her shoulders. It was so light that it seemed to glow, even without the sun shining on it.

"Well, that gives me a little hope."

"What are you expecting out of this, Colby?"

"Expecting? Out of what?"

"Out of you and me being together."

"We're together?"

Her eyes found the icy blue so fast it made his head spin.

"It was a joke, Ivy." He sat up to face her, though he kept a sheet and blanket over his lap.

Her scowl didn't agree. She never was good at recognizing jokes. Reggie could get into it when it was just them and a couple beers, but not Saint Ives. A tease, sometimes, but a joke didn't work for her.

Wait. They did. At least they used to. The only times they didn't work on her was when they mattered—when it was something important. Then she had no sense of humor at all.

She began to back away.

Grabbing her hand to stop her retreat earned him a hard right cross to the gut, or would have if he hadn't blocked it.

At a loss for what else to do, he dragged her into his arms and held her for a moment until she stopped struggling. No head butt to break his nose. No knee to the balls or whatever other lethal mayhem she'd been trained how to deliver. So, just a pissed off woman rather than one who really wanted to get away.

Once she stopped fighting, he eased her back, keeping both hands on her upper arms to at least buy him a moment to speak before she escaped out of his bed and maybe back out of his life.

"Look, Ivy. This is all new to me, too. I wanted you since the moment you stepped off that helicopter. Hell, probably since you were still jailbait sixteen and I was too-old nineteen—even if I didn't know it at the time. It does not mean that I have a clue how to handle whatever this shit is that's going on between us. You are so incredible to make love to, it's like nothing else that's ever happened to me."

She looked down at her clasped hands, shaking her head. It caused a blonde cascade that hid her face.

He risked unleashing one arm to brush her hair aside. The blue eyes that finally looked up at him were softly gray now. Gone was the fury, but the perplexity of the morning's frown had returned.

"It's the best night I've ever had too," her voice was a bare whisper.

He guessed that she was no more in the mood for delving into it at the moment than he was. "How do you feel about mornings?"

With a narrow squint, her eyes seemed to shift back to true blue. Blue backed by a hint of a smile. "Mornings, huh?"

11

"Hell of a smile you've got there, Major."

Ivy tried to turn it down, but Captain Juarez, the flight leader, just grinned at her efforts.

"You should see the other guy," she riposted and did her best to be dignified as she accompanied him to Marine One. She'd fly as passenger on one of the decoy helos, but wanted to make sure everything was squared away on the designated primary bird.

The image of Colby, sprawled beneath her, with his palms cupping her breasts and his eyes practically rolled back into his head with the intensity of his pleasure just wouldn't go away. It was a good image. Rex had popped his head up over the edge of the bed at Colby's groan, then snorted and lay back down on the floor.

Mornings indeed.

But she hadn't felt like laughing. Morning sex with Colby wasn't some quick passage at arms. It was a drawn-out, ecstatic adventure that had left them breathless as they'd finally bolted for showers and rushed to change. Breakfast was a couple power bars and hotel-room coffee as they drove back to the airport.

They hadn't said a word, but there had been a thousand little touches: energetic towel rubdowns that were almost as erotic as the sex they'd just washed away, Colby tweaking the alignment of her oak leaf insignia on the collar points of her camo blouse, both reaching for the elevator button at the same moment.

Though he had teased her as she'd struggled to put her hair up into the accepted donut bun as the car jounced along.

She felt sixteen again. Not the incredibly painful moment of losing her virginity to Gregor on his parents' couch, but the fun, flirting (she could now admit) moments with Colby. These were the teen hormones that had noticed Colby the collegiate athlete and driven her to find new ways to tease him.

It was time to get her head in the game.

"Colby, you're with me." She ignored Juarez's smirk. "I think your best position—" was lying sprawled beneath her "—will be in one of the decoy helos. We'll land ahead of Marine One. That will give you perhaps thirty seconds to test the immediate landing area prior to the President's arrival."

He nodded, "Should be enough."

"Then you can expand into the crowd ahead of the President, which will already have been checked by other dogs, but I'd rather trust you and Rex's nose as a doublecheck."

Again, the simple nod.

No power games with Colby. Which was interesting; there hadn't been any in bed either. It was something she'd come to expect from any lover. They had some need to control or manipulate the petite—gods but she hated that word—Marine Corps officer.

Not Colby.

Not even when he'd grabbed her this morning. She hadn't known what she'd been reacting to, still didn't. But the longer he'd held her, instead of getting angrier, the quieter she'd become. Leaning into him was a place of forgetful peace. Maybe that's why he so confused her. She was Major Ivy Hanson 24/7...except in

Colby's arms when she simply became Ivy the woman. She had no clue who that might be.

He and Rex headed off to recheck all of the helos and the flight crews.

She'd never had much success being a woman. "A Marine with female body parts" had always fit her image of herself. Colby didn't even see the Marine in her. Maybe it was some sort of sick echo of jailbait teen lust on his part that had made him—

That wasn't right either. If it had been that, then he *would* have been that manipulative, controlling jerk she'd met in so many others. Colby was… She wasn't any more sure of what he was than what she herself might be. As much as she hated to admit it, they were going to have to talk at some point. But not too soon, as she had no idea what she wanted to say.

"There," someone called out.

Ivy realized that she'd been studying her reflection in the side of the Marine One aircraft for this first sortie. Trying to see herself in the soft image—wax bright over dark green paint. A dim version of herself. Was that what she was? It wasn't the Marine who looked back at her, but rather a dim reflection of a woman. That was new.

She turned to see where everyone else was looking.

At the far end of the long runway—0900 hours and already shimmering in heat haze—a black dot headed straight in. It rapidly expanded to the massive 747 of Air Force One. A brief puff of smoke as it touched down and the tires jumped from hanging still in the air to spinning at a hundred and fifty knots… and the President was down.

While the plane taxied, her phone rang, it was the WHMO group call.

"Everything fine here on Air Force One," Steve reported.

"Motorcade is good," Tish waved from where she was hanging out with Colby's Counter Assault Team guys—eight tough-as-hell dudes and a slender Goth in equally black clothing.

"Looks like you found some guys."

"Oh, they're *so* sweet!" From what Ivy could see at a distance, it looked as if the most lethal assault team on any security detail anywhere didn't mind at all being called sweet. At least not by a woman as cute as Tish.

"HMX-1 helos are clean," Colby's voice was heavy, like a hammer spiking the last nail into a coffin and ending all further conversation.

They all signed off as the 747 rolled to stop and things began happening very fast.

Before, she'd always been in her place: pilot, crew, something.

This time she could simply stand and watch the logistics with no defined purpose herself.

Almost identical in size, there couldn't have been two more different aircraft.

The Air Force gray C-5 Galaxy's bulk squatted low on its wheels. The high wing reached out from atop the fuselage and angled down, giving the plane a slightly sad and droopy aspect. The tail ramp and nose still gaped open, making the aircraft appear to be no more than a hollow tube. It looked every moment of its thirty years of hard service.

Air Force One might be the same age, but it was in sparkling condition, sporting the brilliant blue-and-white of the presidential livery. Its wings, attached to the bottom of the fuselage, angled up with perky energy still raring to go. It even bore the Seal of the President close by the President's door as a stamp of hard-won pride. The luxury aircraft rolled to a stop near the gathered HMX-1 helicopters and the stairs were lowered as an honor guard formed up around the aircraft.

The press and Secret Service agents poured down the rear stairs like an untidy river that splashed against the pavement. The press hurried to the bottom of the President's forward stairs as if they hadn't just been on a two-hour flight with him. Of course they were only rarely let out of their rearmost compartment in flight and perhaps the President hadn't visited them this time. How much could have happened in a two-hour flight that they demanded a comment since the boarding press conference? This was the leader of the world's most powerful nation, so perhaps a lot.

The Secret Service dispersed in a much more orderly fashion: some to surround the base of the President's stairs, a few to the HMX-1 aircraft, and others to the motorcade vehicles that had been delivered yesterday.

Colby met up with another dog handler near the lead Beast limo. She recognized Clarice Carver, the President's driver. That must make the man and dog beside her Jim Fisher and Malcolm. The English springer spaniel and Rex had a slightly longer conversation than Rex had with the Marine Corps dog at Anacostia, but Rex broke it off first.

Two Secret Service agents and a dog. They made a sweet family…a sweet family that had saved the President's life during an attack on his motorcade.

What had she done so far? Been aboard for the first-ever downing of an HMX-1 helicopter was her high-water mark. So to speak.

"Hi!"

If Ivy hadn't been a Marine, she'd have jumped out of her skin.

"He is awfully handsome, isn't he?" Dilya continued blithely as she looked over at Colby. She'd popped up as if teleported in.

Zackie was circling Dilya's knees, pausing to sniff Ivy's, then circling back the other way once she reached the end of her leash. She vibrated with nervous energy.

"You have slept with him by now, haven't you?" Now those mysterious green eyes were inspecting her.

Ivy nodded before she could stop herself.

"Was it wonderful?" The girl sighed like a hopeless romantic.

"Worth waiting for." An answer which surprised her. She'd barely seen Colby since joining the Marines. But if last night and this morning were any measure, he was absolutely worth waiting for. At least the sex. The man she still knew almost nothing about. Well, she did, but—

"Waiting," Dilya sighed. "I get so tired of waiting. I'm like the only senior girl in the whole high school who hasn't made it with a boy yet. You have no idea how completely scared they are when I tell them I work at the White House with the President. I've barely even been kissed."

Ivy could only raise an eyebrow at Dilya in surprise. First, she was a beautiful and exotic young woman. Second, this was way more information than—

"Not even that, really. A peck on the lips doesn't count, does it? Especially not when it was only an excuse to grab my breasts. Maybe some nicer boy would come near me if I had only sprained Kevin Gerber's wrist," she offered a heartfelt sigh. "But I broke it. Actually, both of them."

Ivy couldn't help remembering Gregor's fumbling efforts during her own first time. If the event itself hadn't been so painful, she might be remembering the fingerprint bruises that had taken days to stop showing on her own breasts, hurting long after any other pain had been forgotten.

Then Dilya's smile turned wicked. "Wearing dual casts, I bet he couldn't masturbate for months."

Ivy could only laugh.

"Did you know it only takes seven pounds of pressure to break a wrist, but nine pounds to break a nose? I looked it up. Maybe if he tries it again, I'll see if fifteen pounds is really enough to break his neck," she continued in a happily conversational tone.

"I'd stick with breaking wrists." Maybe this slender and pretty girl *did* know how to break necks. Actually, by Dilya's age, she was well on her way to a second black belt and had been trained to *not* break someone's neck in sparring practice. How far she'd come from seventeen to arching against Colby's glorious body like a wild thing.

"Right. Less jail time." Dilya nodded as if filing away the information. "Oh! Here we go."

Dilya hopped aboard the helicopter just as the President strode up followed by a pair of top advisors. They were deep in conversation.

Ivy had meant to be gone before the President's arrival, but now she was standing close beside the door of his White Hawk, opposite the Marine Corps crew chief who *was* supposed to be there. Too late to do anything else, she saluted as the President strode up.

"Two Marines," President Zachary Thomas stopped and returned their salutes. "You guys have to stop doing this or I'll get a swelled head."

"Sir, yes, sir," she and Sergeant McShea responded in unison.

Crap! She was in battledress uniform. Not her dress blues. Not even her service uniform. She wanted to melt right into the pavement and disappear. She wasn't supposed to be meeting the President on this trip. She was supposed to be an observer tucked out of sight on a decoy helo. Except she wasn't. She was here.

The President almost stepped past—maybe he hadn't really noticed her and this would pass unremarked.

Then he glanced down at her shoulder boards. "A major guarding my door. To what do I owe the honor?"

"Inattention, sir." *Dumb. Dumb. Dumb.* "I'm supposed to be over there," she nodded toward the second alternate aircraft. "I was distracted for a moment."

"By Dilya, I noticed. She's good at that. The little sprite wanted to see the launch so badly, I couldn't turn her away."

"Something we have in common, sir." And if the President thought Dilya was still some cute little girl, he wasn't paying attention.

He smiled down at her, "Major...?"

"Ivy Hanson, sir. White House Military Office Liaison for HMX-1. At your service." She remained at rigid attention.

"Carry on, Major Hanson. Glad to have you aboard. Wait…" he narrowed his eyes for a moment. They were mid-brown, going with his dark-brown hair. Gray was already starting around his temples. "Hanson? You were on that flight that went down yesterday. Why don't you take the seat opposite me? I'd like to hear about yesterday's events first hand."

"There was only one true eyewitness, sir," she waved toward Colby, who was standing by the helicopter she was supposed to be on.

"Bring him along," the President climbed aboard.

Unsure what else to do, she waved Colby over to join them.

He looked down at Rex uncertainly. She gestured again and Colby finally joined them with his dog leading the way. Rex sniffed the President, accepted a pat on the head, and looked about for something else to find that might earn him a treat. She'd already learned to recognize how he thought. She wished Colby was even half as transparent.

"Special Agent…?" President Thomas greeted him.

Colby, apparently comfortable in any environment, corrected the President. "Lieutenant, sir. Special Agent is for the protection service. I'm just a dog handler for the Uniformed Division of the Secret Service. Colby Thompson, and this is Rex."

"I've seen you on my lawn a number of times."

"Four years, sir. Since it was President Matthews' lawn. Rex and I love that patrol. We're typically out by the fence when you arrive or depart."

"Better than crashing into the Potomac?"

"That had its moments as well, sir."

Wasn't Colby ever nervous? This was the President of the United States he was talking to and he sounded as if he was at a baseball game. Whereas she'd crashed and burned like an early Redstone rocket—which didn't fit the metaphor at all no matter how true.

THE PRESIDENT WAVED them all aboard.

Unlike the Sea King helicopters, where the President had his own entry, everyone except the pilots used the main door. A two-panel swing-aside, like an armored, glossy-green French door, opened in the side of the helo.

Colby waited as if his feet were riveted to the runway. He couldn't seem to lift them as the two advisors and Ivy climbed nimbly aboard and all settled on the bench seat running along the far side of the aircraft. For them it was an everyday occurrence. He'd just met the President for the first time about ten seconds ago.

He checked in with Rex, who seemed to be breathing just fine. *Show off!*

President Zachary Thomas looked at him and smiled. "Nerves?"

"I had them once upon a time, but they don't seem to be working at the moment. I suppose that nervous systems are like that."

"Try stepping on one of these birds as the President. That'll jangle your brain worse than a cattle stampede."

"Suppose it would, Mr. President." Up close and personal he was no less daunting than he was on television or chatting with the press gaggle on the South Lawn. His casual-Coloradan attitude was even more obvious in person. Colby climbed aboard, careful to sit in the armchair facing backward rather than the one with the Presidential Seal. Rex settled on Ivy's feet, as well as those of the other two advisors seated beside her. The aisle was narrow between the sides of the two armchairs and the bench seat; Rex filled it completely and none of them would be moving their feet anytime soon.

The President settled into the armchair opposite Colby's.

Only then did Harvey Lieber, the head of the Presidential

Protection Detail, climb aboard. His scathing look at Colby as he attempted to step over Rex without banging his head on the ceiling, which was only about four-six high, was worthy of a carnival contortionist attempting to turn himself into a pretzel. Then he had to step over Zackie, who had curled up between Dilya's feet directly behind the President.

When he finally made it into his seat at the very rear of the aircraft, the look he gave Colby was unreadable. Did he now work for Harvey and was he now Number One on Harvey's dogshit list? Or was Harvey upset with dogs aboard Marine One in general? Or… Harvey was much easier going than Captain Baxter, but he hadn't risen to the head of the PPD by being a candy-ass either. Yeah, they needed to straighten all this out, but this probably wasn't the moment. No more likely than straightening things out with Ivy…ever.

Last aboard was McShea.

That's what finally broke Colby's petrification.

The crew chief stepped aboard, knelt very formally to close the doors behind him, then attempted to move to his seat at the very front of the aircraft. Rex had only partially blocked the rearward aisle, but he completely filled the forward aisle. The crew chief, so immaculate in his dress blues, had clearly never dealt with eighty-seven pounds of German shepherd cluttering up his aircraft.

Rex huffed grumpily when Colby signaled him to sit up. Then he simply laid his big head in Ivy's lap, huffed out a breath, and waited for the crew chief to get by—the equivalent of an exasperated doggie eyeroll.

McShea balanced himself with one white-gloved hand on Colby's shoulder—that he dug in hard enough to claim payback, but not hard enough to show any real anger.

Everyone finally settled, and the rotors began spinning to life.

"So I hear that you didn't enjoy your first flight on my helicopters," the President began.

"Oh, Rex enjoyed the swim well enough. And we finally found Ivy's cover when they fished the helo out of the Potomac, so it could have been worse, sir." It was a little tricky to recall that the man sitting so casually across from him was the Commander-in-Chief and that Colby would probably be better off if he kept his mouth shut.

Over one of the President's shoulders he could see Harvey watching him intently. Over the other, he could just make out Dilya's grin. That gave him a little courage.

"You saw the F-14 model that took out the helo?"

"Yes, sir. And two people on the jogging path did as well so I'm fairly sure I wasn't hallucinating. It was a quiet morning in the park until we crashed in, so they are the only other witnesses. They saw it moving fast and low, barely five feet above the river. I saw it just for the instant before it smashed into us. Climbing hard from our rear quarter. It was a good line of attack. A real pro job from what I would know. General Arnson agrees with me, especially as we weren't exactly standing still."

"Defense suggestions?"

Colby could only blink in surprise. "Sir, I'm sure that people far more qualified than myself have been studying that closely for the last twenty-one hours."

"They have. Defense suggestions?" And the steel tone of an ex-Air Force CSAR captain turned Commander-in-Chief brooked no evasion. Combat Search and Rescue meant that he'd been as exceptional as the HMX pilots in his way.

Colby watched out the window for a moment as they climbed aloft while he considered it.

The helo tilted its nose down to gather more speed and the President—seated toward the rear from Colby's position—now seemed to loom above him, even larger than life. They turned west and for just a moment he had a clear view of Kennedy Space Center. Scattered around its base were samples of their work. Instead of a car lot, they had massive rockets, as big around as a house and twice as long. His view of the launch pads were fast dwindling in the distance.

He glanced at Ivy, who was twisted around to stare raptly out the window behind her. She really should have gone to space…but then they never would have run into each other again.

Colby did his best to look thoughtful until the space port was dwindling behind them.

"What do you think—Ives?" He barely remembered in time that she hadn't been real happy about his calling her Saint Ives. She'd be even less happy if he did it in front of the President, as her instant scowl proved.

"She's much better at this kind of thing that I am, Mr. President."

Ivy WAS GOING to kill him. She hadn't paid any attention to the conversation. How many times in her life would she get to see Kennedy Space Center from the air? One. And now Colby had hung her out to dry in front of the President—and she was about to make a second impression even worse than her first.

Colby was a dead man. But he spoke again before she could decide whether to go straight to murder or implement some torture first.

"How do you stop radio-controlled models and drone attacks?" At least he gave her the damn question again.

"FCC," she responded without thinking.

"You mean the FAA. The Federal Aviation Administration," Colby tried to correct her.

"No," *Doofus!* Her, not him. FAA was exactly what she'd meant, but that's not what had come out.

Assume your mistakes aren't mistakes until proven otherwise. Admit your mistakes, but a Marine Corps officer's brain is often right for reasons you may not understand at first. McKinnon's Law.

"No, I meant the Federal Communications Commission." Now, why had she thought that? "Restriction and jamming of radio frequencies. The FAA was caught flat-footed when the hobby drone market blew wide open. The old radio-control law— if it's below this size, that speed, so many feet altitude, we're just going to ignore it—was allowed to hold control for too long. Now they're trying to regulate something that has already slipped out of the box. Shut down their frequencies. Jam them just like we do with cell phones in combat areas to keep the enemy from remotely triggering explosives. Same idea, different frequencies."

"Told you she was smart. All I could think to do was sic Rex on them." Colby actually had the temerity to wink at the President.

She'd felt like she was babbling. There was something else there, but for the life of her she couldn't figure out what it was.

The President glanced over his shoulder at Harvey Lieber.

"We already do this on the motorcades," Harvey responded. "The Watchtower SUV that travels second behind the limos serves precisely that function."

"*Shit!*" Ivy remembered what she was missing. She scrabbled at her belt and shoved Rex aside so that she could rise enough to scramble forward to kneel between the pilot's seats.

The crew chief had yanked his sidearm. Before she could reassure him, Colby's sidearm was against the chief's temple.

Rex was now on full alert. His snarl filled the cabin loudly enough to have both pilots looking back at them wide-eyed. Rex was moments from leaping to take out the crew chief's throat.

"Really should learn to trust your own, buddy. Now ease the weapon." Colby's voice was low and sounded incredibly dangerous.

He didn't understand that Marines guarding the President were trained in scenarios where anyone on the team could be a traitor. And that McShea wasn't going to ease off until he'd been reassured this wasn't the start of an attack—not even at risk of his own death.

Time to move slowly. She placed one hand on McShea's sidearm and eased it downward with a light pressure. Laying her other hand on Rex's head quieted the dog. Colby looked at that in surprise, then reholstered his own sidearm with a shrug. Easing forward, she leaned into the cockpit far enough that she could speak to the pilots. The copilot had his own sidearm drawn, held mostly out of sight close by his belly in case he needed it. Out the front windshield, she could see that they were fast approaching their destination.

"Captain Juarez. Can you confirm for me that Marine One aircraft never travel without ECM jamming on? Not even when returning to base?"

"I can confirm that. Full ECM on all official maneuvers."

"Thank you, Captain."

Ivy eased back into the cabin, still moving slowly, making sure to reassure Rex as she did so. She buckled herself back into her seat as everyone watched her closely. She noted that neither the crew chief nor the copilot had reholstered their weapons. She'd have to remember to commend them later on their vigilance. That's how she wanted her Marines around the President, act first and apologize for killing any potential aggressors later.

"So, Major, what is the reason you swore in my face?" The President asked it in a perfectly normal tone.

"I swore in your face, sir?"

"Rather vehemently," Colby was grinning.

Dilya giggled. As she'd proven earlier that she wasn't some bubble-headed teen, Ivy suspected that Dilya had calculated that to be a tension breaker. It seemed to work. McShea, at least, put away his firearm. Ivy deciding against turning around to check on the copilot's actions.

"My apologies, Mr. President. I'd realized something that I should have recalled yesterday. I can't imagine how we missed it. We need to review our debrief procedures, but the F-14 model was a scenario we had never previously anticipated."

"Which is?" Colby prompted.

Right. Get to the point, Saint Ives.

"It was neither an accident nor a random attack. It was a strike by an expert."

"How do you conclude that?" Harvey Lieber's voice was suddenly pure ice. As head of the Presidential Protection Detail, there was nothing that he would find more upsetting.

A random attack was unlikely to succeed because of the security bubble around the President. But a planned assault would take the Secret Service's capabilities into account. An *expert* assault implied that its planning included actual knowledge of those capabilities. It was the nightmare scenario. Even the attack on the Presidential Motorcade in Colorado had been mostly an application of brute force. This was far more dangerous.

"That F-14 model should have fallen out of the sky when it flew so close to us. Our ECM—electronic countermeasures—block almost every frequency, except for a very few that we're using ourselves. Frequencies that we're constantly changing. Pull out your cell phone. You won't be able to place a call. All of those frequencies are blocked within a hundred meters or more of this aircraft. That F-14 should have fallen out of the sky rather than performing a pinpoint maneuver."

"So the drone's transmitter wasn't randomly damaged by the crash with our tail rotor. It was *designed* to self-destruct, to hide how they did that," Colby was nodding. "Slick."

Harvey began to swing up his radio, which *was* on an authorized frequency, but Ivy held out a hand to stop him.

"You were about to call in an abort on the visit?"

"Yes, ma'am!" Harvey snapped out.

"Don't. It almost had to be an inside job. If you perform an abort, they may just go underground. You can't keep the President locked away forever."

"Now," said the President, "I believe it's my turn to curse. My apologies, ma'am, but *damn straight* you aren't doing that, Harvey. I expressly forbid it. We need a solution, not a retreat."

"Sir!" Harvey protested, but the President shook his head.

"I flew Combat Search and Rescue for multiple tours. I'm not getting chased out of the sky by some nutcase, no matter how smart they think they are. Figure something out."

The helicopter flared for its landing before settling gently on its three wheels.

"Please hold your seat for a moment, sir."

When the President turned to Colby, he continued.

"I'm supposed to have landed at least thirty seconds ahead of you, sir. Until Rex and I have secured the area, we're going to ask you to stay aboard. I don't like that Marine One landed without Rex first checking the landing zone. You're not going to die on my watch, Mr. President."

President Zachary Thomas clenched his jaw tightly at the restriction, but finally nodded when Lieber rested a hand on his shoulder to keep him in his chair.

Colby opened only one side of the double door built into the side of the aircraft, keeping the President shielded by the armor built into the other door. Ivy tried to follow Rex out onto the Orlando hotel front lawn, but Zackie raced out first, dragging Dilya in her wake. At least Dilya made it look that way, but the dog weighed so little that the girl could easily have picked up the dog.

"Trust me. I have similar problems with her," the President explained. "She and that dog are always underfoot at the oddest of times."

At times that Dilya finds most interesting. But Ivy kept that thought to herself and instead followed with what dignity she could muster as the President laughed.

To one side stood the Disney Dolphin Hotel, a nine-story, stucco-red edifice that rose another eighteen stories to a triangular pinnacle in the center. Atop either end of the main roof were massive smiling dolphins—each six or seven stories high themselves. To the other three sides of the narrow green lawn sprawled a man-made lake. Wide, low passenger boats carried hotel guests to and from Epcot. And today, each was manned by a team of Secret Service agents. She looked but didn't see any agents in the little swan paddle boats, which would be worth the price of admission.

Colby and Rex had circled Marine One and the second decoy helo that they were supposed to have arrived in. The other decoy remained aloft—better able to react in case of an emergency. A pair of gunships hovered in the distance providing cover.

As Colby and Rex proceeded up to the hotel's entrance, Dilya and Zackie tagged closely behind. Apparently Zackie had a new hero and was mimicking Rex move for move, even if the First Dog didn't know what it was searching for.

Ivy did her best to only show her Marine Corps discipline as she marched up the slight slope from the water's edge to the glass-and-steel main entrance. Past the hovering staff and Secret Service agents, Colby radioed just as Ivy caught up with him.

"Lieber, this is Thompson. Clear."

Ivy didn't have an earpiece, as she was just along as an observer. Colby was her way to stay connected with what was going on. She hated being dependent on him. She still wasn't sure if she was even talking to him.

Then the President, his advisors, and a team of agents brushed by her into the hotel. Into the hotel and out of the bounds of HMX-1 for the next seven hours—which they would spend in intense negotiations with Mexico, Cuba, and the governors of the five Gulf Coast states. All she could do now was wait.

MAY IN FLORIDA was enough to melt a man. And to dissolve a dog.

So he chose one of the deep leather armchairs in the vaulted lobby and listened to the water fountain that splashed merrily into the big sandstone-edged pool.

Dilya had been a distraction for a while. She'd wanted to know everything he could tell her about how to control a dog off-leash. Rex was very mellow when he wasn't under the *seek* command—his elder statesman mode—so they worked with hand signals and voice commands until Rex paid attention to her as well. He wished he could ask Rex what was going on. First, he seemed to have fallen head over all four heels for Ivy. Now, he was accepting commands from a teenager.

Zackie proved to be far less of a bubblehead than the Sheltie had first appeared. Once she understood a command, she followed it every time. Soon, Zackie was trotting about the lobby with a bright click of her nails on the terracotta flooring in patterns that, at least roughly, matched each of Dilya's gestures.

Now they were off practicing their new skills elsewhere in the hotel.

"You know what she's probably doing?" Ivy slipped into the next chair over.

He'd noticed her in the shadowed bar at one edge of the lobby, sipping a Coke. He idly wondered if she still crunched the ice cubes in her teeth—a sound that had always sent nearly-painful shivers up his spine.

He shrugged, unsure of how he was supposed to be reacting to her. Childhood friend? Except they hadn't really *been* friends. They'd been almost enemies—more like adversaries in ways only the closest family members might be. And now that he'd slept with her, the whole "childhood" thing was a moot point. She was more of a woman than…maybe anyone else he'd ever bedded. She took and gave and groaned. She melted and attacked, was vibrant and alarming. Ivy was—

"Dilya is probably sending Zackie running into the President's meetings so that she has an excuse to chase after her and eavesdrop."

He wouldn't put it past her. But it wasn't some teenager and her dog that he was thinking about.

"What's going on, Colby?"

"Me and Rex, we just be hanging." After an hour's exposure to Zackie's high-strung energy, Rex was taking a hard-earned nap.

"Hanging at the Disney's Dolphin Resort doesn't sound like hot babe territory. More like moms with families."

"You're here."

"You calling me a babe, Colby?"

That sounded like dangerous territory. "I don't know what the hell you are, Ivy. Do know that I've never wanted a woman the way I want you at the moment." He kept his voice calm so that he didn't attract the attention of any of the other agents or aides who flowed through the lobby in a near constant stream.

Ivy didn't reply for a long time—long enough for him to look over at her.

"I'm not used to men thinking about me that way," her voice was a whisper.

"Get used to it, lady, because I definitely do. Especially after last night. Hey, this is a hotel. I bet they have rooms. Rooms with beds in them."

"Colby," her tone landed deep in shut-the-hell up territory. Which sounded like an excuse to keep teasing.

"Hot showers. Hell, I'd settle for a broom closet at the moment if it meant I could get my hands on you."

———

AND THAT'S what she was to Colby: some babe to "get his hands on."

Yes, last night *had* been amazing. Colby Thompson was a spectacular lover…yet about as deep as the man-made pond in front of the resort—as in not very.

"There's a whole past family-brother-relationship thing going on that you're not paying any attention to, Thompson."

"I didn't know Marines did that."

"Did what?" She wanted to slouch lower in the soft armchair, Colby made it look so comfortable. She never slouched, especially not in her dress uniform. She should be working. While Colby had been working with Dilya, she'd checked her queue. There were three options for the upcoming trip to the Ottawa trade meeting. Preliminary field work for the Pacific Northwest fisheries tour, including a haul over to Japan to once again try to cut down their whaling activities. And a prospectus for the Quito, Ecuador, Climate Conference.

"I didn't know Marines invited their whole family into relationship discussions."

"What are you talking about?"

"What I'm talking about is you, me, and a comfortable bed. What you're talking about is beyond me. What's your family doing in the middle of this conversation?"

"And your family, Thompson."

"Hey, I didn't invite them into this conversation. I was just thinking about sex with you and—"

"And that's all you're thinking about. A man with a dick where he's supposed to have a brain."

Colby snorted out a laugh hard enough to attract the attention of a Mexican and a Cuban government aide conferring hotly in the next set of armchairs over.

"Been called a dickhead before, but never quite like that."

"Tell me it isn't true."

"It isn't true."

As if she believed that.

"Ivy, all I'm talking about at the moment is great sex. It's not as if we're getting married."

"That's not what you told my brother Reggie." Why was she arguing with him on this? Yes, the sex was great. No, not a chance did she want to be in a relationship with Colby Thompson. So *why* was she arguing that he wasn't being committed enough?

"Okay, fine. Let's invite our moms into this. Mine has asked me enough times about getting together with you that I should have her on a loop recording."

"She did? I didn't know that." How could she not know that? She'd followed Reggie over to the Thompsons' nearly as often as Colby had come to their house.

"I always figured it was just a sign of how disappointed she was in her only child's lack of motivation." Colby seemed to slip even lower. If he wasn't careful, he'd end up on the floor with Rex. "She probably figured you'd set a good example or whip me into shape or something."

"That doesn't sound like her." Mrs. Thompson was a Beltway lawyer, specializing in high profile divorces—known for representing the wives of philandering congressmen, senators, and other officials. Yet, despite that, she always seemed to have such a positive attitude.

"If not that, then maybe it's because our moms are already best friends and just wish they were related. We'd be their only chance unless they switch sides and run off together."

"Doesn't sound like either of our moms, the latter part. You could both switch sides and marry my brother."

"So not. First part is true though. Our moms might as well be sisters anyway." Colby glanced over at her. "Anything your mom says?"

"Not directly."

"She's a Marine. I thought everything Marines did was forthright and direct. What does she say instead?"

"We can be subtle when it's called for. Every now and then she points out how handsome you are."

"How handsome I am?" Colby shoved himself upright and raised his voice. "How *handsome* I am? Your *mom* says that? Shit! It looks like I've been chasing the wrong family member."

She was on the verge of taking him down, hard, even if half the lobby was staring at them. And then she caught on that Colby was teasing her. Somewhere along the way, she'd taken him seriously on the topic of relationships. He was right—she was the one who'd hauled their families into a conversation about casual sex. She hated that she'd fallen for it.

Ivy considered throwing him into the deep end of the dolphin fountain, but her mom was right: Colby was incredibly handsome. And, no, he wasn't chasing the wrong family member.

Besides, the fountain wasn't more than a foot deep.

HARVEY LIEBER MIGHT NOT HAVE BEEN able to send the President home, but he made it clear that he wasn't going to trust him in the air unless he had to. Instead of a twenty-minute helicopter flight, the President took a forty-five-minute, sixty-mile ride in the Beast. The Secret Service punched down a sealed-off corridor at the peak of Orlando rush hour, closed Highway 528, and roared down the empty two-laner and into the twilight at well above the speed limit.

With Jim and Malcolm the springer spaniel covering the Motorcade, he, Ivy, Dilya, and the two dogs were the sole occupants of the three helicopters returning to Cape Canaveral.

"Kept him running, did you?" Colby asked the girl. Zackie was passed out during the flight—a state he'd rarely witnessed the Sheltie in.

"Might have."

"Learn anything interesting?"

Dilya looked at him with a puzzled expression. So disingenuous that he might have bought it if not for Ivy's snort of laughter.

The teen shifted to a bright smile and shrugged off her defeat easily. "Not all that much really. Mexico is still trying to hold on to old styles of energy production; drilling the Gulf is how they've always propped up their economy. Now that we can generate the oil more cheaply and more safely with fracking—that's such an ugly word, isn't it? It's like the word itself causes even more people who don't understand it to hate it. Words are so fascinating that—"

"No one can sidetrack us," Colby warned her and she actually frowned for a moment before giving in.

"Cuba is far too desperate to be concerned with any ecologic considerations. They were more worried about being nice to the governors of the two particular states that border the Gulf. They're nearest to Florida, but their economics minister hovered around the Alabama and Mississippi governors. He wanted to know all about their casino operations and how he could rebuild the old Cuban casinos as if it was still the 1950s and they could get Hollywood and tourism money pouring in. 'Green oil' he kept calling it. 'Green oil for our economy.' I liked that analogy. I think the governors liked it too. As if it made sense to them."

"Are you the one who gave it to him?"

She stumbled to a halt as if she'd just accidentally showed her poker hand. Then she shrugged like she didn't know what he was talking about and became interested in whatever was out the window. He checked, a twilit expanse of Florida's never-ending lakes.

Note to self: never underestimate Dilya.

Ivy unleashed one of those million-watt smiles on him.

Note to self: never underestimate Ivy either.

He wanted to continue their conversation from the hotel lobby, but not with Dilya there.

"Aren't you going to at least talk to her?" Dilya was now eyeing him curiously.

"Yeah," Ivy said, sounding far more casual than her usual Marine Corps self. "Aren't you gonna talk to me?"

"About what? The startling way your eye color seems to shift with your mood? The way your hair catches the sunlight, even when there isn't any? Or, there are other things I could point out."

Ivy actually blushed, so maybe it was a good track to pursue later…in private.

"Duh! Tell her what you like best about her. That's what girls want to hear."

"What I like best about her?"

Dilya nodded.

Ivy set her jaw and glared at him, but the color was still bright on her fair cheeks.

"What I like best about you." There were a surprising number of things to like about Ivy Hanson. But best? "Your absolute and complete determination that you can make the world a better place through sheer force of will. I know it changed my life for the better."

Dilya must have been keeping an eye on Ivy, because she punched him in the arm with a job-well-done gesture.

"Your life?"

"I told you. Would never have amounted to much if it wasn't for you. You made being determined look like it was fun. I've never been a particularly driven guy, I know that about myself. But you've made me want to be a better one and I've tried. You kind of lent credence to the old nickname: Saint Ives, the patron saint of Colby Thompson, the sad sack."

That's the moment that Ivy finally shed the last of her "Old Colby" bias. She could feel it sloughing off and falling out of the helicopter just as she'd considered disposing of Colby's body yesterday over the Maryland countryside.

Colby *embodied* the better man. He still wasn't driven, displaying none of that edge that she knew cut other people away from her side. But he was steady as a rock. Was he also as loyal as his dog? It actually wouldn't surprise her if he was.

And he'd done it because of her? No. Erase the question mark. He *had* changed himself because of her.

"I'm not anything special. I'm…"

But Colby was shaking his head and offering her a smile that she remembered from the bedroom this morning. No, from that very first moment on the South Lawn when she'd turned around and almost fallen over Rex. She hadn't recognized it at the time, but it had reflected a genuine pleasure at seeing her. Despite the teasing, the banter, the fumbling, and even the stupid comments each time he became uncomfortable—he looked at her as if she was a joy to be with.

She definitely wasn't a joy. There had been plenty of grunts under her command who had made that clear. Their opinions were solidly backed up by the abort-style exit strategies of her past lovers. She earned respect. She earned obedience. She rarely earned pleasure at her presence.

Ivy the Marine didn't go away around Colby, but it also wasn't the part of her that he saw. And that scared the crap out of her.

Yes, a Marine never showed fear, never ran from a fight. But this handsome, patient man from her past who had somehow metamorphosed into her present made her want to launch her heart right at him.

Just because the President hadn't ridden in the HMX-1 helicopters didn't mean that they were put away on their return to Cape Canaveral. They would remain parked by the C-5 Galaxy, available on a moment's notice until the President was safely back aboard Air Force One. That had meant that he and Ivy were free to go and watch the launch.

Well, moderately free. Harvey Lieber didn't believe in letting assets sit idle any more than Captain Baxter had.

The public would also be at this launch, so Rex and Colby moved into the crowds ahead of the President along with Malcolm and Jim from the Motorcade.

Ivy trailed along in the wide wake that Rex cut through the crowd. But she was enjoying herself hugely. It felt an awful lot like the way she used to tag after him and Reggie so long ago. She gawked like that little kid as they walked through the dramatically lit Rocket Garden.

"Look! Look! Look!" She tried to point in every direction at once. "Both of the Mercury rockets—the Redstone *and* the Atlas—Gemini, Juno, Titan." She named each like it was her favorite pet ever. "Look at them all standing on their tail fins as if they were still ready to leap into space right now." She slapped her hands together sharply enough to startle Rex, then slashed one skyward as if she could take off like Superman. Or Superwoman.

When they reached the Apollo/Saturn V Center, she practically swooned, sighing like a movie heroine in love. That rocket was so big they had laid it down in a cradle rather than erecting it vertically like the others. And still it dwarfed them. She was right, it was incredible.

"This is when they knew how to dream," Ivy told him. "The shuttle was a delivery van compared to these racing cars. Nixon made us give up space."

"No, he authorized the shuttle. That's what got us to orbit."

"Trust me, Colby. The day we began work on the space shuttle was the day we gave up on reaching the planets. Nixon invested an extra hundred billion—a one-third increase—in 1968 alone into the defense budget to destroy Southeast Asia. At the same time, in just six years, he cut NASA's budget from six billion (which was already the lowest in four years) to three. We were supposed to be on Mars in 1986. I could have gone there if—"

She bit it off hard, looking sour and angry. Like everything else, she took this completely to heart as a personal affront.

He took his attention off Rex long enough to wrap an arm around her shoulder. She leaned into him for a moment as if seeking comfort. He liked that. He liked learning that Saint Ives did have a vulnerability and was even willing to share it with him, however briefly.

He couldn't think of what to say as they made their way to the NASA control room, called a Firing Room.

"Well, they're dreaming again, Saint Ives."

She nodded as fiercely as Dilya sometimes did. Then she gazed longingly with puppy-dog eyes out toward where the rocket would launch later tonight. Why couldn't she see that in herself? *This* was obviously where she belonged. All the echoing silence of the distant runway was vibrantly alive here at Kennedy Space Center, especially in this pre-launch moment.

"How often do they launch here, Ivy?"

"Every twelve days globally. They're expecting growth to one every two days this year or next. A third of that is US, probably growing to half. Most of that from right here," she sounded dreamy. Then blinked at him in surprise.

"That sounds like a lot of launches."

"It does, doesn't it?" And for the first time since they'd rushed out of bed this morning, that smile was back. That smile of hope and what was possible.

They'd arrived in the glass-walled room where the President was the guest of the NASA management team. The floodlights out at the launch pad three miles away shone like a star in the Florida night. He led Ivy over to a corner where they'd still have a view.

"Secret Service trick to being invisible," he whispered to her, "be exactly where everyone expects you to be."

"But not anywhere that they'd normally look," Dilya said as she and Zackie slipped up by Ivy's elbow.

Ivy looped an arm through Dilya's as they both leaned back against the wall, well out of the common sightlines.

They were raptly watching the goings-on.

To their left through an interior wall of glass window, long rows of computer stations were manned by serious, focused personnel. On their level, raised enough to look down over the entire floor, was the primary row of control stations. There were only six seats at the station and the launch director striding back and forth, hovering over their shoulders.

At either end of the upper platform were a pair of glassed-in rooms. On the far side, the Operations Support Team were the top-tier of decision makers. Ivy whispered that they were the senior flight and manufacturing personnel who would give the Launch Director the final go/no go. They themselves were in a similar glass box with all of the officials.

"Nobody in this area has any say-so, but they're too important to shut out." And indeed, the NASA Administrator and his deputy sat to either side of the President while others hovered as nearby as they dared.

Harvey Lieber, far from being inconspicuous, stood in the center of the only doorway into the room. Nobody was getting near the President without going through Harvey first.

It was a real problem here. NASA security was like an itch he couldn't scratch. They were an independent agency, but they needed a serious lesson. Colby figured that even without his badge, he could have entered this room given only minimal planning and a minor dose of razzle-dazzle. Security was still based in old-fashioned metal detector thinking. The White House had a multi-layered defense system far beyond most buildings, but—despite being the center of the American space program—this site was little more secure than a post office. Those guys at least had a healthy paranoia about how unpredictable civilians could be. NASA seemed to think that if you were dressed like an engineer, then you must belong.

If not for Rex and Malcolm, who was also on patrol, he could have walked in with an entire knapsack of Semtex and taken out whole sections of the complex. They'd blocked all of the obvious routes and methods, but the Secret Service had plugged those decades ago. The kind of attacks the Service planned against could breeze in here on a tourist pass.

So Colby kept a careful eye in the one direction that Harvey couldn't see without fully turning around. Harvey spotted that and gave him an infinitesimal nod of acknowledgement. Which, in the grand scheme, wasn't bad. It was more than Captain Baxter had typically offered.

The closer the launch came, the lower the numbers rolled on the countdown, the harder it was to not watch Ivy and Dilya rather than Harvey's back.

The brilliantly blonde Marine Corps major was the same height as the dark teen, but they could almost be mother and daughter with how greedily they both watched the monitors and the small star of light that was the distant launchpad.

Mother and daughter.

Imagining Ivy with her own mother only evoked images of how alike the two women were. Ivy's coloring had come from her father the chef, but her small build and attitude had come straight from her Marine Corps mother.

Watching Ivy with Dilya made it easy to imagine Ivy with a precocious daughter of her own. Of *their* own? Was *that* the image in his head? Despite her mother's decades of service and his own mother's constant tales of high-profile divorce, both of their parents' marriages had been very stable through the years.

Relationships that grew too deep were his excuse to find fresh pastures. But Ivy, who felt like the freshest ground of all, also dated back to his first memory. What was up with that?

The clock was finally released from the final planned hold at nine minutes. The other glass cubicle, filled with its specialists, must have given approval for the launch. The excitement grew palpably as single-digit minutes became double-digit seconds and ultimately they turned single-digit as well.

Three.

Two.

One.

At zero, the star of nighttime floodlights was suddenly overwhelmed by the brilliant glare of the rocket. The clock reversed.

One.

Two.

Three.

On four, the tiny rocket balanced atop the huge ball of light climbed impossibly slowly out of its own steam cloud. But climb clear it did, clawing aloft until it seemed to find its gait, then it roared aloft.

But it wasn't the rocket's glare that captured his imagination. It was the fire's glow on Ivy's shining face as she tracked it upward with her whole being.

Somewhere in the background, the announcer declared they were five-by-five and continuing on profile. All good to go. Cheers broke out around the room. The NASA administrator and the President were trading solid handshakes of congratulations.

And Ivy stared aloft with tears streaming unwiped down her cheeks and a smile bigger than all of space lighting her features.

He liked his life just fine, but he'd never felt the way she looked. No woman, anywhere, had ever looked that happy.

He'd thought Ivy was done with changing his world, but he'd been wrong. He wanted to be a part of that joy so badly it almost hurt.

vy wasn't used to waking in a man's arms, but she could get used to it quickly if it kept feeling like this. And despite its newness, she felt instant awareness about the identity of the man holding her. Perhaps it was because of the massive dog lying by her feet like the world's best foot warmer, but she didn't think so. She leaned into Colby's smell, so unchanged from when they were younger yet completely different.

In their youth, he'd sometimes carry her piggyback, at least until she'd started tickling him whenever he did—she hadn't been able to resist. He'd reluctantly agreed to be her sparring partner when she needed to practice a judo move, at least until she'd misjudged a grapple and throw, bloodying his nose so badly that it had taken hours to fully stop.

Breathing him in now, he smelled like home. As familiar and safe as her childhood room.

Safety.

Colby Thompson?

That part of him wasn't completely new, but most of it was. It was like the transition from a Bell TH-57 trainer (the 206 to civilians) to the majesty and power of the MV-22B Osprey. It was bigger than the transition from a solo Mercury rocket barely reaching low Earth orbit to an Atlas V moon rocket. Younger Colby and the man presently sleeping with his arms still wrapped around her couldn't be more different. He was the Falcon Heavy rocket, the biggest rocket since the Saturn back in the 1960s.

She'd been emotionally exhausted after the long day and the launch. Riding back to the C-5 Galaxy within the President's Motorcade, the President and Dilya were quickly airborne and headed back to DC on Air Force One. It was midnight when they began breaking down and loading the helos. Three a.m. before they unloaded at Andrews Air Force Base back in DC. At four a.m., they'd crawled into Colby's bed. She had no real memory of her arrival here. Up the stairs, through a darkened room, shed clothes, and pass out curled up in his arms.

Now, she was awake, realizing how spontaneously she had gotten where she lay and feeling a bit wanton. She hadn't even asked, but then again, neither had he. She'd simply climbed into the taxi with him and ridden back to his place.

This wasn't confusing enough, let's go back to bed together because the sex was better than having a warp drive in her own personal starship.

Real deep, Ivy.

Who needed deep when it felt and smelled this good?

She snuggled back in and let the exhaustion take her back under.

He'd felt her wake up, but hadn't said anything at first. And then when she didn't, it finally became so awkward that he wasn't sure what to say so had kept his mouth shut.

Colby had spent the entire night in uncharted territory. Rex hadn't tested it for safety with his nose, wasn't even trained to help him detect potential hazards and traps. Colby was out here on his own, stumbling into pitfalls and triggering explosions all on his own.

In the middle of the night, Rex had snuck up onto the bed, and Colby couldn't figure out how to stop him without waking Ivy. Now, his feet were numb and tingling below where Rex lay across them. They had so little blood flow that they could probably be amputated without him even noticing, until Rex moved and the nerves all came roaring back to life.

That's what Ivy had done to him. She made it feel as if he was roaring back to life—a life he'd never known he was missing in the first place. And it hurt!

He'd named the uncharted territory somewhere around dawn. It was the land of the *What If* in the future possible lives of one Colby Thompson. Definitely not a place he'd ever been before. Thinking ahead wasn't a major pastime for him or Rex. He liked that about his dog: they were both very present-tense sort of guys.

Ivy was anything but that.

What if Ivy wanted more than a fast fling for old times' sake? But there was no "old times' sake" between them for that to happen. She wasn't some sexy, ex-girlfriend looking for a one night revisit to old triumphs. She was... He didn't know. So he'd continued the game as its sole and unwilling player.

What if she *didn't* want more than a fast fling? That didn't sound like as much fun as it usually did.

What if it became *more?* What if they both let that happen, then she left the Marine Corps to pursue a job in space? She'd end up in Cape Kennedy or Houston, or, God help him, maybe she *would* walk on the surface of Mars someday. Meanwhile, what would Colby be doing?

Walking the South Lawn.

Rex still had a couple good years in him if everything went well. But eventually Rex would be retired. And then one day his pal would go to sleep and never wake up...not a prospect Colby could even face.

When had he become emotionally dependent on a dog? Attached? Sure. He loved the furry beast. But to have Rex as the deepest emotional relationship of his life sounded pretty lame.

And he was flung back into the land of *what if.* What if this fling-that-didn't-feel-like-a-fling turned into more than a fling? What then? He and Ivy?

Reggie would kill him, that was a given.

Their moms would probably be thrilled. Their dads...well, they'd be dads. They'd raise a beer and call it a job well done.

What would Ivy do? What would he do?

It was better not to tell anyone...especially himself. The less he knew about this, the happier he'd be. But he couldn't seem to get there. Not with Ivy curled in his arms as if she'd never belonged anywhere else. Her hair, so light he could barely feel where it lay upon his chest and cheek, smelled of springtime and that joy that she wore like an inner skin—letting it shine through her fair outer skin whenever the mood struck her.

He wanted to hold on *and* run away both.

He felt her go back to sleep. He considered waking her, because maybe it *was* time they had a talk. Tried to figure out what was—

The phone by his bed rang so loudly that he felt as if he'd been plugged into an electric socket. He was—normally—a very deep sleeper, so he kept it loud.

By the second ring, several things had happened.

Rex leapt to his feet on the bed.

Only by quickly scooting sideways was Colby able to avoid being castrated by one of Rex's massive paws.

Ivy jolted awake.

Having learned a thing or two, he managed to get a hand

between her and his solar plexus to block any random incoming elbows. He even managed to get his face out of her hair and turned to the side so that he didn't get headbutted as she too jolted to life.

His balance tipped precariously at the edge of the mattress, but he held on.

Until Ivy dove for the phone on the nightstand, placing a breast squarely in his face.

That did it.

All balance and control gone, he tumbled down onto the carpet, where Rex and Ivy both looked down at him in surprise.

"Hello?" Ivy answered his phone. At least she said something like that, her voice was still thoroughly sleep-fuzzed.

"It's for you," she handed it down to him.

"It *is* my phone."

She blinked her eyes hard a couple of times, looking around the room as if uncertain quite where she was. It was Saturday morning. The only person who called him on Saturday morning was his mother. They usually checked in with each other about whether they could fit in a family meal over the weekend.

And *Ivy* had answered the phone. This was bad in so many ways.

"Hi, Mom." There had to be some way to avoid explaining the woman in his bed. No, that wasn't the problem—Mom was used to that. There had to be some way to avoid explaining quite *which* woman was in his bed.

"Not your mom, Thompson," General Arnson snarled into the phone. "Was that my best officer who answered?"

"Um, yes, sir." This was even worse than Mom.

"And what did I say about you messing up my best officer?"

"You didn't say anything about *mussing* her up though." Not his best comeback, but he was lying naked on the floor with an equally naked Ivy looking down at him quizzically and that was a very distracting vision. Her hair was loose and tangled, making a charming golden halo about her face. It was a vision he wouldn't soon forget.

There was a stony silence on the phone.

For lack of anything else to offer to keep him out of the future job of dogshit cleaner, he kept his own silence.

"Why aren't you at the White House?"

"Because we—" should have said *I* "—got in at four a.m. And perhaps I should mention that it's Saturday."

"You don't understand the trouble you're in, Thompson. Neither does Major Hanson."

"Trouble, sir?" *We're both in trouble?* Colby mouthed the question to Ivy.

She furrowed her brow for a moment, then shrugged. Which set off some very nice secondary effects down her body that he did his best to ignore. At least until he got off the phone.

"Harvey Lieber is unwilling to place the President's life in *my* helicopters until we have a solution. HMX-1's next mission is supposed to be Ottawa. That's Monday morning. You and Major Hanson have forty-eight hours to solve this. I expect you to arrive in the White House Military Office in twenty minutes and not move your asses a single inch until you get this done."

"I live thirty minutes door-to-door from the White House."

"Make it in twenty-five," he snarled, leaving no doubt that it was the limits of his patience.

"We aren't even dressed," some idiot part of himself just couldn't resist. But the instant he said it, he knew he was a dead man.

"Twenty-*four!*" And the line went dead—thankfully before he could think to point out that Rex needed a morning walk as well.

IVY'S ATTEMPT TO detour to the Navy Mess to get coffee and

something breakfasty was blocked when General Arnson spotted her coming through the West Wing lobby.

"Where are your dress blues?"

"Still water-logged from my swim in the Potomac." All she'd had in her go-bag were battledress uniforms. And her spare blues were in her apartment on the other side of town from Colby's apartment. It was embarrassing to come to the White House dressed so casually, but she hadn't had any other option. The general was immaculate in his uniform.

"Where's Thompson?" The general looked ready to commit murder.

"Taking Rex for a quick walk," she nodded toward the West Wing's entrance. "He thought it might be better if his dog didn't pee on the lobby security desk." They'd split tasks to save time—he'd walk Rex and she'd get breakfast—but her part of the job wasn't working very well. She tried leading the general over to the mess, but he didn't appear to be in the mood to move so she was stuck.

"Thompson." He said it completely deadpan. "You have a history?"

"Not the way you mean. We grew up next door to each other."

"Assessment? And don't give me any happy smile crap. I can see that part of it all over you already."

Ivy had been sure that her best deadpan was firmly in place. "I —" she tried to start, but Arnson's scowl stopped her and she had to try again. *Happy smile crap all over her?* He was right, that couldn't be what was happening. Except she could feel that it was.

"Colby Thompson. If ever there was an unambitious man, he's it. Always was. However, he has risen to his current position through skill and hard work. It would never enter his mind to maneuver or be a political animal."

"A top soldier, but no officer."

"A natural leader, but no cutthroat attitude to match."

"How many throats did you cut before you came to my attention at HMX-1, Hanson?"

"As few as possible," she risked a smile.

The general returned it readily enough before continuing in a softer voice. "Being a Marine officer means that you toed the line —and you toed it hard. You know and I know that anyone who waivered from the standard of the Corps was *meant* to be left in the dust."

"Yes, sir."

"Do you think you and your unambitious lover can get my helos back on the job?"

She wasn't comfortable with the word lover, but that wasn't something to point out to a pissed-off general.

"If we fail, it won't be for lack of killing ourselves, sir."

His grim nod said she'd better come back dead if she failed.

"Any assets you need, *any*, get them. Call my cell at any hour if some dead man tries to stonewall you. And Hanson…"

"Yes, sir."

"You cut any throats you have to. Even dog boy's. I want my birds back in the air."

"GOT ANY THROATS I CAN SLIT?" Ivy lay her head down on the desk, not even bothering to shove aside any of the paperwork.

"How about mine?" Colby was too exhausted to slouch and barely managed a slump in his own chair. Three shifts had cycled through the WHMO without making them much wiser.

The organization chart of who was informed of flight operational frequencies hung on one wall. They'd managed to reduce the list by a third—General Arnson's approval for that had arrived less than six minutes after they'd sent him the proposal.

Three different radio experts had reviewed the operations frequency selection methodology—the White House Communications Agency was a part of the WHMO, so they didn't have to go far to find the top people in the field. Between them, they generated an entirely new set of protocols that required half as many frequencies and actually improved operations and crisis communication efficiency. Because that one was more convoluted and had broader ramifications to HMX procedures, it required Arnson *nine* minutes to approve it. Harvey Lieber's approval—as the Presidential Protection Detail was also involved—arrived six minutes later with the note: *Good work. But it's not enough yet.* That had sapped what little energy had sustained them through the round-the-clock shift.

"Twenty-four hours down," Colby rubbed at the back of his neck, but that didn't help either. "Twenty-four more to go before the President is on the move again. You know, if you'd gone to space, neither of us would be in this pickle."

"Next time he goes into the Oval Office, let's sneak upstairs and padlock all the doors shut from the outside."

"Nah," Colby forced himself not to lay his head down on the table right next to Ivy's. "Then Harvey Lieber, as head of the protection detail, would have to shoot us. And that would lead to all sorts of awkward problems."

"Like the general not being able to kill us himself for not fixing this problem."

"Right. Besides, being killed twice doesn't sound like much fun from our end of it either."

"I'm hungry," Ivy told the diagram of the F-14 model's flight path and attack line that her head lay on.

"I'm too tired to be hungry," Colby agreed. The only one who'd eaten regularly had been Rex. Colby looked at his watch. "It's 0600. Sunday, I think. The Navy Mess won't open for a while."

"The White House has a kitchen. I know because my brother works there."

And the chances of running into Reggie at this hour on a

Sunday were thankfully very low. "We'll circle out across the South Lawn for Rex to do his thing."

It still took them a couple of minutes to generate enough enthusiasm to stand and another to get moving. Once he was outside, Colby felt as if he could breathe again. This is what he and Rex were used to. Walking the lawn, out in whatever the weather was. This inside desk work just wasn't right for a man and his dog. But that was a problem for another time.

"I love this time of day." The dawn had painted the entire sky in roses and pinks. Blues were still several minutes away and for the moment there was a hush on DC. Too early for the traffic or the protestors, even the birds seemed to be holding their breath.

Rex piddled on a couple of rose bushes on their way to enter below the South Portico. The ground level entrance passed through the Diplomatic Reception Room.

"Are we even supposed to be in here?"

"Sure. I'm Lead Dog. Clearance to go anywhere, even the Residence if I could justify the need." Though he'd only been through this entrance a few times over the years.

"I thought you weren't Lead Dog anymore."

Colby felt the gut punch. Ivy rested her hand on his arm in immediate sympathy.

"I'm sorry. I wasn't thinking."

"It's okay. I've got to get used to it."

"I feel like I'm making the room dirty just by breathing in here." She tucked her hand around his elbow as they stepped further into the room. After that, he didn't care if they were supposed to be here or not.

It was one of the four oval rooms in the White House, all roughly the same size. Predating the one in the West Wing were the three in the Residence. Stacked up, one per floor, the Green, Blue, and Yellow Ovals formed the grand curve of the South Portico giving the White House its distinctive shape.

The Green was a pristine space. Its elegance so extreme that

Colby had always felt it was stark. The rug was a vast terrain of pale blue and gold with the emblems of the fifty states worked into its perimeter. White doors, white walls, white ceiling, crystal chandelier.

"It feels chilly," Ivy's voice was barely a whisper.

"Elsie, uh, this woman I knew, would have liked this room." Several of his former girlfriends would have. The high-end furnishings, the obvious history of it all. He liked that Ivy would be more comfortable in a room with a battered but comfortable couch and a coffee table you could prop your feet on rather than one you'd be afraid to brush against.

"Did you dump her or she you?" Ivy missed nothing, of course.

Colby ignored the question and instead looked at the wallpaper mural. Zuber wallpaper, he'd been told, worth over sixty grand and put in place by Jackie Kennedy who had salvaged it from some mansion about to be demolished. He'd never really had time to look at it. Stylized scenes of nineteenth century America, back when there'd been much less of it. Boston Harbor, Niagara Falls, New York Bay—with a skyline that looked nothing like in the movies by about a hundred stories. It wrapped all the way around the room from waist height to eight or nine feet.

He looked at Ivy and she was as wide-eyed as he felt.

"Yeah, out."

She nodded quickly and they exited the far side of the room. The Central Hall had none of the pomp. Red carpeting, massive white arches supporting the upper three stories of the Residence that felt a little too low just because of the arches' heft. It was immaculate, but far less scary.

"Maybe I'll avoid that entrance in the future."

"Good idea."

He dropped Rex off on the dog bed that was kept in the corner of the small Secret Service Ready Room before ducking down the hall to the kitchen. At this hour, there should only be one of the staff chefs manning the place. They could grab whatever was at hand and get right back to work. Stepping in the door, he was almost run over by Chef Klaus, the executive chef—who didn't even bother to slow down, assuming the world would get out of his way.

The kitchen was in full swing.

Klaus strode up to a chef surrounded by massive crates of vegetables. He might be a Teutonic hardass, but he was also an amazing chef. He stopped beside the chef surrounded by crates of peas still in the pod, tiny brilliant green zucchini, and bright yellow, star-shaped pattypan squash.

"It is not some hammer you are beating them with. It is a chef's knife. It is a tool of art, not war. One extra ounce of pressure and we see it mar the flesh," he watched the poor chef make another cut. "No! No! No! Do not slow down. Slow is as bad as too hard. Gentle and fast. Then you get smooth slice. *Jawohl?*"

The chef nodded as Klaus continued to watch his every motion.

Colby was glad that he hadn't followed Reggie into being a chef. Reggie had tried to nudge him that way, but Colby had never had the deep passion about food that his best friend did. He was a better-than-average cook from all the meals they'd made together, but that was a long way from being a chef.

Reggie was studying one of the massive soup kettles as if it was a set of nuclear launch codes.

"Maybe if we step away quietly," Colby whispered. "He won't notice us. Then we can run for our lives."

Ivy LOOKED at Colby in surprise.

"You're afraid of Reggie?" But they were best friends.

"We're in a kitchen filled with knives and cleavers. Consider it the better part of discretion."

"We're armed too," she patted her sidearm and dragged him the last step into the kitchen. "What's that, Reg?"

There was no reason for Colby to be worried, her brother didn't even look up from his soup. There was no heat coming from it. In fact, the air felt cooler near it. Chilled pureed soup of some sort. Colby would probably know what it was just by looking at it, but she didn't have a clue other than it looked creamy, smooth, and green. Maybe a space ooze that would leap out of the pot and turn them all into pod people.

"Watch." Reggie picked up a squeeze bulb attached to long rod. He squeezed the air out, dipped it in a bowl of an orange liquid, and sucked some of it up. Then he turned to his soup and, pressing the bulb once again, slowly formed a small orange globe that bobbed on the surface. He then stabbed it with a syringe of something dark green. Setting his implements aside, he picked up a soup spoon, scooped up the orange globe with some soup, and held it out for her to taste.

She took it off the spoon. Bright mint was the first flavor to hit. She might not know how to cook oatmeal, but living with Dad and Reggie, she'd learned how to eat and taste. Waiting past the initial surprise of mint, the smooth depth of fresh peas rolled over her tongue. But there was a citrus tease from the globe that had her biting down on it. In a minor explosion of flavor, bright orange sunshine flooded her mouth, finishing with just a hint of original mint and lemon that he'd injected into the center of the globe.

"Oh. That's wonderful. Spring in a spoonful. Make one for Colby."

"For Colby?" Reggie almost jumped out of his shoes when he looked around to realize that Colby was standing close beside her. Shocked out of his chef mode, his eyes immediately tracked down to where her hand was still looped around Colby's elbow. It felt so natural there, she hadn't thought anything about it. Well, to let go wasn't going to happen. She wasn't doing anything wrong.

Reggie slowly made another and held a spoon for Colby.

She watched him as he tasted. It was as if she could see so much more of the dish just watching his face than tasting it herself. The balance of the salt and pepper. The choice of chicken rather than vegetable broth behind the primary pea flavor. And when he bit into it, the smile that touched his lips made her want to kiss him so that they could share that taste. They had been together for just two nights and again she was imagining intimate, sharing moments with him. And where might *those* moments lead? To equally connected and intimate sex. It wasn't a question; it was a given with how it felt to lie against his body. How it felt to simply hold his arm.

"A little more lemon in the mint center," Colby suggested.

"Then a little more pepper in the soup—no, just on the surface," Reggie concluded. "The pepper will accent the lemon, bringing the final taste to life but I don't want to unbalance the soup for today's Rose Garden luncheon." Which explained why the kitchen was so busy at such an early hour.

They watched him in silence as he made another pair of globes. Scooping them onto fresh spoons, he ground the tiniest bit of pepper on each before handing them over.

The globe now burst to life in her mouth, "Oh my God!"

Colby just offered a thumbs up.

Chef Klaus joined them. This time Reggie selected a small sundae glass from the shelf above his station. He poured in a ladleful of the soup so carefully that it didn't splash the sides. He then floated another of his orange-mint-lemon balls in the middle, topping it with the tiniest amounts of pepper, sour cream, and chives.

The chef inspected it carefully, perhaps for visual effect, then tasted it, showing absolutely no reaction.

Ivy wanted to beat up on him for not loving her brother's beautiful soup.

He took another spoonful, of just soup this time, and waited for a full thirty seconds after tasting it again. Then he set the glass down, nodded, and walked away.

"Wait! What about—" but Chef Klaus had moved on.

"That's high praise from Klaus, Ivy." Reggie actually smiled. "High praise indeed."

"Because he didn't say anything awful?" Ivy was still outraged.

"Yep."

"Well, ignore him. That was really something special, buddy," Colby slapped Reggie on the shoulder.

Which once again drew Reggie's attention back to them. Somewhere in the tasting, she'd let go of Colby's arm, but that didn't change what her brother had seen. He looked back and forth between them. Maybe Colby was right and they should have run when they'd had the chance. Did the energy between them sizzle so brightly that it glowed like some force field? If so, she should feel much more impervious than she did. Instead she wanted to stare at her feet like a bad little girl.

"How did this happen?"

"How did what happen?" And there was the Colby she knew. His subtle tease, forcing Reggie to actually state what he meant.

"You two. I should beat the shit out of you, Colby. That's my little sister."

"Hello, standing right here. I'm not in the third person."

Reggie ignored her and glared at Colby and looked as if he actually might try to tackle him right here in the kitchen. "Together. How?"

Ivy and Colby glanced at each other. And again there was that hint of a smile that told her Colby was about to zing his best friend.

Even better to zing in stereo.

They turned to Reggie in unison, then, as if they'd planned it and practiced it, they both shrugged and said, "No idea."

"He didn't look very happy." Even by the end of the breakfast he'd served the three of them, Reggie had still been grumpy. Maybe because Ivy had kept poking at him throughout the hurried meal of cheese and mushroom omelets with a blueberry marmalade scone and hot chocolate.

Colby had focused instead on enjoying a White House breakfast as fast as he could. He knew that, with Reggie, it was best to just let him stew on things a while. Despite being his sister, Ivy had never learned that lesson.

"I can't see why it matters to him," Ivy grumbled as they retrieved Rex. He scarfed his egg-and-cheese doggie omelet off the paper plate in two gulps. "It's *my* personal life, not his."

"When it comes to protective older brothers and their little sisters, it's very personal."

"Well, it shouldn't be."

"It would help if I wasn't his best friend."

"Why? He already likes you. Better than me sleeping with some stranger."

"It doesn't work that way between guys. Besides, I'd rather you didn't do that."

"Sleep with strangers? Why?"

"Becoming rather partial to sleeping with you myself, Saint Ives."

She rolled her eyes at him.

"Missed sleeping with you last night."

"We were working side-by-side all night. Straight through. And we—" she unleashed a tonsil-deep yawn "—have to get back to it."

"Sure, but I liked the sleeping together part." And he had—even if it was now most of two nights he hadn't slept. Holding Ivy was a real treat. If he'd ever dated a snuggler before, he didn't recall it. Sleeping with Ivy made a man feel as if he was somehow more than a man. Ivy gave a hundred percent of her attention to sleeping beside him just like she did everything else.

"I'm done in. We've got to get *some* shuteye. I'm unsafe to fly at this point."

"I'll keep you out of any cockpits."

Rex had stopped without Colby noticing. Colby hit the end of the leash and still Rex didn't move, forcing Colby to a halt. His dog was staring down the long Central Hall. They'd progressed most of the way from the midpoint where the Secret Service Ready Room was, back to the Palm Room to return to the West Wing.

Behind them, trotting along by herself as if she hadn't a care, Zackie came silently toward them over the red carpet.

Ivy laid her head on his shoulder, not even bothering to turn, simply falling asleep because they'd stopped moving.

Zackie traded nose sniffs with Rex, turned around, and trotted back the way she'd come.

Normally Colby would shrug it off. The dog was Dilya's problem, or the First Family's. But the little Sheltie was moving with purpose just as she had at the conference center in Florida, after the training Colby had given to Zackie and Dilya. Then the Sheltie sidetracked to sniff a potted plant before cutting over to the other side of the hall.

Colby caught the barest glimpse of dark hair peeking around the corner, then a whispered command echoed down the odd acoustics of the long hallway. Zackie snapped to and continued on her way back to Dilya.

It was too early to play games, but she probably hadn't sent Zackie to them just as a game—nothing was ever that simple with Dilya. Besides, he liked the kid. The kid who might never have been a kid according to the stories he'd heard about her war orphan past. Despite his exhaustion, he was intrigued.

He unclipped Rex's leash and gave him the hand sign to move ahead fast.

"*Geh Herum! Links!*" *Go around! Left!* He added the whispered command as a last minute thought.

Rex swung left into the first corridor at a fast trot.

Colby began his countdown. *Seven.*

Zackie disappeared around the far corner where Dilya waited. *Six. Five.*

Colby made a point of turning the near somnambulant Ivy toward the exit, but kept his head turned just enough to see down the Central Hall in his peripheral vision. "Wake up, Ives. You don't want to miss this."

Four. Three.

The top of Dilya's head peeped around the corner once more, with Zackie's nose down by her knees.

He had to pinch Ivy to get her attention.

Two. One.

Ivy startled and turned just as Rex caught up with his target.

With a loud *"EEP!"* Dilya stumbled out into the middle of the hall. Zackie launched forward as well. Then Rex, emerging from where he'd circled around and run down the back corridor, stepped on Dilya's foot and leaned into her. She tumbled to the carpet and Rex proceeded to sit on her before looking happily down the hall toward him. He completely ignored Dilya's protesting laughter and Zackie running excited circles around the pair offering bright yips that echoed painfully down the hall.

He and Ivy strolled back, but he didn't give Rex the heel command. It was another new behavior, pinning Dilya in place. Apparently you *could* teach an old dog new tricks.

"Good morning, Dilya."

She managed a gasped, "Morning," as she shoved ineffectively at the dog who probably weighed as much as she did.

Rex apparently decided it was a back scratch and began wagging his big tail, beating her about the head and shoulders with it.

"What trouble are you up to?"

"Brea-thing." Her gasp had devolved to a wheeze as she gave up and crossed her arms over her face protectively.

Colby slapped his thigh and Rex trotted over, eliciting a final "Oof!" as he pushed off. He gave Rex a couple of well-earned treats.

Dilya sat up rubbing her belly. "That was…so cool. I never saw him…coming. If Zackie hadn't turned…at the last…second, Rex might have…run me…over." She spoke quickly despite her breathlessness.

"No. I didn't give him an attack command. So he just tries to corner the prey, not disable it."

"That's good I guess."

"Why were you stalking us?"

THAT FINALLY WOKE Ivy up the rest of the way.

Apparently this wasn't some amusing dog test. Dilya had wanted their attention for a reason—even if she'd earned more of it than she'd counted on.

"I was told to find you. Quietly."

"How's that working for you?" Colby offered her a hand up.

Dilya shrugged uncomfortably as Ivy glanced up and down the long central hall. No one around, even though they could still hear the controlled mayhem coming from the kitchen at the far end of the corridor. Rex's run and Dilya's half-choked giggles hadn't attracted anyone else's attention.

"Now that you found us," Ivy turned back to the girl, "care to tell us who told you to do so?"

Dilya shook her head as she attempted to get control of her hair that Rex's tail had completely tangled. "It's better if I show you. She's not the sort of person who is easy to describe. She keeps…changing."

Colby waved for Dilya to lead the way.

Ivy couldn't think of who she meant. First Lady Anne Darlington-Thomas was a very steady person—at least on television or when aboard HMX-1. She seemed the unchanging type, actually, very consistently herself. But Dilya didn't lead them up the main stairs. Instead she cut through the Curator's Office. Ivy barely had time to take in the space—four desks and floor-to-ceiling bookcases. Ever since the Kennedys' declaration of the White House as a museum, the office of the curator had become the repository of all historical items and in charge of all displays—from the portraits of the Presidents on the wall of the Oval Office to the furniture in the Lincoln Bedroom.

In moments, they were out the other side of the empty office and into the back corridor. From there, the staircase narrowed and led downward. She had no time to see anything of that level, as Dilya led them down once more.

Ivy noticed that Colby had signaled Rex ahead of them and he suddenly veered into a doorway. All she could smell was cleaning products. The steady thrum of massive air conditioning units seemed to echo along the white walls and bounce off the concrete floor like it had been slapped away. But Rex had picked some thread out of the Residence's lowest reaches.

Dilya stopped at the door Rex had entered.

The German shepherd was sitting in front of an old woman. She sat behind a battered steel desk in a tiny room surrounded by dusty bookshelves. Lit only by a down-focused desk lamp, she should look like an evil spider lurking in the shadows. Instead she looked to be a dotty librarian who had absentmindedly wandered in off the street and never been heard from again.

The walls of books were much more tightly packed than the pleasantly jumbled shelves of the curator's office. Here they crammed into any available space in apparent disarray. The few titles she could make out in the dim light reflected off the desktop were even more of a misfit than the woman in the basement: *The Military Cipher of Commandant Bazeries, Caesar Cypher Quick Reference, and Polygraphiae.* Other titles often included: *Code, Crypto,*

Analysis, Enigma... She was in a spy library in the White House basement.

Strange objects hung on the walls above the cases, some even dangling from the overhead pipes that gurgled with rushing water every now and then. Wrong sound for flushing toilets. Maybe they were below the dishwashing room—she didn't know anything about this part of the White House.

A number of the wall "decorations" were strange, clandestine-looking weapons that she was amazed had made it in through security. Actually, it was a surprise that the *woman* had been let in through security. Mother Hubbard and her knitting belonged in fairy tales, not a clandestine library on...being clandestine. Except for her eyes—which seemed to miss nothing.

The room shifted Ivy over into Marine Corps officer defensive mode. Something about it sent a chill up her spine. She stepped away from Colby so that they'd have two angles of fire if necessary.

"Oh, no need for that, my dear," the woman said in a surprisingly pleasant voice for an alien impossibility lurking in the dark of the Residence's lowest basement. The small desk lamp illuminated almost nothing other than a multicolored sock she was knitting and her bright-blue eyes.

Colby's arms were crossed casually over his chest, his hand nowhere near his sidearm.

"I expect you'd like a dog biscuit," the old woman addressed Rex. Then she looked up at Colby. "If you would be so kind as to call him off, Mr. Thompson. I'm not likely to explode, but there are many smells in this room he won't like."

Colby glanced down at Dilya, who held up her hands in denial.

"I didn't say a thing. Miss Watson knows everything."

Colby tapped his thigh and gave Rex a treat when he returned to his master's thigh.

Too trusting! Ivy kept her position in one corner and did her best to ignore the prosthetic arm that dangled just over her head.

Miss Watson rose, proving that she was actually quite tall for a dotard granny. Then she and Dilya approached one of the bookcases and pushed on the middle. The cases swung back to either side, revealing a long and cheerfully lit parlor, complete with armchairs, little side tables, and a snug fireplace crackling away beneath a solid marble mantel. The walls were covered with photographs of women, mostly in military uniforms—though not all US military.

Ivy glanced up the moment before she stepped forward to inspect the room more closely. The brighter lamplight from the cozy sitting room illuminated the prosthetic arm above her head. A glint of steel and she was focusing on it differently—not stainless like an armature, rather gunmetal gray. There was a rifle embedded in the structure of the arm, with a barrel that ended flush with the palm. A deadly handshake.

Someone had written across the arm, in neat strokes of violet nail polish, *Mission accomplished! All my love, Binky.*

Ivy checked quickly, but the strange Miss Watson appeared to have both hands as she lifted a pair of dog biscuits out of a Snoopy cookie jar and offered a big one to Rex and a smaller to Zackie. Apparently she wasn't Binky herself.

"It's a pity you've already eaten as I just made a lovely quinoa and salmon breakfast torte, but I'll fix you some tea. I'm sure your nerves are far too jangled from the last few days' experiences for coffee."

They were soon settled in chairs clothed in delicate sepia-toned fabric of world maps. With a set of colored pushpins, they'd make fine diagrams for mission planning or mapping out global geopolitical dynamics.

The tea was served in delicate porcelain cups adorned with sweet peas. Dilya, perhaps as part of some innocent-teen-girl disguise that she'd long since blown, was sitting cross-legged on the floor between the two dogs, a hand resting on each as they settled in for a nap. All three of them appeared to trust Miss Watson, which was interesting in itself.

"I expect that you are tired enough that we should postpone any pleasant chit-chat until some later opportunity. You must both come back when you have leisure time and perhaps some more recent shuteye."

"So, why are we here?" Ivy didn't like this. She appeared even more grandmother-kindly in the parlor than she had at her desk, but knew far too much. After a long hesitation and a tiny confirming nod from Colby, they settled into the luxurious wing-back chairs close by the gas fireplace. Ivy did her best not to imagine that colored pushpins weren't poking into her own back as her life changed more every minute.

"Terribly difficult to have logs delivered here, so I've had to accept a gas artifice," Miss Watson seemed to be pursuing point-less chit chat despite her prior comment.

Ivy resisted the mild hypnosis the jumping flames offered. It was easy to forget first impressions in this cozy space. Perhaps she'd have a space like this in her and Colby's house...though without the rifle prosthesis. And— Without Colby! She really must be tired to think such things.

"On December 4th, 2011," Miss Watson continued her very pleasant tone, "control was lost of a Lockheed RQ-170 stealth drone named the Sentinel—a flying wing model—while it was patrolling over Iranian airspace. Our government has, naturally, insisted that it was over Afghanistan when it malfunctioned and crashed. The Iranians have insisted that they interrupted its control-and-guidance system deep within their own borders and landed the drone themselves. It took them three years to reverse engineer and copy the aircraft."

Not so much with the chit chat apparently—unless this was Miss Watson's idea of charming conversation. Besides, Ivy knew about that drone. There were some who argued that they had simply done a nice job of plastic work for the published photographs but didn't yet have a working model.

Though it seemed an odd tale for Mother Hubbard to be telling. Or was she Mother Goose? Ivy wasn't sure. She had grown up on science fiction and dreams of space—which hadn't helped her fit in with little girls at all. They played with dolls and she built intricate scale models of the LEM lunar lander and the *Serenity* spaceship from the *Firefly* TV show.

No. Models that Colby had helped her build. Did he remember that? She hadn't. Not really. She looked over to see if Colby remembered, but he showed no signs of it. Not that she'd said anything aloud. The flickering fire, hot tea, and lack of sleep were ganging up on her.

"The Iranian's copy is fully functional, in case you are interested. Not as refined perhaps, but still, very effective."

So much for the plastic theory.

"Seven days after its initial loss, the President of the United States requested its return. He was very polite, though he was careful to admit no wrongdoing or to apologize. Iran offered to return it free of charge. Actually an Iranian *toy manufacturer* offered to return twelve of them—in 1/80th scale rubber toys." She waved a negligent hand toward one corner of her dingy inner office visible through the swung-aside bookcases. Dangling from one of the pipes was a hot pink model of a flying wing drone about a foot across. "You have an interest in drone control systems, Ms. Hanson."

Ivy startled upright and almost slopped her tea in her lap. The few people who knew that should not include some odd woman in the deep basement.

"More specifically, how to block them."

Ivy's hand drifted to her sidearm. Colby casually dropped Rex's leash. His dog popped up his head from his pending nap and looked at him. So, Colby wasn't as excessively trusting as he appeared—apparently ready to unleash the lethal weapon that was his dog.

"My, but you two are so cute together. They make such a charming couple, don't you think, Dilya?"

Dilya squinted up at them from her spot on the floor. "Seem like an odd couple to me."

"Oh, now there was a charming code breaker if ever there was one." She freshened everyone's tea and set out shortbread cookies in the shape of cherry blossoms. Did their shapes change with the seasons?

"Who?" Ivy bit her tongue too late to keep the question from slipping out. She didn't like this Miss Watson commenting on a relationship she didn't understand herself. Maybe if she *had* gone to space the way Colby had suggested, she'd not be here and then this wouldn't be half as confusing because she wouldn't know about it.

"Tony Randall. He starred in the television serial entitled *The Odd Couple* for years as an intelligent, but rather fussy gentleman who is burdened with the slovenly Jack Klugman as a roommate. Tony was also an exceptional code breaker for the United States during the Second World War. Although that role is one of his least known."

"Anything you want to be telling us?" Colby actually teased her in a somewhat suggestive tone.

"Oh dear, no. I wasn't even born yet, Mr. Thompson. Besides, Mr. Randall was happily married well before he was recruited to the Army Signal Corps. But most of the codebreakers were women and my mother said that Tony was particularly charming, always doing his best to make everyone he came in contact with laugh as it was an arduous and stressful occupation. Apparently he was also a wonderful dancer. He was a semi-professional ballerino for a time."

Ivy was wondering if it was the exhaustion or if she'd fallen down some White House rabbit hole into an alternate reality.

Miss Watson leaned forward so abruptly that Ivy slammed into the back of her chair. The woman's voice shifted to surprisingly sharp and businesslike—not befitting an old grandmother at all.

"You are missing the most simple fact that apparently eluded the mechanics of the RQ-170 as well. Minimizing frequency selection mitigates the problem, but doesn't solve it. The problem is that the moment you broadcast on a frequency, any electronics store scanner can overhear that. Yes, the Sentinel drone had an inertial guidance system in addition to its GPS guidance. But it also had a command-and-control frequency. Once used and identified, it was simply a matter of beaming a stronger signal at the drone and overwhelming more remote, less powerful instruction sets."

"Encryption?" Colby asked.

Miss Watson waved her hand at the open bookcases. "Codes, ciphers, cryptograms: they all have their place. But a sufficiently powerful computer—or rather a sufficiently powerful network of computers—can overcome that. Electronics have made codes both more secure and more predictable."

"Then what's the solution?"

Miss Watson sipped her tea and eyed Ivy as if willing her brain to solve it for herself. But struggle as she might, there was still a need to communicate between pilots, ground teams, overwatch patrol, and so on. They even had to keep the channel for the President's personal panic button open at all times.

"Don't transmit?" Dilya guessed.

"Close," Miss Watson acknowledged with a smile.

"Don't transmit in any way that can be detected," Ivy knew the answer, but wasn't sure—

"Give the girl a gold star."

"But how can we…" But Ivy could see it. Transmit, but never from the Presidential aircraft. Use a laser-encoded communication system for point-to-point communication with another helo

—one outside the ECM-suppressed area. And let them relay transmissions. This setup would provide an undetectable point of communication without impeding its efficiency by more than any other electronic relay. All possible with standard equipment already aboard the HMX-1 one aircraft.

Colby and Dilya were watching her closely. Why? She looked down at her own hands and realized that she had frozen in place with the teacup half raised to her lips. She made a point of completing the gesture and sipping the sweet peppermint tea before replying.

"Thank you, Miss Watson."

13

"We still don't know who she is," Colby fumbled for his apartment keys with little luck. It had taken only minutes to get Arnson's and Lieber's approval. But then they had to rush out to Anacostia and work with the pilots to perform test flights and work out a dozen unanticipated bugs with the plan.

The three HMX-1 helicopters of any Marine One mission were always shifting in position. If they shifted so that one helo was above the rotors of another one, the blades chopped up the laser-based transmission.

And the interface between the radio and the laser system wasn't direct. It required a human relay because the data bus interfaces on the voice-to-laser transmission systems were not CAAS compatible. And that had only been the beginning.

The problems dragged on through most of the day, and his hands were no longer working well enough to unlock his own door. With two hands, he finally managed it and they stumbled into his apartment in the middle of Sunday afternoon.

"Dilya's trust is a good sign though, don't you think?" Ivy was still riding high on finding the solution. She was bubbling with energy. If a person could effervesce, then Ivy was the woman on the planet closest to doing it.

The signs of their hurried departure thirty-six hours ago were everywhere. Grabbing his vest from the closet had dislodged several jackets, which spilled onto the floor and caught under the door. Rex tried to jam through the narrow gap right after Colby stepped into it. The door didn't budge, which stuck the two of them fast.

Ivy shoved against the middle of his back and he tripped over coats and dog to land squarely on the middle of the living room carpet.

She yanked her jacket and blouse off with a single hard, overhead yank at her back collar.

"Get naked, Colby. I'm in the mood to celebrate."

He was in the mood to pass out cold as he'd now missed two nights sleep. Then she dropped her weapon's belt—her sidearm thumping down with a heavy weight—then shed the rest of her clothes. The woman was an amazing sight. This wasn't some darkened hotel room. Or some half-awake glimpse of her while he stumbled through a phone call with General Arnson. This was Ivy Hanson, far more glorious than he'd ever imagined her, wearing nothing but her dog tags.

"If I must," he conceded. But he wasn't fast enough for Ivy, who had his boots and socks off and was working on his pants before he managed to undo his vest. He had it off, but still wore his t-shirt by the time she got the rest of him naked.

Then…she dove on him. Landing no more gently than she had on the South Lawn, at least this time she didn't inadvertently punch him in the solar plexus.

But the impact was no less.

She was everywhere. Nuzzling his neck one moment. Digging her hands hard into his butt the next while making a happy humming sound.

Thankfully, she'd kept some protection handy from last night, stashed in a back pocket for something. She straddled him then, in a total shift from wild to still, she eased down on him so slowly that it seemed there was time for the afternoon sunlight to shift across the carpet before they fully came together.

Her eyes were closed long before she completed the move, but he couldn't look away.

He and Saint Ives. Sex on the living room floor. It was beyond awesome.

Her back arched, then her head bowed down until he was surrounded by the long fall of her blonde hair as she ever so slowly reversed the process.

Cupping her face, he pulled her down enough to kiss her as he almost slid out of her and she began the impossibly slow return. He swallowed her deepest groan of pleasure and did his best to hold on, because—while her slow movements were absolute torture—they were *exquisite* torture.

And with each movement, with each moment, he knew that he'd never find another woman like her. No with her dedication, her passion for her job, and definitely not the way she felt and smelled.

She added a side-to-side gyration to the beat of a very slow drummer that blanked his mind until all he could do was give up what little control he had and take the ride with her.

When she finally let the release take her, take them both, he wondered if he'd ever seen anything as amazing as the smile of ecstasy painted across Saint Ives' features.

<hr>

IVY DIDN'T REMEMBER MOVING to the bed. Maybe Colby had carried her. Never in her life had there been such a release. It was as if she'd been filled with pure light. Turned into a being of nothing but light.

It was too bad, really.

Could a being of pure light still have sex with Colby's incredible body? It would be very sad if she couldn't. Could a being of pure light ever move again? Her limbs felt disconnected, her body floating.

It was just dark and Colby's steady breathing told her he was close beside her and out cold. She dug her toes through the covers into Rex's side for a moment and received a happy sigh.

Good.

That meant beings of pure light *could* still interact with those of mere mortal stuff. Based on that encouragement, she rolled over until she lay fully on Colby's back.

His breathing grew a little more labored, but didn't change particularly. For a while, she was content to ride up and down with each cycle of breath—a languid but deliciously comfortable carousel horse.

"Colby Thompson," she whispered in his ear. "Wake up, Colby Thompson."

"Why?" The softest grunt of a reply.

"Because…I'm hungry." For more Colby Thompson.

He reached out a hand for—his phone. He punched in a number.

"Hey Jake, this is Colby. Yeah, Unit 42. The usual, but make it a large. Yep, a side of bacon, too. Thanks, you're a champ." And he hung up the phone, burying his face back in his pillow.

She lay there, and it seemed he was falling back asleep. "Wake up, Colby Thompson."

"No," his reply was muffled.

"Sex. Colby Thompson."

He made a thoughtful hmm sound that rippled down his back and into her chest.

"Must be quick, Colby Thompson," she shifted to whisper in his other ear. "If you just ordered pizza."

"Might have."

"Sex. Colby—" was all she had time for before he rolled over, pinning her beneath his back.

With the smooth grace of an athlete, he twisted about and pinned her in place with his hands and lips. He never gave her a chance to even sigh in happiness: not during a hand brush over her breast or a kiss planted firmly between her legs. Unable to find protection in the bedside table, he slung her over his shoulder with all the ease of a beach towel and headed into the bathroom. When she struggled, it earned her a sharp slap on the buttocks—not hard enough to do more than sting.

Before she could retaliate, he found protection, sheathed himself, and shifted her until they were chest-to-chest. He never let her feet touch the floor, instead slamming her back against the cool tile between a towel rack and the door. As perfectly gentle as this afternoon's lovemaking had been, tonight's was anything but. With her legs locked around his waist and his palm supporting her behind, he took her.

There was no other way to describe it, he simply took her.

And she was powerless except to give. She'd always made sure that she was in perfect control during sex. Had even convinced herself that she could only find release if she was.

Colby proved she was completely wrong and he took her body, her kiss, her very breath, until she really was just a vessel of light absorbing his unquestionable corporeality.

Sex doesn't equal love. Reminding herself of that wasn't having any particular effect. She was swooning. In moments she'd be completely gone.

Then her first release slammed away all thoughts.

Still Colby didn't relent.

Even as the shudders rolled through her, he took her higher and higher, even better than the rocket launch. His final liftoff tipped her into a second-stage burn that she hadn't known she possessed. She had to pound her fists against his shoulders because the power slamming through her body couldn't be contained, not even within a body made of pure light.

And when the mad pulsing waves finally eased, his kiss was gentler and deeper than the deep rumble that had reached them from the rocket's launchpad a full twenty seconds after they'd witnessed liftoff. It didn't matter that it was an unmanned satellite launch, her heart had gone aloft with it into the fiery heavens. She had wanted to be there like an ache in her body.

At the moment, she couldn't imagine wanting to be anywhere else. Ever.

Colby held her gently as he carried her back to bed and deposited her there with a kiss. Moments later, he yanked on a pair of sweatpants and headed for his door. Doorbell. Pizza. How mundane after a lover had just launched her right through the stratosphere.

When the phone rang, Ivy answered it without thinking.

"Hello?"

"Is…ah, Colby Thompson there?" A woman's voice this time. She'd recognized General Arnson last time and handed off the phone as fast as she could hoping that he hadn't recognized hers. This time she'd be a Marine and take the challenge head on.

"Mrs. Thompson?"

"Ivy? Well, I certainly didn't expect to hear your voice on my son's phone. Oh! *Especially* not sounding so languid. I'm so pleased for both of you. That's simply wonderful. Oh, your mother and I always hoped the two of you would get together. How long has this been going on? I'll just strangle him for not telling me sooner." Her voice rose higher and accelerated with each statement acting like a fresh booster rocket.

"We didn't—"

But they totally had.

"We aren't—"

But what if they were? "Together" implied things that they hadn't discussed even a little.

Colby stepped back into the room carrying a large pizza box and two beers, with a roll of paper towels tucked under his arm. His sweatpants rode low and his bare chest looked awesome. He hesitated in the doorway and offered her a puzzled frown.

"The sex is amazing, Mrs. Thompson." She offered Colby her best radiant smile as he gawked at her and lost the paper towels, which bounced onto the floor. Hopefully he'd be more careful with the pizza. "Don't know why we didn't think of doing this sooner."

"It's just the way of it. I did the same dance with his father for months. Then *pow!* And I never knew why I made him wait so long. An engineer. I *never* expected to be swept off my feet by an engineer."

"Literally, I hope."

That earned her a knowing laugh followed by a happy sigh. "He still does. Tell Colby I was just worried when he didn't come over for Sunday dinner. He usually calls if he's not going to make it. Even at his age, mothers worry."

"I may have been busy distracting him. But he's standing here half naked and carrying a pizza."

"Ooo. Why didn't I think of doing that? Tomorrow night. Definitely tomorrow night. Wearing nothing except one of Steve's shirts."

"Or maybe just one of his ties and nothing else."

Colby's face went white and perhaps even a little green. Apparently guys didn't talk about sex with their moms.

"Even better. I like the way you think, Ivy. I'll leave work early to make sure I'm home first. Have fun, dear." And she was gone.

Ivy hung up the phone, well aware that she was still completely naked and lying back on Colby's pillows, still in sex-magazine-model-in-training mode apparently.

"Your mom says hi."

When he still didn't move, she clambered out of the bed, bent down to fetch the paper towels, and couldn't resist running her hand up the inside of his sweatpants and cupping him.

"Yummy. Maybe later. Pizza first, I think." She secured the box with a slight tug and carried it back to the bed with a happy swing to her hips.

Colby didn't make her feel like a Marine with inconvenient woman parts. He made her feel like the luckiest woman on this planet. And since the rest of the planets appeared to be unpopulated—except maybe whatever hid under the ice on Europa, besides it didn't really count even if there were females of some weirdo sub-ice species—she decided to stake claim to the entire solar system while she was at it. And that was mightily lucky.

14

$\mathcal{C}$olby had never been comfortable in a suit. Wearing one of the President's suits and walking across the White House lawn only worsened the sensation.

Harvey Lieber was trusting of their communications solution, but not *very* trusting. So Colby was playing body double, having donned one of the President's cowboy hats (he didn't wear them often, but today "he" did). With a pair of sunglasses and Ivy in her dry-cleaned dress blues talking to him intently so that he had an excuse to keep the brim of his hat down low because of their difference in heights…

"You make a good decoy for the President, Colby."

"That's Mr. President to you."

The Motorcade had left the basement of the Treasury Building very quietly fifteen minutes earlier, without sirens and only a minimal police escort. They'd be most of the way to Andrews Air Force Base by now. If everything went right and no one tried to kill him, they and the President would be arriving to board Air Force One at roughly the same moment.

Rex hadn't liked the idea of traveling with the President. It had looked like the whole plan was going to go awry on that point

189

alone until Dilya trotted out of the tunnel that connected the White House East Wing basement to the Treasury Building garage. She'd had Zackie and a day pack, and without even hinting that she hadn't been invited on the trip to Ottawa, she strode up to Rex. She'd given him a good head rub, taken the leash from the President's hand, and done exactly as Colby had taught her—leave no doubt about who was in control.

"C'mon, Rex. Time to go." She'd climbed into the Beast limousine and, after one bewildered glance back at Colby, Rex had followed her in and lain down on the floor. Zackie was ecstatic—even by Sheltie standards—to have her big buddy Rex along for the ride.

The President had merely shrugged at Dilya's abrupt appearance, shaken Colby's hand, and said, "Good luck, Mr. President." That was fifteen minutes ago.

Now, it was just him and Ivy coming down the front lawn. The press had been told that there'd be no statement or time for questions on the South Lawn. The fourteen reporters lucky enough to get a seat on Air Force One were following the fake Motorcade. Everyone else had left an hour ago—taking vans out to Anacostia to board a greenside MV-22. Air Force One would reach Ottawa in under an hour, the slower Osprey needed almost two.

So there were only a few stringers left at the White House. None had bothered to come out for a photo of the Marine and the imposter walking down the lawn. Even if they didn't know that's what was going on.

He saluted the Marine standing at attention by the helo's door. Not McShea—he'd gone ahead with the other helos shifted up to Ottawa for transportation to the meeting. The Marine saluted back, then did a sharp doubletake.

"Carry on, Sergeant. It's all with good reason."

The Marine glanced at Ivy. No, he looked at Ivy like she was a side of meat he wanted to take home. The man was too damn handsome for his own good and knew it.

"Stow it, Sergeant Mathieson," Ivy said in a tone that implied things Colby didn't want to be thinking about Ivy and other men.

"If you say so, ma'am." He actually gave her a leer. If he really was President, Colby knew who his next appointment to Nome, Alaska, would be.

Colby clambered aboard, forgetting about the hat. He almost knocked it off, revealing his hair, which he wore much shorter than the President. He made a point of avoiding the President's chair until Ivy grabbed his arm and shoved him into it. She sat in the armchair directly across from his.

When the Marine sergeant boarded after folding away the stairs, hc offered a glare that could scorch Colby's image irreparably into the fabric of the seat. Apparently all Marine crew chiefs were very protective of the President's seat. With this asshole, he was fine ignoring the man.

"It's for security, Sergeant. The President is traveling by another route." Ivy's reassurances did little to assuage the man.

"At least I have you here to protect me," Colby told her once the crew chief turned to other duties.

"Tell me why I should bother," Ivy made a point of yawning as if bored, but it carried longer than fit the joke. They'd slept through the afternoon and evening, but somewhat less during the night after they eaten most of a large pizza.

"Because you already can't live without me," he teased.

"I thought it was the other way around."

"Well, could be," he had to admit as they finally lifted off the South Lawn.

Ivy twitched and collapsed deeper in the seat opposite him.

"Ivy," he signaled for her to lean in close, as close as the seatbelts allowed.

She watched him the way cats watched Rex—with a great sense of caution and some alarm. Rex hadn't even sniffed at one since a long ago feline had tried to quarter and section his nose with a swipe of claws.

And that was when Colby knew. Dad had always said that Mom had simply taken his heart and run away with it after their first date. He didn't know if a swim in the Potomac, a space launch in Florida, and tackling a major security problem was the kind of thing Dad had meant. But Colby understood *what* he'd meant.

After his parents, the number of people on the planet he cared about as much as he cared about Ivy Hanson totaled precisely zero. Her first homecoming was his first memory. He remembered her dogging his and Reggie's footsteps, but he also remembered an awful lot of good moments.

She was a voracious reader. With her Marine Corps mom often overseas and her father running a restaurant and a household, Colby was the one she came to when she didn't understand a story. He'd been the one stuck trying to explain the cruelty of twelve-year-old boys to her.

If she'd been a remarkable kid, she was an astonishing woman. A woman he hadn't known he was waiting for.

It was as if the focus shifted as they lifted up and over the National Mall. Maybe it was sitting in the President's chair, but he could see more clearly now. He'd climbed up out of the weeds and, looking back, could see that he and Ivy had a common path that went back a long way. And it was so easy to imagine what that path looked like going forward as well—without the duckweed.

Ivy finally leaned closer as the helicopter's rotors, finally up to speed, lifted them off the South Lawn. The seat belts let them lean just close enough to whisper despite the pounding rotors.

"What?" Her caution ran even deeper than his.

"Could be that I can't live without you. Maybe. Maybe not. But I do know one thing." Did she remember all of the good times as well as all the teasing?

"What's that, Thompson?"

"I have no idea how I lived without you this long." Not what he'd been intending to say. He'd started out to say something about how he couldn't live without the awesome sex. But it had shifted, morphed by the President's chair, into some strange, impossible truth.

"Get a grip, Thompson." Ivy's expression definitely agreed about the strange and impossible.

For the first time in his life, it felt as if he actually had one. "I've got a grip. Trying to live up to your standards, you've already made me a better man than I ever set out to be, Ivy. And while I do love your body, it's nothing compared to how I feel about you."

"Whoa!" Her eyes went as saucer wide as the day she'd asked him where babies came from and hadn't let him escape answering. He could still feel the heat in his cheeks from that long-ago conversation. Or maybe it was the heat from what he'd just said.

"Whoa!" Colby said himself and flopped back in the President's chair. "I didn't just say what I think I just said. Did I?"

"Not unless I heard what I didn't just hear. Or didn't hear what I just heard. Or..." She took a slow, deep breath before asking softly. "Did you just say you...loved me?" She mouthed the last two words silently as if even the sound of them had been scared away.

"Uh," Colby looked around the helo, but he couldn't even pet Rex as a distraction because Rex was in the Beast with the real President.

Love was a word for moms and dads. It was a word for a man's best friend—at least of the four-footed kind, not for Reggie. But was it a word for someone he'd known his *whole life?* And for *her* whole life?

He didn't think so. Yet maybe it was.

"Colby?" He could hear the strain in her voice.

He tried to look away. He really wanted to watch the approach to Andrews Air Force Base. He wanted to look down on Air Force One from the sky.

But he couldn't look away from *her,* from Ivy.

There was the right question. Was love a word for describing Ivy Hanson?

"Yes."

"Colby, what did you just say?"

"Yes." He'd just said yes.

"What are you saying yes to, that I just said your name?"

"Yes," he teased her, which wasn't at all what he'd meant.

She scowled at him as the wheels settled on the pavement close beside the shining bulk of Air Force One. They taxied forward, entering the massive hangar that could hold all four of the big executive jets: the identical pair of 747s used for Air Force One, and the pair of 757s used for Air Force Two duties for the Vice President or when the First Lady traveled alone. The shadows seemed to bring them even closer.

Sergeant Mathieson lowered the forward door and descended to stand at his station as the engines wound down to silence. The helo pilots were busy with their logbooks. He and Ivy were alone for just a moment.

"And yes, I said what I said."

"Which was?" How typical of Ivy to not let him off the hook.

"Yes, I can't think of a better word to describe how I feel about you." He tugged on the President's cowboy hat and clambered out of the Chair of Truth before something else slipped out, like how easy it was to imagine spending the rest of his life with her.

"Typical, Colby," she muttered to herself as she descended the stairs behind him. "Can't even say the word."

He decided against pointing out that she hadn't said "the word" either.

***

Ivy was in a bad reentry burn. Her heat shield—the shield that kept men away from meaning too much to her—was badly cracked and burning away. Would it last long enough for her to survive whatever this newest game of Colby's was?

The Motorcade raced into the hangar and stopped on the back side of the helicopter, out of everyone's view. When the President emerged, Colby handed over hat and sunglasses, then shrugged off his jacket and flipped it over his shoulder. Taking up Rex's leash, Colby now looked much more like himself.

He had looked important, even daunting in the President's seat on Marine One. And so sure of himself. So…impressive. As impressive as the President in his own way. When had that happened?

Never avoid the question! One of Drill Sergeant McKinnon's Laws. *If you're asking it, there's a reason. Be damn sure you figure out the answer…preferably before it kills you.* And this one definitely possessed lethal qualities—like death and destruction to her sanity.

"Okay," she muttered to herself as she followed Colby and the President out of the hangar. "Do I love Colby Thompson?"

"Duh!" Dilya said from close beside her. "Dumb question."

"Why is it dumb?" Even with Zackie in tow, the girl had a serious stealth mode.

"He isn't just amazing. He's amazingly amazing."

Ivy couldn't believe that the kid was quoting *Hitchhiker's Guide to the Galaxy* at her about being in love.

"It isn't *possible* that I love him."

"Why not?"

"Because he's like a big brother to me. Maybe even more than my own brother."

"But you had sex with him. You told me that."

The President headed for Air Force One's forward stairs—the entry for the President, special guests, and senior staff—to greet the press and then climb aboard. Colby led them toward the rear stairs that had lowered from the center of the tail section for everyone else to use.

"I did." Not that she was comfortable discussing her sex life with a teenager—though she didn't seem to have much choice at the moment.

"Was it good sex?"

Ivy eyed Dilya, but the teen didn't blink. Not hiding behind any facade at the moment, Dilya was daunting as well.

"It was *amazing* sex," Ivy did her Marine Corps best to answer honestly.

Dilya sighed happily. "I knew it. I just knew it. That doesn't sound like you're thinking of him as a brother very much."

She wasn't at all, was she. Meaning that had been a lame excuse.

Never use an excuse. They just hide the answers.

She wished McKinnon could have been a *little* less helpful. Then maybe she could have avoided all of this.

But she hadn't.

Maybe if she'd gone to space as Colby suggested. Or left for space right now…

But she didn't want to avoid Colby. Didn't want to miss out on all they could have shared.

Did she love the boy who had let her weep out her first-ever fifteen-year-old heartbreak on his shoulder? Did she love the man who kept trying to convince her that it was never too late to pursue her real dream of space? Did she love the man who saw past the uniform? Colby saw *her*. He was incapable of seeing her any other way because he knew her too well.

"You know what true love is?" Dilya asked without a hint of teenage innocence.

"Uh… Why don't you tell me? Then I'll see if I agree."

"First Lady Anne Darlington-Thomas told me it was two things. First, you can't imagine *not* living your life beside someone. She said that test worked for both men and women. But she said women were lucky, because they had an even better measure."

"What's that?" Ivy climbed the stairs into the back of Air Force One. Thankfully Rex had pulled Colby up well ahead.

"Can you imagine giving birth to any man's child other than his?"

Ivy didn't need to think about it for a second. Not an instant. She'd give anything to be able to hold Colby's child in her arms. Dilya was right; it was the gut punch question when the answer couldn't be denied. But could she stand to live with him for all the years to come? That was a much harder question.

Ivy sat beside Colby in the Secret Service section at the tail of the airplane. Dilya used her First Dog privileges to head forward as if she hadn't just dropped a ticking time bomb in Ivy's psyche.

Colby didn't even seem to notice as he slid his fingers through hers and took hold of her hand. It was so natural.

She was so screwed.

15

One hour to Ottawa. One hour in which not a single word had passed between them. Colby was cool with that.

Ivy had asked for no more impossible confessions—thank God. Nor had she offered any of her own. But it was clear what she was thinking by the way she fell so quietly asleep on his shoulder, never breaking their handhold.

He could do this all day, every day.

And apparently he was comfortable with it—as the impact of landing startled him awake with his cheek resting on her hair.

Their fingers were still slipped together.

And Harvey Lieber was glaring down at them.

"You two think this is going to work." He made it a demand rather than a question.

Colby looked at Ivy. Was it going to work? He didn't know. But he knew he'd be an idiot if he didn't try.

Except why was Lieber asking about his relationship with…

Oh. He wasn't. He was asking about the HMX-1 helicopters.

"Nothing is ever a hundred percent certain," Ivy stated as if she was quoting someone.

Harvey harrumphed.

Colby could feel his pain. From Ottawa's Macdonald-Cartier International Airport to Harrington Lake—the Canadian PM's retreat—was forty kilometers through the very heart of Ottawa city past a million people along unfamiliar roads and bridges. Or an eight-minute flight on an HMX-1 aircraft out over sparse suburbs. Less exposure in time. Far more hazardous if attacked.

"Okay, here's how we're going to play it." And he began to explain. Colby could only groan.

AIR FORCE ONE parked at the south end of Runway 32, well away from any of the passenger or cargo handling areas.

Two large hangars faced the area where Air Force One, several helicopters, and the backup Presidential Motorcade had all been parked. Between the hangars, a barracks building that would have housed the pilots and mechanics had been appropriated as an operations center. A lone, bright orange helicopter was parked off to the side by a building with a medical transport sign.

"It's an old QRA," a Canadian security agent informed her before continuing his patrol.

"A what?" Colby—again clothed as the President—whispered his question in her ear as they crossed to one of the HMX White Hawks that had been moved up the previous night. The President, wearing a Secret Service vest and leading Rex, along with Dilya and Zackie, headed toward one of the backup helos.

"Quick Reaction Area. It was where they staged emergency alert fighters at the peak of the Cold War in case of a Russian attack. They could be airborne over the capital in less than three minutes. Those square blocks we spotted out behind the hangars, those were probably missile silos, which I'd guess were nuclear armed back in the day."

The airport itself was strangely quiet, as there would be no takeoffs or landings while the American President was on-site.

"Let's get a move on, 'Mr. President'."

"Lead the way, Major Hanson," Colby said with all the graciousness of the President himself. Banter with Colby had always been fun—he was just as quick to hand it out as she was. Something she'd found far too rarely.

The two of them climbed aboard one of the White Hawks. This time it was again Sergeant McShea waiting for them—the crew chief they'd gone swimming with in the Potomac four days ago.

Four days? *Four days!* Ivy was clearly losing her mind and it was all Colby's fault.

"Um, Colby?" McShea asked.

"Salute when addressing the President, Marine!" Colby snapped it out but backed it up with a big smile. Because of the last-minute change, she hadn't thought to warn the Marine crew. Her area of responsibility.

Tish was loading up in the Motorcade and had probably kept her Motorcade people in the loop just fine.

McShea saluted automatically, probably Colby's intent. Then he'd offered a slight, but very amused smile. "Welcome aboard HMX-1, sir!"

"Carry on, Sergeant!" Then Colby banged his hat and head hard against the White Hawk's low entry. It took everything she had not to laugh in his face as he collapsed into the President's chair.

"Ow!" Colby reached up to remove his hat.

"Don't! The press corps are watching. Look at me." Ivy clambered over to the bench seat that would force Colby to look away from the open door. His face wasn't *that* good a match for the President's.

"Sure, just as soon as my eyes stop swimming."

McShea had them locked in moments later and they were quickly aloft.

"Now we hold our breath."

The eight-minute flight was uneventful, but she couldn't relax until they were on final approach to Harrington Lake—which was the name of the mansion, not the lake it commanded. The helicopter circled once over the big house, the luxurious lawn, and the lake shore. What she saw were the security checkpoints, the patrols, the Emergency Response Team van parked near the entry to the grounds.

The Prime Minister's country getaway lay northwest of Ottawa. The mansion sat by itself in the only cleared area along a quiet narrow road. Over three thousand acres of forest surrounded the lone residence. A few cottages and outbuildings, and a large vegetable garden dotted the clearing. The house faced a grassy beach and a stunning view of Lake Mousseau complete with a pair of boat docks. The lake itself was long and narrow, stretching out of sight between darkly green, towering conifers on steep shores.

The three helos of the HMX flight settled onto the broad lawn in back of the house. The two overwatch Black Hawks circled above.

Ivy watched carefully, but during the unloading, none of the Canadians appeared to notice that she and a Secret Service agent —without his cowboy hat—stepped out of one helicopter while a teenage girl led his dog out of the one the President had flown in.

Under the auspices of trade negotiations, they had eight hours to wander the grounds.

Ivy was at a loss of what to do with herself. It was late morning. A lone heron flapped lazily by overhead. A small contingent of Canadian geese had stopped off on their northbound journey and were fishing quietly along the shores of the lake. Otherwise, the wildlife had been scared off by the sudden invasion of two countries' security forces.

The President, Prime Minister, and their advisors had settled in comfortable chairs in the front garden. The house itself was a two-story colonial revival with steep roofs, generous windows, and a large sunroom topped by a balcony. It was very pretty, for a twenty-room "cottage." For her and Colby, she'd prefer a cozy house where they were always in each other's way. That's how they'd both grown up: bedrooms for sleeping or teenaged pouting and a merry great room that always had puzzles, cats, cooking, and maybe a game on TV.

She wanted that closeness again (though it had often irritated her as a teen—hence the pouting part of bedroom usage). And she *did* want it with a man like Colby.

A man *like* Colby? Was there such a thing other than the original?

Ivy watched him as she chatted with the flight crews. They'd staked out one of the docks closest to their helos to enjoy the sunshine. Their easy laughter had sent the geese farther up the lake for peace, so the only sound was the soft lap of tiny waves against the rocky verge.

Colby circulated with the other dog teams, patrolling the perimeter.

She could see him gathering up respect as he progressed, along with the occasional baggie of dog poo.

The respect came naturally to the man. The sense of play from his boyhood was still there, but the rest of it was a hundred percent self-made. But it was a self-made that she completely recognized because it was so based in who he was.

Now, if only he hadn't instilled those doubts in her.

She was a Marine. Five tours, ten years. It had earned her a role at the White House Military Office. Someday, it might even earn her the lead. Would she become as bitter and stodgy as Major General Markham and his two-minute-and-no-seconds welcome lecture?

"WHAT HAVE you done to me, Colby?"

He looked up at Ivy in surprise. "Nothing. You've been avoiding me all morning."

"No, I haven't." To prove her point—because she always had to—she sat down next to him on the grassy beach. She held a piled-high picnic plate from the spread the Canadians had set out for lunch that was at least as generously mounded as his own.

"Sure you have. You've kept your pilots wrapped around you like a security blanket. So, what could I have done to you? Nothing. They would have sunk my body in the lake if they knew that I'd touched so much as a hair on your head. See," he nodded at the nearby dock before forking up a maple-flavored meatball. "Even now they're planning my demise should I even look at you inappropriately."

"I mean, you have me questioning my whole career." She sounded grumpy, but bit into her chicken-avocado sandwich so she couldn't be too upset.

"Just trying to keep you on your toes, Ives. How did I do that?"

She glanced up at the sky without looking at it. Glanced up as if…looking at space.

"Oh. So go for it."

"Just like that?"

"Just like that."

"Don't be an idiot, Colby."

"Can't help it. Comes with the territory."

She shook her head and set down her sandwich. He knew the look. It had to be something bad to kill off Saint Ives' appetite—she'd always been a hearty eater. Which was a good thing, because with her metabolism she needed to be or her blood sugar plummeted through the floor.

With two fingers, he gave a meatball to Rex. Rex approved and licked his fingers completely clean. Then he picked up his own sandwich, trying to set an example for Ivy, but she wasn't buying it.

"It's already passed me by," her voice was the barest whisper.

"You said that before, but you're wrong."

"No. You are." Of course nothing with Ivy was simple. She had a persevere-against-all-odds streak so wide that it was sometimes hard to tell it apart from stubbornness.

"I'm not wrong, Ivy. You can do anything you set your mind to. You are five-foot-four and barely crack a hundred pounds. Yet you're a highly decorated Marine Corps pilot. You qualified for HMX-1—which I have on the best of authority is almost impossible to get into. I know this because you told me yourself. And you're so exceptional that a man of General Arnson's caliber selected you to represent his outfit at the WHMO. Go ahead, tell me there's something you can't do."

She didn't respond, but she started eating again, which he took as a good sign.

The silence stretched out between them. Birds fluttered down to see if they were offering any treats. He tossed a twist of pasta salad out toward a red-winged blackbird, but Rex's lunge for it spooked the bird away. A flock of black-capped chickadees settled for a moment but were gone before he could break off any bread-crumbs for them. Even after they finished and Rex had licked their plates clean, they sat quietly and watched the wind ruffle across the lake's surface.

"There's one other problem," Ivy said at length.

"What's that?"

"Say I did go for the astronaut program or even volunteered for a Mars mission and was accepted. I'd be in Florida."

"I wasn't a big fan of that heat wave, though the evening was nice enough. I'll bet the winters are great. Seems all right to me."

"You'd be Washington."

Colby hadn't thought about that. There was no way he could leave Rex to some other agent. Not even for Ivy Hanson.

But that wasn't the right answer either.

Now he knew where her appetite had gone.

A CHILL WIND was making up along with the thick clouds to the south by the time the meeting wrapped up. The meeting had moved inside after lunch and the agents on the grounds were soon scrounging up jackets. The pleasant day had decided that May wasn't quite done with winter yet. Weather services reported that the cloud ceiling was still acceptable for the flight back to the airport but that bad weather was moving in fast.

Everything kicked into high gear.

Crews were pre-flighting their helicopters.

Tish stopped by to check in, wearing a massively oversized USSS jacket that one of the assault team must have loaned her. She confirmed that the Motorcade, which had traveled empty across Ottawa just in case they were needed, was ready to roll.

Security agents from both countries gathered up their gear.

Ivy had taken advantage of the quiet afternoon to log some flight time with Captain Juarez so that she could stay current. Circling above the Canadian lakes and forests had served as both a wide-area patrol and a bit of welcome distance from Colby.

Once she was back at Harrington Lake, she'd sat alone out at the end of the farthest pier and no one had disturbed her except the waves starting to kick up in the contrary wind.

She'd only ever wanted one thing: to be the best Marine Corps officer.

And she'd achieved that in so many ways. She'd met her goals.

So set a new one.

It sounded like a McKinnon Law, but it felt as if it came from her.

The problem was that she now wanted multiple things.

She loved the Corps. There was a reason that there was no such thing as an ex-Marine—it was going to be a part of her forever.

Colby had reawakened her dream of space. And he was right.

She just might have a chance. Even her few days so far at WHMO would put an indelible stamp in her file that said she had the organizational skills to be of use as a mission planner, perhaps even a mission commander. And while an MV-22 Osprey might not be a jet, it wasn't a helicopter either. It was an immensely technical hybrid that brought far more skills to the cockpit than the simple little White Hawk she'd just logged a couple hours in. That should look good as well.

And she wanted one other thing. One that made the second dream impossible. She wanted Colby Thompson. Not for a night's tumble. Not just for that. His mere presence brought a piece of her to life that she'd forgotten, or perhaps never understood. Ivy wasn't used to being a woman as well as everything else. But also…

She'd been happy as a Marine. It had fit her well.

But Colby had brought her back to the feeling of pure joy. To a thrill that had made her want to tease him, to interact with him.

But he was—

But *she* was—

She'd gotten nowhere but flying in circular orbits all afternoon that had insisted on looping back over themselves faster and faster.

And now she was standing in the middle of the Prime Minister's backyard all alone. If she didn't hustle, she was going to miss her flight back and be *stuck* in the middle of nowhere during a chill downpour. The Motorcade had already rolled out, headed back across Ottawa. If you weren't ready when the President was, you got left behind.

Colby, Dilya, and both dogs were aboard one of the decoy birds.

She wasn't ready to face either of them.

The President's staff were already aloft in the second decoy.

That only left her one option—Marine One. Thankfully, the

President waved for her to hurry, so she clambered aboard just moments before McShea closed the doors.

The only other person aboard was Harvey Lieber, seated behind the President.

"Glad you decided to join us," the President's voice sounded hoarse.

"Did the meetings go well?"

He nodded as he leaned back tiredly in his seat. It made his cowboy hat, which Colby had once again returned when they landed, slide down over his eyes. The man wanted his privacy, that was his option, so she focused her attention out the window.

Racing from the countryside back toward the airport under the edge of the darkening storm, the trees gave way to housing. Soon they were over thick suburbs with the city lights ahead. They were approaching the Ottawa River. Curiously, they passed over a sprawling golf course—though at a thousand feet up there was little chance of disturbing the few remaining golfers trying to finish a round before the storm hammered in. Darkly massive thunderheads marched in from the east—garishly lit by the last of the sunlight cutting in below the cloud cover to the west.

Looking down at the golf course gave her both a shiver and a smile. Remembering the helo pilots messing with the golfers. And Colby and Rex taking a helicopter crash so professionally—dealing with a situation that threw untrained people into panic.

Colby was *highly* trained. The Secret Service were at least as selective as the Marine officer corps—the Presidential Protection Details equivalent to Whiteside operations of HMX-1. Yet, Colby had made the grade. If ever there was a man to match her, impossibly it was her childhood nemesis. If ever there was a man to push her ahead, it was oddly enough the man who never pushed himself.

She *was* a Marine.

She *wanted* space.

But she *needed* Colby. The woman that she'd almost lost, Colby had found and brought back from the brink. She could have ended up like General Markham—entrenched at the WHMO, bitter and old before her time. Colby would never let her get away with that. Just by being himself.

Her escape from a similar fate had been so close. Now if only she could figure out—

She didn't see the attack coming any more this time than she had last time.

16

There was no crunch and cry of rending metal.

A shattering crash sounded from the cockpit. Then a scream that could only be human as the helo lurched badly.

Some body memory had Ivy diving into the cockpit even faster than Crew Chief McShea.

The windshield was gone. Juarez was dead. He had to be with half of a model jet smashed into his chest.

His copilot had his hands still on the controls, but he was screaming from a face half torn off by one of the model's wings.

She slapped the seatbelt release on Juarez and tried to yank him clear. He outweighed her by at least double. McShea reached over her shoulder and grabbed Juarez's collar. With a single yank, he hauled the pilot across her lap and into the back.

Diving into the seat, Ivy grabbed the controls. No time to move the seat forward or put on a seatbelt, she perched at the forward edge of the seat and stretched her toes out to reach the rudder pedals. The Captain's headset was gone, so she took a moment to reach out and grab the one off the copilot's head. The muffs thankfully cut off most of his on-going cries.

The controls fought her as she struggled to gain control of the spinning helicopter.

The copilot—why couldn't she remember his name?—clutched his duplicate of her controls with a death grip.

"McShea. Get him off the controls."

Rain and snow drove into her face, forcing her to squint. Combined with the cloud cover, it was so dark it might as well be night for all she could see.

McShea made a grab at the copilot, but the man—Merton—didn't let go. Instead, the controls jerked hard and almost flipped them onto their backs, driving the nose aloft. She slid back into the seat. Without her feet on the pedals, they spun in a hard circle counter to the spinning rotors.

There was a sharp crack as McShea broke Merton's arms with a powerful blow, then hauled him out of the way.

Ivy struggled to right the aircraft. The centrifugal force of the spin was strong enough to slide her forward once she leveled out the nose. It was almost enough to fling her out the missing windshield, but she managed to regain control before that happened.

The ground was—where?

There. On the right. They were falling sideways out of the sky.

She keyed the mic switch on the back of the cyclic control.

"Mayday! Mayday! Mayday! This is—" she shouldn't identify that the President was in trouble "—HMX-1 going down."

"Roger that," someone replied calmly. They'd know that she was past their help until she was down, so there was only silence on the airwaves. They could be calling in rescue and aid units on another frequency, but as long as she was in the sky, this frequency was now hers.

She got them upright, but something else had been damaged and they rolled hard onto their left side. Each attempt to correct their position with the cyclic joystick between her knees was met with odd jerks and jumps. Linkages were broken or damaged.

A glance at the altimeter. Three hundred feet. In the heart of the Death Zone.

Except on the radio there wasn't only silence.

There should have been. The laser transmitter should be dead silent without input.

A high-pitched tone warbled at the upper edge of her hearing, like a supersonic dentist's drill.

"Carrier wave. Someone tell Colby. Carrier wave!"

olby could only watch in horror as Ivy's helicopter pitched and rolled its way out of the sky.

"Colby!" The pilot was shouting at him. "Colby!"

"What?" He'd sat close beside the crew chief. That placed him near the cockpit.

"Major Hanson said to tell you 'carrier wave.' That mean anything to you?"

Carrier wave? For a moment it didn't, then he remembered a discussion they'd had with one of the WHMO's radio communication specialists. In an instant, he knew she'd used the radio.

No, they—the bad guys—had *been using* the radio.

And a carrier wave meant that the attacker wasn't using some empty frequency, as their new protocols had peeled most of those away. Nor were they using a high blast of power to override the jamming on any one frequency. Instead, the attackers were using the *primary* communication frequency, but only using the very highest part of the signal as a carrier for their control commands.

Communication hadn't been the problem.

Their problem had been identifying which of the three shifting helos was the actual Marine One with the President aboard.

By launching that initial attack over the Potomac, they must have known that the Marines would eventually stumble on the idea of not letting Marine One ever transmit by radio. Instantly, its simple silence on the radio would identify which helo carried the President.

But that meant—

"Set your electronic countermeasures to broadband. Block all frequencies," he shouted to the pilot.

"Are you crazy? If I do, no one can communicate."

"Exactly! Including the attacker with his aircraft. Do it. *Now!*"

The pilot snarled and made some adjustment to the radio console between the two pilot seats.

Moments later, a large model aircraft impacted their helo's steel nose directly below the windshield. Colby had seen it falter with the loss of a radio signal and lose the crucial meter or so of altitude that was all that kept it from coming in through the windshield.

That's what must have happened to Ivy.

He looked out the window for her helicopter. It took him a moment to find it, and when he did, his heart stopped.

IVY FOUGHT THE CONTROLS, but it wasn't doing her much good. Each moment she managed level flight, she added all the lift she could manage to slow their plummeting descent.

But those were stolen moments.

They spent far more time tipped onto their side, once even flailing through a full roll.

Setting up an auto-rotation was out of the question. She still had some power to work with—in engine Number Two. She'd been forced to pull the fire T-handle on Number One as the turbine must have ingested something nasty. She had enough power to maintain level flight, but not sufficient control.

Where to land? Assuming she could find any control to make a choice even possible.

The snow now blasted through the missing windshield. It stung worse than a Libyan sandstorm.

The golf course was out of reach.

In fact, either shore was out of reach. They were going down in the Ottawa River. But it wasn't some gentle flow like the Potomac. There would be no giddy banter as they raked handfuls of duckweed out of each other's hair.

Here, the Ottawa River was over two hundred meters wide and narrowing rapidly for the hard pinch at the heart of Ottawa. She'd seen the Remic Rapids south of the Champlain Bridge before. They weren't a waterfall, but she had no desire to be beaten against those rocks.

***

"FOLLOW THEM DOWN!" Colby shouted.

The pilot half-turned to face him, then nodded and turned back. The upward slam of Colby's gut into his chest told him they were dropping altitude fast.

He began stripping off his jacket and vest. He dumped his sidearm as well.

"What are you doing?"

Damn it! He'd forgotten about Dilya. He turned to console the frightened teen, but that's not who was looking at him. No. The girl who now faced him was the war orphan he'd heard about— the one who had seen a *lot* of war before being picked up and adopted by one of the military's top snipers.

With the facade ripped away, he now saw that she'd never been young.

"I have to go in to save them." Because he had to save the President. No matter what. And if he didn't save Ivy, there wouldn't be any point in any of it. Next time he had a chance, he wasn't going to fool around with any word games—that was for damn sure.

"I..." Dilya hesitated, then suddenly looked ready to cry. "I'm a lousy swimmer. Oh God. I should have learned better. You don't swim in Afghanistan's rivers. Especially not girls. I have to help. If you think I can, I'll go in. But I don't—" Her voice remained calm and steady even as tears started rolling down her cheeks—tears of anger at her own shortcomings.

He bent down to quickly unlace his boots. A good trick against the bucking descent of the helo.

"You can do two things, Dilya. First, once I'm in the water, I won't be able to see very far. I'll look to you to point me toward anyone who is washed away. Don't lose track of anyone. Can you do that?"

She nodded fiercely and he didn't doubt her for a second.

"Second, make sure Zackie doesn't try to follow Rex and me into the water."

That got the choking half laugh he'd been hoping for.

He swung open the two doors until they latched off to either side, then leaned out and looked down.

Ivy's helo was so close that it felt as if he could reach out and touch it. But she was even closer to the river.

IVY FOUGHT FOR A LEVEL SPLASHDOWN. They'd be jarred harder, but it might give them a moment of float time to escape the helo before it sank. It might not. White Hawks weren't big on floating.

Twenty feet up, whatever damage she'd been fighting in the control system finally gave way.

She'd been dragging the cyclic back and to the right when it simply let go and she slammed her elbow into the edge of her seat back.

No time to curse or compensate, she was flung up and forward as the nose dropped out from under her.

Weightless, with no seatbelt to hold her, she was flung out through the missing windshield. How close she came to the spinning rotor blades she'd never know. She slammed into freezing water and was driven under.

Good idea.

She dove as deep as she dared to get away from the churning blades that should be shattering themselves against the surface of the water.

Unable to hold her breath against the freezing cold any longer, she fought to the surface. The rain-shrouded darkness was lit by brilliant punches of two spotlights. Both were aimed behind her at the floating wreckage.

Even as she watched, one of the helos slowed to hover above the scene and a swimmer jumped off the side. A massive dog followed close behind, removing any doubt as to the swimmer's identity.

The water was moving—she could see the Champlain Bridge coming up at warp speed. The rocks of Remic Rapids lay not far beyond the bridge.

Ivy knew she should be doing something, but the water was so cold that it was hard to concentrate. Dunk training had taught her what fifty-degree water felt like—this was definitely colder.

Swim. That was it. That's what she was supposed to be doing.

She tried to stroke out with her right arm—

Pain screamed up from her elbow.

Not so much with the swimming.

<hr>

COLBY SWAM through the bits of floating wreckage.

No one. No one.

Then his next stroke slammed onto someone's back.

The President.

"Mr. President?"

"Uh-huh!"

Dazed, but conscious. He kept staring up at the spotlight centered on him, blinking hard but not thinking to look down.

Colby pulled his head down. A big hard bump on the back side. Maybe a concussion.

"Look at me, sir."

He managed that.

"Don't look at the light. Look at me. Got it?"

"Okay."

Rex swam up at that moment.

Colby took the President's hands and wrapped them firmly around Rex's harness.

"Hold onto Rex, sir. Hold on hard."

"Okay," the President squinted his eyes as if it took all of his concentration to do so, but he seemed to have a handle on it.

When Colby swam away, Rex dutifully followed in his wake, dragging along the President.

The next body he rolled over had a massive hole in his chest. One of the pilots by his gear. The next body he rolled over coughed and sputtered as soon as he rolled into the air.

"McShea. Buddy! Good job getting the President out. Where's Ivy?"

"Uh-huh," he was no better off than the President.

Then he grabbed Colby's shoulders and shoved him underwater.

Colby knew that drowning men would climb atop one another to save themselves. Colby prepared to hit McShea in the gut to force him to let go when the man released him back to the surface.

"Sorry. I had to push off. To get…this." His voice was still wavery, but he held a lifting collar in one hand, dangling on a line from the hovering helo. In moments they had the President's head through it and the helo crew was winching him aloft.

Together they found Lieber in rough shape and got him winched aloft after the President.

McShea was flagging badly. It took little argument to convince him to go aloft as well.

"Ivy!" He shouted at McShea as his feet cleared the river.

McShea shook his head, then raised his arms in an I-don't-know gesture that almost slipped him free of the collar tucked under his arms.

Then Colby remembered. Dilya was his eyes tonight.

He had to backstroke out of the spotlight. The snow shifted to rain and pummeled down on him hard.

There! Dilya squatting in the doorway of the helo hovering above him.

Her arm was out, pointing firmly downriver.

IVY LEARNED many things about herself as she flowed between the pylons of the Champlain Bridge, which shuttered the bridge's roadway lights into a surreal strobe light.

One, she was going to dress far more warmly in the future.

Two, she'd never again complain about how cold the ocean was by the family's Maryland beach cabin.

Three, there was only going to be one real tragedy if she died tonight. If she did, she was going to lose a lifetime with Colby.

No way was she going to let that happen. She tucked her injured arm into the half-zipped front of her light jacket. The shivers were continuous now as she heard a growing roar.

She could almost see her brain shutting down, the life signs on the med bay monitor drooping lower and lower with each pulse.

The helicopters weren't the roar. They were still on the upstream side of the bridge, illuminating whatever was in the water.

An eddy flung her around and she saw the cause of the roar.

Even in the darkness, the whitecaps of the Remic Rapids caught the glow of the bridge's streetlights.

This was going to really hurt.

She braced herself just as something slammed into her from behind and forced her face underwater as if she wasn't wet enough already.

Wet enough already?

She surfaced to a mouthful of wet dog fur just as a strong arm wrapped around her waist.

Colby. She wanted to burrow up against him. Hide, just for a moment.

But there was something important.

And it was happening soon. Really, really soon.

If only she could remem—

"The rapids!"

"Hang on!" Colby shouted back.

COLBY DUCKED down under the water, grabbed Ivy's thighs, and with all his strength, heaved her upward.

Someone on the White Hawk helicopter hovering right at water level must have grabbed her, because she kept going upward after he'd lost all momentum.

Kicking hard, he surfaced again with a shoulder under Rex and heaved him up and through the door as well.

But he himself had run out of time.

Heaving Rex aloft had driven him back under.

Just as he surfaced once more, the helicopter lifted abruptly out of reach. He could see Rex's rear legs still dangling out the door as water poured out of the helicopter's cargo bay.

Then Colby felt the blow to his chest as he was flipped head over heels by the rapids.

1 8

*I*vy had never in her life screamed in fear.

And she didn't this time either.

It was stark terror that erupted from her throat as Colby slammed into the rapids. She didn't even care when Rex made it to all fours and sprayed everyone with a massive shake of his coat.

The searchlight swept back and forth over the white caps. Colby's passage through the rapids should only have taken seconds, but she couldn't see him anywhere. Had he survived it?

It was the sharp-eyed Dilya who spotted him. Some swirl of the current had dragged him sideways in the river. Her limbs were shaking too hard with the cold to throw herself in to save him. The helo swooped in close and everyone leaned out to pluck him from the racing water.

In moments, he too was aboard. Blood was streaming down his face from a scalp wound. But it was easily staunched by her palm, so it couldn't be too deep.

Dilya had her fists in both dogs' collars. The President lay along the bench seat with McShea and the rescue helo's crew chief checking him over.

Colby lay back against her knees as she sat in the President's seat. "Let's not do this again, Saint Ives. Deal?"

"Deal!" And she wanted to laugh. Is that how his marriage proposal would sound? Casual, a little teasing and whimsical, both backed up by a smile for humor? She'd be disappointed if it didn't.

She watched out the still open door as they gained altitude over the river.

Piercing the sheeting raindrops, she spotted a series of red dots. A line aimed right at…

She twisted around and saw the dot—on the President's chest.

A rifle's aiming laser.

She instinctively dove forward enough so that the light was on her own chest instead. Then braced for impact…

No bullet slammed into her. No wound erupted in the middle of her chest, geysering blood.

If it wasn't a guiding laser for a bullet, maybe it was guiding—

A fast-moving shadow in the rain.

No time to act, a shout erupted from her.

COLBY TRIED to sit up as Ivy shouted, "Rex! Fetch!"

Rex pushed off the far bench, breaking free from Dilya's grasp and slamming Colby aside.

He launched out the door and into the air.

What Colby saw should have been impossible.

Fifteen feet out from the side of the helo and thirty feet above the rushing darkness of the river, Rex's jaws clamped down on the wing of a model plane that was rushing straight at the helicopter's side door.

It was moving fast enough that it would have wounded or killed anyone in the flightpath.

Rex was snapped around cruelly, but he hung on to the model's wing and together they plunged down into the river.

Even as Colby scrambled to look down, there was a roar like a buzz saw. One of the overwatch helicopters must have traced the origin point of that laser. Whoever the attackers were, they were done for as the minigun unleashed on them.

Their gripe with the President, whatever it was, had just been definitively settled. And if there was anyone behind them, he'd trust the Secret Service to ferret it out.

19

____

vy was touched that the President had sent a jet at his own expense down to fetch them from the Cape for the ceremony.

"Not Air Force One," Colby noted, "But a Gulfstream is still a class act."

General Arnson personally flew their helo from Andrews to the South Lawn.

Ivy noted that even he wasn't above messing with the golfers as he climbed out particularly low over The Courses at Andrews that lay behind the Air Force One hangar.

But once again she didn't get to see the approach to the South Lawn. She was far too busy staring at the incredibly handsome man beside her. They both sat on the side bench—they certainly weren't going to sit in the President's chair, not even with her bridal gown as an excuse.

She had debated about wearing her Marine Dress uniform, including the Congressional Medal of Honor she'd been awarded for managing to only somewhat crash the Marine One helicopter with the President aboard. But that wasn't how Colby made her feel. He made her feel like a hundred percent woman.

"I didn't go overboard-girlie, did I?" She brushed a hand over the dress that was the first she'd worn in at least a decade.

"No one would ever make that mistake about you, Saint Ives." Colby leaned in and kissed her very convincingly. The dress wasn't bouffant—though it wasn't a bad word for the kiss that sent happy sighs rippling all through her. It had no great gobs of taffeta all over its surface. Instead, she'd chosen a sleek dress, but with a lace over-collar that made her seem more curvy than she was. The skirt had a lovely flair and swoop to it that somehow made her look taller. She'd tried heels once, for almost ten feet in the wedding store, and almost insisted on Army boots after the experience.

Colby had opted for a tailored suit. His own Director's Medal of Valor had been left in a drawer at home. At home. Not quite her cozy cabin on the Maryland beach dream—that would come later. For now they had a small house close by Cape Canaveral. It *was* right on the beach so that they could go swimming together every morning before work. After her swim in the Ottawa River, she never complained about the overly warm Gulf Stream current that flowed by their beach. The chill of thinking she'd lost Colby to that cruel water had never truly left her.

She still couldn't believe she'd made the astronaut corps. Maybe it was NASA's access to the tape of her plunging flight. Or maybe when dredging up the helo had revealed the extent of the damage she'd fought against—it shouldn't have been able to fly at all, but she'd fought it down out of the Death Zone all on her own. Piloting wasn't just about jets, and NASA had finally seen that.

Life had seemed so short in that moment and it made every moment since twice as precious.

"You shouldn't have let him see the dress," Dilya greeted her the moment Master Sergeant McShea opened the helicopter's door. Then her maid of honor squealed like the teenage girl she sometimes was and threw herself into Ivy's arms. "You look beyond amazingly amazing. He's so lucky! You get that, don't you?" she asked Colby over Ivy's shoulder.

"Maybe," Colby shrugged noncommittedly. Dilya barely had time to frown before he simply bent down and scooped her into a hug that left her feet dangling well above the ground.

Dilya hugged him back hard and seemed reluctant to let go.

"Hey, he's mine," Ivy reminded her. "You don't get to keep him."

Dilya nodded, but sniffled a little once her feet were back on the ground. And did her best to glare at Ivy. "You get how lucky you are too, right?"

"I'm going to say 'I Do' when it matters. Does that count?"

The girl nodded fiercely and again teared up. To hide it, she knelt down to greet Rex.

"Hey, boy." She gave him a big hug. "Zackie will be so glad to see you, c'mon."

Rex limped alongside her as she led the way up to the White House Rose Garden. Rex's limp didn't pain him but it would never fully heal, disqualifying him from the Secret Service. His fall with the model plane had cut a tendon that the surgeons had to shorten to put back together. But he was certainly plenty healthy to fulfill his role beside Colby as the new Lead Dog of NASA's security.

Colby held Ivy's hand, keeping her back for a moment.

Together they looked at what awaited them. A full Marine Corps Honor Guard, so beautiful in their dress blues, with swords. She would get to walk through an arch of swords after the ceremony because even though she was an astronaut now, there was no such thing as an ex-Marine.

Their families and much of the administration, including the First Family, were chatting together on the front lawn. No sign of Reggie, probably off making some last minute adjustments in the kitchen before serving his Best Man duties.

A tall, elegant woman, with lovely long gray hair and wielding a camera, came down the lawn. Miss Watson—who, as Dilya had said, kept changing—snapped a photo of them, winked, and moved on.

Ivy realized that it was the photo she'd always wanted but never imagined. Her, on the South Lawn, in front of an HMX-1 White Top helicopter, but in a way she'd never imagined. Wearing a wedding dress with the man she'd always be able to say she'd spent her whole life with.

Colby squeezed their joined hands. "Luckiest man alive, Saint Ives."

"You are," she smiled up at him.

At his laugh, she leaned her face into the center of his chest.

They had the whole universe ahead of them.

M.L. BUCHMAN
3-time Booklist Top 10 Romance Author of the Year
Off the Leash
WHITE HOUSE PROTECTION FORCE
POLICE
#1

OFF THE LEASH (EXCERPT)

"You're joking."

"Nope. That's his name. And he's yours now."

Sergeant Linda Hamlin wondered quite what it would take to wipe that smile off Lieutenant Jurgen's face. A 120mm round from an M1A1 Abrams Main Battle Tank came to mind.

The kennel master of the US Secret Service's Canine Team was clearly a misogynistic jerk from the top of his polished head to the bottoms of his equally polished boots. She wondered if the shoelaces were polished as well.

Then she looked over at the poor dog sitting hopefully on the concrete kennel floor. His stall had a dog bed three times his size and a water bowl deep enough for him to bathe in. No toys, because toys always came from the handler as a reward. He offered her a sad sigh and a liquid doggy gaze. The kennel even smelled wrong, more of sanitizer than dog. The walls seemed to echo with each bark down the long line of kennels housing the candidate hopefuls for the next addition to the Secret Service's team.

Thor—really?—was a brindle-colored mutt, part who-knew

and part no-one-cared. He looked like a cross between an over-sized, long-haired schnauzer and a dust mop that someone had spilled dark gray paint on. After mixing in streaks of tawny brown, they'd left one white paw just to make him all the more laughable.

And of course Lieutenant Jerk Jurgen would assign Thor to the first woman on the USSS K-9 team.

Unable to resist, she leaned over far enough to scruff the dog's ears. He was the physical opposite of the sleek and powerful Malinois MWDs—military war dogs—that she'd been handling for the 75th Rangers for the last five years. They twitched with eagerness and nerves. A good MWD was seventy pounds of pure drive—every damn second of the day. If the mild-mannered Thor weighed thirty pounds, she'd be surprised. And he looked like a little girl's best friend who should have a pink bow on his collar.

Jurgen was clearly ex-Marine and would have no respect for the Army. Of course, having been in the Army's Special Operations Forces, she knew better than to respect a Marine.

"We won't let any old swabbie bother us, will we?"

Jurgen snarled—definitely Marine Corps. Swabbie was slang for a Navy sailor and a Marine always took offense at being lumped in with them no matter how much they belonged. Of course the swabbies took offense at having the Marines lumped with *them.* Too bad there weren't any Navy around so that she could get two for the price of one. Jurgen wouldn't be her boss, so appeasing him wasn't high on her to-do list.

At least she wouldn't need any of the protective bite gear working with Thor. With his stature, he was an explosives detection dog without also being an attack one.

"Where was he trained?" She stood back up to face the beast.

"Private outfit in Montana—some place called Henderson's Ranch. Didn't make their MWD program," his scoff said exactly what he thought the likelihood of any dog outfit in Montana being worthwhile. "They wanted us to try the little runt out."

She'd never heard of a training program in Montana. MWDs all came out of Lackland Air Force Base training. The Secret Service mostly trained their own and they all came from Vohne Liche Kennels in Indiana. Unless... Special Operations Forces dogs were trained by private contractors. She'd worked beside a Delta Force dog for a single month—he'd been incredible.

"Is he trained in English or German?" Most American MWDs were trained in German so that there was no confusion in case a command word happened to be part of a spoken sentence. It also made it harder for any random person on the battlefield to shout something that would confuse the dog.

"German according to his paperwork, but he won't listen to me much in either language."

Might as well give the diminutive Thor a few basic tests. A snap of her fingers and a slap on her thigh had the dog dropping into a smart "heel" position. No need to call out *Fuss—by my foot.*

"Pass auf!" Guard! She made a pistol with her thumb and fore-finger and aimed it at Jurgen as she grabbed her forearm with her other hand—the military hand sign for enemy.

The little dog snarled at Jurgen sharply enough to have him backing out of the kennel. "Goddamn it!"

"Ruhig." Quiet. Thor maintained his fierce posture but dropped the snarl.

"Gute Hund." Good dog, Linda countered the command.

Thor looked up at her and wagged his tail happily. She tossed him a doggie treat, which he caught midair and crunched happily.

She didn't bother looking up at Jurgen as she knelt once more to check over the little dog. His scruffy fur was so soft that it tick-led. Good strength in the jaw, enough to show he'd had bite training despite his size—perfect if she ever needed to take down a three-foot-tall terrorist. Legs said he was a jumper.

"Take your time, Hamlin. I've got nothing else to do with the rest of my goddamn day except babysit you and this mutt."

"Is the course set?"

"Sure. Take him out," Jurgen's snarl sounded almost as nasty as Thor's before he stalked off.

She stood and slapped a hand on her opposite shoulder.

Thor sprang aloft as if he was attached to springs and she caught him easily. He'd cleared well over double his own height. Definitely trained…and far easier to catch than seventy pounds of hyperactive Malinois.

She plopped him back down on the ground. On lead or off? She'd give him the benefit of the doubt and try off first to see what happened.

Linda zipped up her brand-new USSS jacket against the cold and led the way out of the kennel into the hard sunlight of the January morning. Snow had brushed the higher hills around the USSS James J. Rowley Training Center—which this close to Washington, DC, wasn't saying much—but was melting quickly. Scents wouldn't carry as well on the cool air, making it more of a challenge for Thor to locate the explosives. She didn't know where they were either. The course was a test for handler as well as dog.

Jurgen would be up in the observer turret looking for any excuse to mark down his newest team. Perhaps teasing him about being just a Marine hadn't been her best tactical choice. She sighed. At least she was consistent—she'd always been good at finding ways to piss people off before she could stop herself and consider the wisdom of doing so.

This test was the culmination of a crazy three months, so she'd forgive herself this time—something she also wasn't very good at.

In October she'd been out of the Army and unsure what to do next. Tucked in the packet with her DD 214 honorable discharge form had been a flyer on career opportunities with the US Secret Service dog team: *Be all your dog can be!* No one else being released from Fort Benning that day had received any kind of a job flyer at all that she'd seen, so she kept quiet about it.

She had to pass through DC on her way back to Vermont—her

parent's place. Burlington would work for, honestly, not very long at all, but she lacked anywhere else to go after a decade of service. So, she'd stopped off in DC to see what was up with that job flyer. Five interviews and three months to complete a standard six-month training course later—which was mostly a cakewalk after fighting with the US Rangers—she was on-board and this chill January day was her first chance with a dog. First chance to prove that she still had it. First chance to prove that she hadn't made a mistake in deciding that she'd seen enough bloodshed and war zones for one lifetime and leaving the Army.

The Start Here sign made it obvious where to begin, but she didn't dare hesitate to take in her surroundings past a quick glimpse. Jurgen's score would count a great deal toward where she and Thor were assigned in the future. Mostly likely on some field prep team, clearing the way for presidential visits.

As usual, hindsight informed her that harassing the lieutenant hadn't been an optimal strategy. A hindsight that had served her equally poorly with regular Army commanders before she'd finally hooked up with the Rangers—kowtowing to officers had never been one of her strengths.

Thankfully, the Special Operations Forces hadn't given a damn about anything except performance and *that* she could always deliver, since the day she'd been named the team captain for both soccer and volleyball. She was never popular, but both teams had made all-state her last two years in school.

The canine training course at James J. Rowley was a two-acre lot. A hard-packed path of tramped-down dirt led through the brown grass. It followed a predictable pattern from the gate to a junker car, over to tool shed, then a truck, and so on into a compressed version of an intersection in a small town. Beyond it ran an urban street of gray clapboard two- and three-story buildings and an eight-story office tower, all without windows. Clearly a playground for Secret Service training teams.

Her target was the town, so she blocked the city street out of her mind. Focus on the problem: two roads, twenty storefronts, six houses, vehicles, pedestrians.

It might look normal…normalish with its missing windows and no movement. It would be anything but. Stocked with fake IEDs, a bombmaker's stash, suicide cars, weapons caches, and dozens of other traps, all waiting for her and Thor to find. He had to be sensitive to hundreds of scents and it was her job to guide him so that he didn't miss the opportunity to find and evaluate each one.

There would be easy scents, from fertilizer and diesel fuel used so destructively in the 1995 Oklahoma City bombing, to almost as obvious TNT to the very difficult to detect C-4 plastic explosive.

Mannequins on the street carried grocery bags and briefcases. Some held fresh meat, a powerful smell demanding any dog's attention, but would count as a false lead if they went for it. On the job, an explosives detection dog wasn't supposed to care about anything except explosives. Other mannequins were wrapped in suicide vests loaded with Semtex or wearing knapsacks filled with package bombs made from Russian PVV-5A.

She spotted Jurgen stepping into a glassed-in observer turret atop the corner drugstore. Someone else was already there and watching.

She looked down once more at the ridiculous little dog and could only hope for the best.

"Thor?"

He looked up at her.

She pointed to the left, away from the beaten path.

"Such!" Find.

Thor sniffed left, then right. Then he headed forward quickly in the direction she pointed.

CLIVE ANDREWS SAT in the second-story window at the corner of

Main and First, the only two streets in town. Downstairs was a drugstore all rigged to explode, except there were no triggers and there was barely enough explosive to blow up a candy box.

Not that he'd know, but that's what Lieutenant Jurgen had promised him.

It didn't really matter if it was rigged to blow for real, because when Miss Watson—never Ms. or Mrs.—asked for a "favor," you did it. At least he did. Actually, he had yet to meet anyone else who knew her. Not that he'd asked around. She wasn't the sort of person one talked about with strangers, or even close friends. He'd bet even if they did, it would be in whispers. That's just what she was like.

So he'd traveled across town from the White House and into Maryland on a cold winter's morning, barely past a sunrise that did nothing to warm the day. Now he sat in an unheated glass icebox and watched a new officer run a test course he didn't begin to understand. Lieutenant Jurgen settled in beside him at a console with feeds from a dozen cameras and banks of switches.

While waiting, Clive had been fooling around with a sketch on a small pad of paper. The next State Dinner was in seven days. President Zachary Taylor had invited the leaders of Vietnam, Japan, and the Philippines to the White House for discussions about some Chinese islands. Or something like that, Clive hadn't really been paying attention to the details past the attendee list.

Instead, he was contemplating the dessert for such a dinner that would surprise, perhaps delight, as well as being an icebreaker for future discussions. Being the chocolatier for the White House was the most exciting job he'd ever had. Every challenge was fresh and new, like the first strawberry of each year.

This one would be elegant. January was a little early, it would be better if it was spring, but that wasn't crucial. A large half-egg shape of paper-thin white chocolate filled with a mousse—white chocolate? No, nor a dark chocolate. Instead, a milk chocolate mousse but rich with flavor, perhaps bourbon.

Then mold the dark chocolate to top it with a filigree bird, wings spread in half flight, ready to soar upward. A crane perhaps? He made a note to check with the protocol office to make sure that he wouldn't be offending some leader without knowing it.

"Never underestimate the power of a good dessert," he mumbled one of Jacques Torres' favorite admonitions. This was going to work very nicely.

"What's that?" Jurgen grunted out without looking up.

"Just talking to myself."

Which earned him a dismissive grunt, as if he was unworthy of the agent's attention. It wouldn't surprise him. Clive was not trained like a Secret Service officer. His skills lay in his palate and his fingers for shaping the very finest chocolate work. He knew his big frame and good looks said easy-going and, while his size wasn't quite to oaf, people always assumed he was just a big and clumsy guy.

Clive often felt defensive about being a chocolatier when he was so dismissed out of hand. He had spent years learning his skills. And to be invited to join the White House kitchen…well, he couldn't think of a higher accolade. The fact that his father would agree with Jurgen didn't help matters. However, Lieutenant Jurgen didn't look like the sort of man to risk upsetting.

His own father had been a quiet, drunken merchant marine who rarely spoke when he was ashore—except for grumblings about his only child's lame excuse for a choice of profession. The one blessing of having Nic Andrews as a father was how much of Clive's life the man had spent at sea. In between, Clive and his mother had lived together in Redwood City very quietly and with some small degree of content. Their apartment had a view of the brilliant colors of the Cargill Salt Flats of San Francisco Bay. He often used their colors in his chocolates.

"They're starting." It was clear by his tone that Jurgen could break Clive over his knee like a piece of sugar work despite

Clive's size and would be glad to demonstrate at the least provocation.

"Oh, thanks," seemed to be an acceptable response.

A "you're welcome" grunt sounded softly.

Miss Watson had told him to watch, so he closed his notepad and tucked it in his shirt pocket.

"Any suggestions on what I'm looking for?" Miss Watson had *not* been clear on that point. He looked down at the new officer and the small dog entering the far end of the course. He picked up a pair of binoculars from the window ledge but the dog was still small, barely reaching the officer's knees.

He scanned upward.

A woman. For some reason he hadn't expected that. Of course with the silly little dog, that somehow fit. However, officer or not, the woman offered a great deal to be looking at. Five-seven or eight. Medium chocolate brunette, about a fifty percent cocoa, with a nicely tempered shine like a fine ganache. It fell in a natural flow down to her shoulders, slightly ragged rather than in some DC socialite perfect coif. A thin face without being gaunt. Perhaps intense would be a better word.

Her jacket hid her shape, but she wore no hat or gloves despite the cold. Tan khakis hinted at nice legs. Army boots declared definitely not DC socialite.

"Well, for one thing, she's not following the damned course," Jurgen sounded puzzled.

"Is that a bad thing?" Clive could see the worn track and that they definitely weren't on it.

Jurgen made a sound that was neither yes or no.

"What's her name?"

"Linda with Thor," as if it was a single name.

Clive couldn't stop the laugh. "*That* scruffy little mutt is named Thor?"

Jurgen's grin would look appropriately nasty to be carved into the flesh of a Halloween pumpkin.

The woman had transformed once she started the course. Pretty and intent had transformed to focused to the point of lethal. She moved with all the efficiency of a fine-honed knife blade. Maybe she was Thor and the dog was Linda.

With a series of hand signs—Linda's mouth rarely moved though he did spend some time watching it—she directed the dog along a storefront. When she disappeared inside, he turned to watch the camera feeds on Jurgen's console.

"It isn't just the dog," Jurgen volunteered. "The dog has the nose, but the handler guides the dog to make sure no area is missed. Neither one can do it alone. Hundred percent a team effort."

Inside what might have been a real estate or travel agency, the dog sat abruptly and looked back at Linda. The officer stuck a red Post-it on one of the desk drawers.

"PETN. Very hard to find. Under half of the dog teams find that one," Jurgen didn't sound pleased. Maybe he was one of those people who was only happy when someone was suffering. Clive had worked for more than one chef like that.

"Linda with Thor"—or "Thor with Linda," he wasn't going to commit on that one yet despite Jurgen's evil grin—were on the move again.

Just as they stepped out of the office, Jurgen flipped a switch on his console.

Clive jumped as the blast of sirens sounded from a police car parked at the curb, even though they were muffled by distance and the observer station's windows.

It must have been painfully loud right next to the car, but Linda and Thor both merely looked at the wailing vehicle, sniffed their way around it, then continued along the street.

For an hour they left behind a trail of red Post-its and for the most part ignored sirens, gunfire, and other distractions. Once an actual explosion spattered them with dirt. For that, Linda had wrapped her arms around the dog and huddled in a bookstore doorway with her back turned toward the worst of it. Moments later they were back at their task.

Clive could look down in wonder. She'd positioned herself so that if the explosion had been lethal, rather than merely a training distraction, she'd have given her life to save her dog. Maybe the guys on the Presidential Protection Detail really would step in front of the bullet if given the chance. Would he himself step in the line of a rogue chocolate shard? Perhaps, but only because that didn't sound terribly threatening.

When they reached the end of the course, they stopped in the center of the intersection. From a small pack, she pulled out a fold-up bowl and poured some water into it for Thor before drinking herself. Then a doggie treat. Nothing for the handler.

With a tip of his head, Jurgen indicated that Clive should follow him down.

As they stepped out onto the street themselves, she was tossing a bulbous Kong toy for Thor. He'd once more turned into the dog most likely to belong at a little girl's tea party, eating all of the cookies whenever the hostess wasn't looking.

"You missed two," Jurgen snapped out his form of a polite greeting, not bothering to look at his clipboard.

Linda flinched as if she'd been slapped and her shoulders sagged.

But Clive had learned some things about Jurgen's expressions: there was a sourness there like bitter chocolate. "What's been your best score by any other team?"

"Five misses," Jurgen's scowl now included him since Clive had just spoiled his fun.

Linda still didn't look any happier. That told him a lot about her—this was one seriously driven woman. Anything less than perfect was a hundred percent failure. Which he supposed was true when your job was to make sure that no one blew up the President.

At that moment Thor stopped playing with his toy, trotted up to Jurgen's feet, circled him once, and sat abruptly with his nose aimed at one of the lieutenant's shoes.

"Damn it," he growled. "Okay, that makes one miss."

"Let me guess," Clive could get to enjoy this after all. "The observer's station also has an explosive." Then his breath caught in his throat. He wouldn't put it past Jurgen to have him sitting on an explosive the whole time he'd been in the observer's chair.

JURGEN'S EXPRESSION said it all.

"Of course," Linda couldn't believe she'd missed it. "It is always the person and place you least suspect that gets by you." *That* was certainly never going to happen again.

She was furious with herself for missing that but wasn't going to show any weakness. It was one of the great traps of serving in the military. If a woman showed the least weakness, she'd forever be tagged as unable to perform. If a guy showed ten times as much, he'd be tagged as being tired and probably told he'd done a good job. The military had taught her how to hide *anything* she was actually feeling—often until she barely felt it herself.

It was even more galling that some stranger had to be the one to point it out. He didn't sound or act like Secret Service, making it even worse.

"Usually takes a new dog-handler team weeks of hard work to get even close to that kind of performance. Fine!" Jurgen's tone said it was anything but. He yanked a sheet from his clipboard, scrawled a signature, and handed it across. "Oh eight hundred tomorrow. Report to Captain Carl Baxter at the USSS office in the West Wing of the White House. Take that damn dog with you. I've got a meeting to get to." Then he stalked off. A trumped-up meeting, because earlier he'd said he had all day.

Linda could only look down at Thor in amazement. She squatted down and gave him a big scritch. It wasn't Thor's fault that she'd screwed up and not led him into the control center to sniff around and she had to make sure that he knew that. She'd never before worked with such a well-trained dog. He flopped onto his back and presented his belly. As she rubbed it, his back leg began kicking spasmodically in joy.

"You did so good, Thor. You are such a good doggie!" She used that ridiculous high-pitched voice that so many dog trainers used. She was long past being embarrassed by it. Mostly. She couldn't care less about Jurgen, but something about the other man who'd stayed behind made her less sure.

"Maybe I should leave you two alone." He had a nice deep voice, befitting his large frame.

Linda glanced up at him. Her automatic profiling assessment kicked in: Caucasian male, closecut dark hair, dark eyes, built big like a wrestler—enough so that he'd look heavy if he wasn't six-four. Instead he looked like the guy most likely to wrap you up in a friendly bear hug, which would force her to flatten him if he tried. His standout feature was powerful hands well marked with small cuts and burns. That and an amazing smile, which lit up his whole face. He wore a fleece jacket over a maroon turtleneck and a knit scarf in a blocky pattern of brilliant colors that made his brown eyes even warmer.

"Hi," his pleasant tone not the least diminished by her own silence, which was now growing awkward.

Thor had rolled to his feet, sniffed around the man, then looked up at him wagging his short tail.

He knelt down and reached out to scratch the dog's ear.

She snapped her fingers to get Thor's attention and made the hand sign for "enemy" as a test.

He looked up at her in surprise as if she'd lost her mind.

She sighed and whispered, "*Spiel.*" *Play.* The dog could do what he wanted.

He nosed out and slipped his head under the stranger's half-extended hand. Without a moment's hesitation, the man began to rub the offered ear. Easy for the dog.

Not so easy for her. Well, she had to start somewhere and he looked kindly enough.

"Nice scarf."

He looked down at his chest. "Oh, this one. Thanks. My mom knit it for me last Christmas. It's the colors of home."

"Where did you grow up, in a kaleidoscope?"

"Almost. South of San Francisco there are these huge salt flats that turn wild colors as their salinity increases. This is the last scarf she ever knit for me. I made one of cherry blossom colors for her that same year." His smile was wistful, which was more than she'd ever feel if her mom died.

"You knit?" She couldn't imagine how with those big hands of his.

"Doesn't everyone?" But his smile said that rather than an actual expectation, it was some form of humor—not one of her strengths. It was getting strange, not knowing if he was someone to salute or not, so she held out a hand.

"Sergeant Linda Hamlin. New to the Secret Service—as of today, I suppose."

"Clive Andrews," which still didn't tell her who he was. He reached up from where he still squatted by Thor. His hand was warm—her fingers were freezing—and as powerful as it looked. His massive hand completely enveloped hers. That's when she realized that he wasn't merely big, he was immensely strong. If he was trained, she might have trouble taking him down—though she'd learned more than a few dirty tricks fending off unwanted attentions in her decade of service.

There was an easy roll to his voice that hinted at Scottish, overlaid with a soft American accent that she couldn't pin down— which must be San Francisco. It made him sound as much of a mutt as Thor.

"Not *Agent* Hamlin?"

"*Special Agent* is separate from the Uniformed Division. The canine teams are UD; we use ranks."

"Oh."

Great way to build a friendship—her first potential one outside of the military in a decade—by correcting him. It did tell her that he wasn't Secret Service or he'd have known that. Which raised the question of what he was doing on their secure base.

"And this is a White House patrol dog?" He rubbed under Thor's chin.

She looked down at Thor's shaggy appearance. Despite his exceptional performance, it was clear that she was going to be endlessly harassed about him. She sighed and changed the subject.

"And you are…?" Best way to appease a man, talk about *him*.

"The White House chocolatier." His cheery wince said that he too was expecting a certain dismissive reaction.

When she didn't take the bait, he merely acknowledged it with a shrug.

Again the silence was stretching… "Is there a reason a chocolatier is here at James J. Rowley Training Center?"

This time the shrug looked a little awkward as he rose back to standing, much to Thor's dismay.

She was an expert on reading a dog's body language. Men were a mystery to her. Well, except for a few obvious nonverbal messages that she had made it a rule to ignore. But she wasn't getting those from Clive the Chocolatier.

"Grown men actually make their living with chocolate?"

That earned her another of his dazzling smiles, "Only the lucky ones."

"Chocolate was never a big motivator for me."

He slapped a hand on his heart and staggered backward as if she'd knifed him with her Benchmade Triage foldable. "You have set me a challenge, madam. I shall expect you to visit the White House Chocolate Shop at your first convenience so that I may convince you otherwise."

"The White House has a chocolate *shop?* Like where you buy chocolate?" She was definitely back in civilian land. The places she'd been operating, a chow tent was a luxury and a mess hall mostly a distant dream.

He sighed and hung his head as if she was a hopeless case, which wouldn't surprise her for a moment. But then he smiled down at her again, as cheerful as ever. He and Thor were apparently two of a kind.

"Actually, in the world of chocolate, a chocolate shop can be either a place of sale or a kitchen. Mine is a actually a chocolate kitchen. We just call it a shop."

"Okay. Sure. Whatever. I'll look you up if I get there." A chill breeze flapped the piece of paper directing her to report at the White House tomorrow and made her shiver. "Okay, *when* I get there."

Clive cast off his fooling around. His friendliness actually made her feel warm despite the freezing temperature. She really needed to get some gloves. Did he know how powerful that smile was on his handsome features?

Her jerk-o-meter wasn't twitching either, which was unusual.

Then, of all unlikely things, he bowed deeply—once to her and once to Thor, the second bow accompanied by a brief head pat—before turning and heading for the parking lot.

A nice guy. One who remembered her dog. She didn't like being charmed by any creature with less than four legs, but he'd somehow managed it.

Available at fine retailers everywhere

ABOUT THE AUTHOR

M.L. Buchman started the first of, what is now over 50 novels and even more short stories, while flying from South Korea to ride his bicycle across the Australian Outback. Part of a solo around the world trip that ultimately launched his writing career.

Three times, his titles have been named "Top 10 Romance of the Year" by the American Library Association's *Booklist*. NPR and Barnes & Noble have named other titles "Top 5 Romance of the Year." In 2016 he was a finalist for Romance Writers of America prestigious RITA award. He also writes: contemporary romance, thrillers, and fantasy.

Past lives include: years as a project manager, rebuilding and single-handing a fifty-foot sailboat, both flying and jumping out of airplanes, and he has designed and built two houses. He is now making his living as a full-time writer on the Oregon Coast with his beloved wife and is constantly amazed at what you can do with a degree in Geophysics. You may keep up with his writing and receive a free novel by subscribing to his newsletter at: www.mlbuchman.com

Join the conversation:
www.mlbuchman.com

Other works by M. L. Buchman:

SIGN UP FOR M. L. BUCHMAN'S
NEWSLETTER TODAY

and receive:
Release News
Free Short Stories
a Free novel

Do it today. Do it now.
www.mlbuchman.com/newsletter

www.ingramcontent.com/pod-product-compliance
Lightning Source LLC
Chambersburg PA
CBHW060539190726
48283CB00003B/786